A CHRISTIAN STONE THRILLER

SEAT 3A

T0282092

ERIC SUGRUE

GREENLEAF
BOOK GROUP PRESS

Published by Greenleaf Book Group Press
Austin, Texas
www.gbgpress.com

Distributed by Greenleaf Book Group

For ordering information or special discounts for bulk purchases, please contact Greenleaf Book Group at PO Box 91869, Austin, TX 78709, 512.891.6100.

Design and composition by Greenleaf Book Group
Cover design by Emily Burns
Cover images used under license from
©Shutterstock.com/Peshkova; ©Vecteezy.com/jrslompo71921403

Publisher's Cataloging-in-Publication data is available.

Paperback ISBN: 979-8-88645-183-2

eBook ISBN: 979-8-88645-184-9

Hardcover ISBN: 979-8-88645-198-6

To offset the number of trees consumed in the printing of our books, Greenleaf donates a portion of the proceeds from each printing to the Arbor Day Foundation. Greenleaf Book Group has replaced over 50,000 trees since 2007.

Printed in the United States of America on acid-free paper

24 25 26 27 28 29 30 31   10 9 8 7 6 5 4 3 2 1

First Edition

CHAPTER ONE

It's a perfect day for flying. A seasonal fifty-seven degrees. Cloudless sky. No wind to speak of. My fellow passengers are chatting a mile a minute on their phones as we stroll down the accordion tunnel connecting the terminal and the plane. Their spirits are high, and why not? Soon enough they'll be sipping frozen drinks in Miami Beach.

I'd be right there with them if it weren't for the fact that I'm already a bit hungover. That's the danger of owning the restaurant where you do your drinking: It's easy to forget that you're draining your own supply.

A cabin attendant whose name tag reads GENNA greets me as I step on board.

"Nice to see you again," she says, nodding to the loyalty stickers decorating my shoulder bag. "Let me know if I can do anything to make your flight more enjoyable."

There's a faint pulsing in my temples, and my tongue keeps sticking to the roof of my mouth. "I'd love a bottle of water," I say.

I stuff my bag under the seat in front of me and settle down beside the window. This is my third trip to Miami in as many months. My brother Michael moved down there roughly a decade ago. My biggest regret is that I didn't begin visiting him right away.

For years, my fear of flying kept me anchored to a one-hundred-mile radius around Wilmington, Delaware. Then Michael totaled his Jeep, and I had to be at the University of Miami Hospital ASAP. The only seat available on the next plane out was 3A. I took two Xanax and white-knuckled the armrests. And a miracle happened: 100,000 pounds of metal successfully defied gravity. Soon after, Michael's collapsed lung righted itself and 3A became my safe zone. As long as I'm sitting in 3A, nothing bad can happen.

Since Michael's accident, Miami has been my second home. I bought a one-bedroom condo three buildings down from his place. The small balcony has the kind of ocean view that brochures are made of. Sitting out there with my morning cup of coffee, I feel the backlog of sixteen-hour days melt away. And now I get to see my brother whenever I want without cramping his independence or mine.

Genna brings my bottle of water. I guzzle half of it in one go, and my tongue turns instantly more nimble. The dull throb in my skull grows a bit duller. If I can catch a few winks, I might just arrive in Miami feeling like new.

A woman plops herself down next to me, then flashes a neighborly smile. She's wearing a Phillies hat, and her canvas bag has the words *Betsy Ross House* embroidered in red, white, and blue across one side. A tourist on her way home, no doubt bursting with stories to tell. I'd guess she's in her early forties, like me. Tall and toned and still carrying traces of the tan she must have brought with her from Florida to Philly. Normally I'd be eager to chat, but not today.

Today it's more than just the hangover itself; it's my reason for being hungover. Quinn left me. Our yearlong cohabitation went bust last Friday. Her parting words were "I didn't move in with you so that I could live alone." Those sixteen-hour days took their toll. She was offered a job in Chicago and couldn't see any reason to turn it down. I didn't want her to go. I don't want her to be gone. But my hours will only get longer with a new location opening next spring, and I'm not about to make promises I can't keep.

"Beautiful fall day," my seatmate says. "We don't really get seasons in Florida."

I nod, then deflect her icebreaker by sliding a manila folder from the side pocket of my computer bag. *Sorry, can't talk. I'm Christian Stone, important businessman reading important papers.* It feels slightly less self-involved than the truth: *I'm Christian Stone, currently lovesick and unavailable.*

The important papers I'm pretending to read are specs for the new restaurant. It didn't help my case with Quinn that the latest installment of Big Ocean Bar & Grill will be located on the ground floor of a Dax Morelli property.

"The man's a thug," she said. "He belongs in jail."

"Those are just rumors," I told her.

But as rumors go, they're pretty compelling. Dax has spent the last half decade buying up most of Wilmington. Nobody knows for sure where the money comes from, but the loudest whispers suggest mafia ties. Dax, with his slicked-back hair and impeccably tailored Armani suits, does his best to look the part. Still, his latest venture seems more than legit; it seems downright well-intentioned. Morelli Capital is revitalizing three square blocks in the heart of downtrodden Wilmington. Planned renovations include a public arts project, a performance complex modeled on Lincoln Center, solar-powered affordable housing, and a slew of sleek new storefronts. Big Ocean will claim a 5,000-square-foot space in the lobby of a sprawling, state-of-the-art convention center. Yes, Dax stands to make a lot of money, but it's hard to argue that the people of Wilmington won't profit too.

The cabin doors draw closed, and then the passengers all make a show of ignoring the flight attendants while they demonstrate vital safety procedures. Once that's out of the way, our captain jumps on the intercom and declares that we're ready for takeoff, an announcement that always sounds to me like a threat. I glance over at my seatmate. I must have been wrong about her eagerness to chat. She's donning a pair of noise-canceling headphones and has her arms folded across her chest. She wants to be left alone, like me. I wonder what else we have in common. Maybe I was too hasty. Maybe I should strike up a conversation when the snack tray comes around. But I know that I won't. I'm still in that phase where talking to other women only reminds me that I'm not talking to Quinn.

We start down the runway, then pick up speed. The vibration kicks in—that feeling like you're fusing with your seatback as the plane tries to suck you out through its underbelly. I grip my armrest and force myself to look out the window. Sitting in 3A is only the first of my survival rites. Between liftoff and cruising altitude, I have to keep my eyes glued to the earth. I have to mentally catalog every receding object. If I face my fear, then it can't sneak up on me. No pilot would dare crash while I'm holding vigil.

As we begin our ascent, I see a golf cart ferrying ground crew back to the terminal. A US Postal Service plane coming in for its landing. A canopy of red-and-gold leaves at the edge of the airport. A traffic jam on the highway. Rooftops that must quake as we pass overhead. Boats docked at a marina on the Schuylkill River. Tires and oil drums and plastics of every size and shape gathered on the bank just beyond the marina.

And then, lying atop the reeds in the middle of all that trash, I spot an object I'm slow to identify. Something long and elastic and curvy. I press my face against the glass like I'm trying to zoom in.

Or maybe I just can't believe what I'm seeing. It's . . . a man. A man wearing a tent-sized Eagles jersey. Except my eyes *must* be playing tricks on me, because who would lounge out in the middle of all that debris? And who would contort their limbs like that, with one arm wrapped awkwardly around his head and his legs splayed? I squint and crane my neck, searching for a better angle. But then the nose of the plane jolts skyward, and the body's gone.

That's what it was—not a living being, but a body. A dead man washed up on shore with the beer bottles and soup cans and other detritus. As though someone threw him away. My head is pounding, and my vision has blurred more than once since the alarm went off this morning, but I know what I saw. A dead man in an Eagles jersey. There isn't a doubt in my mind.

Or is there? Could I really have made out a body from so many feet above the earth? Then there's the question of my state of mind. No one who knows me would say I've been doing my clearest thinking lately. Mistaking a green Hefty trash bag for a corpse in an Eagles jersey would fit right in with my recent blunders. In addition to drinking more than usual, I've lost my temper with staff, shown up late to meetings I called, let my voicemail sit full for days on end. I've been generally unavailable to anyone who has my best interests at heart. That's why I decided to take a full week off. A rare extended break. Claire, vice president of Big Ocean and my closest confidant, says she's never seen me so distracted. She stopped short of calling me a liability. "Get your money's worth out of that condo," she told me. "Come back refreshed." Translation: Come back when you have your shit together.

Since I can't trust my own judgment, I'll have to rely on someone else's. I hesitate, then lean forward and tap the shoulder of the woman in 2A. She turns and peers over the back of her seat.

"Yes, dear?" she asks.

She has short gray hair and deep smile lines. The "dear" is more genuine than condescending. She strikes me as someone whose thoughts bend toward kindness, someone whose first instinct is to want to help. I start to answer her, then realize I haven't thought things through. I can't just come out and ask this pleasant stranger if she happened to glimpse a cadaver lying among the trash on the riverbank.

"Sorry to bother you," I tell her, "but I was looking out the window just now, and I thought I saw something strange near the marina. I couldn't quite make it out. I was wondering if maybe you saw something too?"

The question sounds ridiculously vague, even to me. Vague, and also pointless. If she'd spotted a corpse, then she wouldn't be so calm and composed.

She holds her Kindle up for me to see. "Sorry," she says. "My eyes were glued to this thing. I run through cozies like they're candy."

"No worries," I say. "It was probably nothing."

She turns back around. I feel suddenly very alone. *Just drop it, Christian*, I tell myself. But I can't. My body won't let me. There's a tightening in my chest, and my right knee is bouncing up and down like I swallowed a bottle of NoDoz. I need to move, but the seat belt sign above my head is still ordering me to stay put. When it finally goes dim, I free myself and get to my feet. But there's another obstacle blocking my path: 3B's legs. Either she's dead asleep or she's doing a great job of pretending. Her jaw's hanging open, and she's making a high-pitched whistling noise with every exhale. She must have spent her last night in Philly painting the town. Our hangovers are one more thing we have in common. The prospect of disturbing her brings on a fresh wave of doubt.

Let the woman be, I think. *Her rest is more important than your delusions.*

But then a second little voice asks, *Of all the things you might have imagined, why a dead guy in an Eagles jersey?*

I have to know for sure. I clear my throat, but 3B doesn't budge.

"Excuse me, miss?" I say.

Nothing. I prod her arm with one finger. Her eyes pop open. She looks embarrassed, like there was something else she was supposed to have been doing and now I might tell on her.

"Sorry, I just need to use the restroom."

"Of course," she says.

She stretches and yawns, then steps into the aisle so I can squeeze past. I walk the short distance to the front of the cabin. Genna is standing near the exit, stocking a tray with cheap headphones. She sees me coming and smiles, but her eyes aren't so welcoming. As someone who's worked in the service industry his whole life, I know that look—Genna's flagged me as high maintenance.

"Everything okay?" she asks.

"Yes, thank you. I . . ."

I stall out. It's the same problem I faced with 2A. How do I ask what I want to ask without sounding like a lunatic?

"I saw someone, just now, when we took off," I tell her. "A man. By the river. He didn't look right. I think he might need help."

She rearranges my fragments into a complete thought: "You saw a man by the river who might need help?"

I nod. "He was wearing a green-and-white jersey."

"Okay."

"I was wondering if maybe you saw him too?"

She points to a fold-down seat beside the coffeemaker. "I didn't see much of anything."

The fact that she tells me *why* she couldn't have seen a distressed man lying by the river feels encouraging. She must think I'm something less than a total crank.

"Listen," I say, "I know this sounds nuts, but would you mind asking the pilot if he noticed anything out of the ordinary?"

Now she looks amused. This is clearly a first.

"Why not?" she says. "Just wait here a moment."

I stand with one hand pressing against an overhead bin for balance while Genna knocks on the cockpit door, then steps inside and shuts it behind her. I wonder how she's framing the question. *I'm sure it's nothing, but this needy passenger paid for a first-class seat, and he wants to know if . . .* I picture them sharing a joke at my expense. Meanwhile, a potential murder victim is decomposing back at sea level.

Genna reemerges, shaking her head. "Sorry, but he didn't see anything unusual. Neither did the copilot."

"All right," I say. "Thank you for checking."

The sign on one of the two front-end bathrooms reads VACANT. I step inside and lock the door behind me. Nature isn't calling, but I need a minute to myself. We hit a pocket of turbulence just as I start to splash some water on my face. I manage to wet the top third of my sweater in the process. I mop the cotton dry with a handful of stiff paper towels, then look at myself in the mirror. I look surprisingly normal. I have a face you can trust. A face *I* can trust. I know what I saw. My mind isn't the type to play tricks.

So what's your next move? I ask myself.

The woman from 3B is waiting for me in the aisle. Her smile, like Genna's, is a cover. I can feel her thinking, *Once is enough, buddy.* I nod as though she's said it out loud, then slide back into my seat. I pull my laptop from my day bag and open it on the tray in front of me. If no one else can confirm what I saw, then I'll have to do it myself.

I start by searching the Philadelphia Police Department's Missing Persons Blotter. There's a whopping forty-five pages to scroll through, though only the faces featured on the first six pages have disappeared within the last month. None of them is even a ballpark match with the man I saw. Most are children, a mix of adolescent girls and boys. The rest are elderly. Even from that distance, I could tell my floater was a full-grown man with a healthy head of dark hair. Fully grown and in his prime. An Eagles fan. Those are all the facts I have to work with.

Maybe it's just too soon for him to have been reported missing. Maybe the very people who might have reported him missing are the ones who killed him. His wife. His lover. His father or mother, brother or sister. Or maybe he isn't so much missing as abandoned. A drug addict. An escapee from the nearest mental hospital. The kind of person who gets discarded. Whoever he is, my job now—the job I've assigned myself—is to cut through all the maybes. I'm the one who saw him. That's enough to make him my responsibility. I know what happens when the dead are left to fend for themselves. The guilty go unpunished. Loved ones stumble around in a fog that never really lifts. I was just eleven years old when my friend Jon was murdered, but I swore I'd never look away again.

I type *Schuylkill marinas* into a search engine, then click on the entry from Google Maps. There's only one in the right vicinity. The body I saw is lying less than a mile north of the Schuylkill Marina.

I navigate over to the American Airlines website. We're scheduled to land at 11:32 a.m. That means I'll have a half hour to kill in MIA before the next flight back to Philadelphia. I can't believe I'm seriously considering this—scrapping a week's vacation to follow some kind of gut instinct. But then the universe gives me a clear signal that I'm supposed to be on that flight: Seat 3A isn't booked.

CHAPTER THREE

"It's work, isn't it?" Michael says. "It's always work."

I'm in my car, heading to Schuylkill Marina. I-95 is a parking lot. I've been driving for half an hour and can still see the airport in my rearview mirror.

"I'm sorry," I tell him. "Something came up. I need a couple of days to sort it out."

His silence means he knows I'm withholding. I don't tell him that I was just a few miles from his condo earlier this morning. He'll think I'm nuts.

"Look, I'll be there," I say. "The trip's just postponed."

"I don't know, Christian. I'm worried about you. Quinn's right— you push yourself too hard."

"I'm fine. I promise."

I can feel him scowling into his phone.

"How about this?" he says. "If you're not here by Friday afternoon, I'll catch the next flight to Philly and drag your ass down here myself."

Now it's my turn to go quiet. Michael's famous for his follow-through; if he says he'll come get me, he means it.

"Do we have a deal?" he asks.

"Look, I can't promise Friday," I say. "But soon. I can promise I'll be there soon."

It's vague, but it's the best I have to offer. Michael grudgingly accepts. Twenty minutes later, I'm pulling into the marina. I called ahead and secured Schuylkill's cheapest rental, an aluminum fishing boat with a tiller steer outboard. A middle-aged man in a pale blue polo shirt with the letters *SM* embroidered above the right pocket greets me in the parking lot. Once I've filled out some paperwork, he walks me over to the rentals dock. On the way, we pass by a glass-walled restaurant and a VIP pier where the moored boats look like small-scale yachts. Both the restaurant and the marina are all but empty on a weekday afternoon.

"This beauty's all yours," the man says.

We're standing in front of a sleek and shiny skiff that looks more like a convertible race car than the motorized rowboat I'd been picturing.

"Ever used a tiller before?"

I tell him I have but don't mention that it's been more than a decade.

"There's a life jacket under each seat," he says. "It's a little nippy out there. I wouldn't be surprised if you have the river to yourself."

I bump hard into a pylon on my way out of the dock, but by the time I'm on the open water, I've started to feel confident at the helm. This is the kind of day people imagine when they dream of autumn in the East. Cold, yes, but the clear sky has held up, and the leaves along the banks have hit their peak shades of yellow and red. I feel worlds away from the Miami beach I'd planned to be lounging on right about now.

I doubt I've been on the water five minutes when I turn a bend and spot an oil drum sticking up out of a bed of phragmites. The surrounding water is littered with glass and plastic bottles, and the nearby shore is hidden under a dumpster's worth of trash. I slow the boat to a crawl and steer toward the reeds. I'm sweating despite the temperature, and I can feel my pulse throbbing in every corner of my body. No doubt about it—this is the spot.

But then where is the body?

I inch right up to the reeds and cut the engine. I stand in the boat to see over the tops of the stems. The man in the Eagles jersey is gone. But there is what looks like a body-sized depression in the center of the reeds. As though something heavy was lying there not so long ago.

I switch the engine back on and maneuver around the periphery of the trash, then step out and drag the boat on shore, far enough so that I'm sure it won't slip back into the water and drift away. I climb higher up the bank, kicking aside cans and bottles as I go. Already, my sneakers and the cuffs of my jeans are covered in a swampy muck. Once I've reached the summit, I turn back and face the water. From my new vantage point, I can see straight down onto the reeds. Now I'm sure. It's clear from the way the reeds are folded over, like they're anxious to unfurl again. Something—or somebody—was pinning them down.

I scan the water and land in every direction, but the man in the Eagles jersey is nowhere to be found. The question is, Where did he go, and how did he get there? Was he carried away by a shifting tide? Do rivers even have shifting tides, or is that only for oceans? I'll need to do some research. And if the body was carried away, then why not the rest of the trash? Why not the oil drum? Or that tire resting right at the lip of the water?

Is it possible that he wasn't dead? Could he have gotten up and walked away under his own power? Did he wake up from an overdose? Was he knocked unconscious and prematurely left to die? But if he did walk away, then what path did he take? Just mooring the boat and crossing roughly thirty yards, I've blazed a visible trail through a thick bed of detritus. I run my eyes back and forth over the bank and find no sign that anyone but me has been here. One thing's certain: The man I saw was in no condition to swim. Did someone on a passing boat spot him and drag him on board? I doubt it. Between the reeds and the trash, he was awfully well hidden. Unless, like me, you happened to be looking down from above.

I revisit one of my original hypotheses: He was never there to begin with. Like Claire said, I've been distracted. Distracted, and stuck in my own head. I've been looking at the world the way people look at Rorschach tests, projecting whatever's stewing in my brain out onto the picture. Is my unconscious fixated on death? Have I flooded it with too much *Law & Order*? Or maybe Michael and Quinn are right, and I've pushed myself to the point of snapping. What was it Quinn said to me the night she left? *You work for the sake of working. Your heart isn't even in it anymore. It's like you're afraid that if you stop, you'll die.*

I take a step back. I stare down at that flattened patch of reeds and do my best to see something other than the imprint of a body. I squint and cock my head, but nothing changes. There's a definite human-sized depression in the reeds.

What I need now is proof, evidence that I did or didn't see what I believe I saw. Whether the body washed up here or was placed here, whether someone killed him or knocked him unconscious or he harmed himself, there's a strong chance that the implement used is lying nearby. A knife or a gun or a baseball bat. A syringe or an empty pill bottle.

I wade out into the refuse, looking for an object that doesn't belong, the thing that isn't like the others. The trash is more diverse than I'd thought, and there's more of it than I would have expected to see so close to a luxury marina. It isn't just plastic bottles and tin cans. I find a cut of drainage pipe. A stubby piece of driftwood. An old-fashioned rabbit-ears TV antenna. Back by the trees, I find a long swath of canvas tarp and a set of dented metal poles lying under a rusted shopping cart. The combination makes me wonder if there'd been a homeless encampment nearby. Maybe the man in the Eagles jersey was one of its residents. Maybe he wound up on the losing side of a territorial dispute. I check the poles for traces of blood but don't find any. I keep one pole in my hand and use it to dig through the surface layer of trash. I scatter countless bottles, thinking maybe the clue I'm searching for is buried closer to the ground. Mostly, what I uncover is more trash. Mottled sheets of newspaper, a chewed-up tennis ball, disposable cutlery, the head of a broom.

I glance down at my clothes. The muck and slime have climbed up my jeans, almost to my knees. My hands are a color I don't recognize. What will the folks at Schuylkill think when they see me? I feel like my sanity is in question. If there's something here, then I have to find it. But time is running out. The sun has already started to dip. I'm supposed to have the boat back by dark.

Just a little longer, I tell myself.

I give a fat plastic jug a hard whack and send it flying. And there, underneath, is the thing that's not like the others. At first, I'm not sure what it could be. It's the size of a library card or a driver's license, but its surface is partially obscured by mud. I pick it up and wipe it off on my already-sullied jeans, then examine it more closely. My heart rate careens back to peak levels. It's a laminated lanyard containing a ticket for last Sunday's Eagles game. Part of a season pass. I give it a more thorough cleaning, then stick it in my pocket.

I saw an Eagles jersey from the sky. I found an Eagles ticket on the ground. Coincidences don't come that big. This is real. There was a man's body lying in those reeds. Somewhere out there, someone who loves him is wondering why he didn't show up for dinner. Why he hasn't returned their phone calls or texts. Whoever he was, wherever he is now, something horrific happened to him. It's up to me to figure out what that something was. I won't leave him to fend for himself. As a kid, I had no choice. But I'm not a kid anymore.

CHAPTER FOUR

I pull into my driveway in Rehoboth Beach at a little after eight. The day began fourteen hours ago, when I rolled out of bed feeling queasy and hungover. Since then, I've driven to Philadelphia and back. I've flown to Miami and back. I rented a boat and went searching for a dead man. I should be ready to sleep for a millennium, so how is it I'm wide awake?

I drop my keys on the kitchen counter and run for the shower. I let the water beat on me for a good long while, then slip into an old pair of jeans and a baggy T-shirt and walk out onto the bedroom balcony. The ocean is just thirty yards away, but if it weren't for the sound of the waves and the flickers of moonlight, you wouldn't know it was there. I take a few deep breaths, then step back inside.

It's time to get a little research done. I pull the Eagles ticket from the back pocket of my muck-stained pants and carry it with me downstairs. My laptop is sitting on the kitchen island, surrounded by empty coffee cups and snack bowls. I have a small office overlooking the garden, but since Quinn left, I have no desire to use it. The back rooms of a house feel even more isolated when no one else is home.

I take a minute to straighten up, then pour a glass of Goldeneye Pinot Noir and tap the computer's space bar. I begin by touring

Philly's most recent crime blotters. There are two new missing persons since I checked this morning—one a juvenile, the other an octogenarian. There was a stabbing death in the sixth district and a shooting death in the twenty-fifth. Both bodies are accounted for. I find no hint of foul play anywhere near the river.

I open a fresh tab and Google *Schuylkill tides*. A local weather station features a graph that looks like it was drawn by hand using a stencil kit. Measurements in feet are written down the left side and hours of the day across the bottom. According to the wavy line in the heart of the graph, the tide switches from low to high every five to seven hours. Today's first low tide hit at roughly 7 a.m., with high tide following at a little after noon. It's possible, then, that the body landed on those reeds in the morning, just before I spotted it during takeoff, and washed away again by the time my second plane touched down at PHL.

I navigate over to Craigslist and click on Lost & Found. At first glance, there's a lot of *lost* and very little *found*. Cats, dogs, and jewelry make up the bulk of what's missing. I scroll past listings for a stolen Shih Tzu, an escaped calico, a gold-diamond engagement ring lost somewhere in the vicinity of Dickinson Square Park. I read the titles of all seventy-six entries. No mention of an Eagles ticket. But then how could there be if the ticket holder is dead?

I hold the laminated case up to the light like there might be a clue I've missed. The ticket is standard Eagles fare. There's a seat number and a date. There's a cartoon drawing of an angry bird encircled by the phrase *Est. 1933*. All it tells me about its owner is that he must have been old-school. Most people opt for digital tickets these days.

But I do know something else about him. Something important. He won't be using his season pass next Sunday. The seat he's left empty could be surrounded by his friends and acquaintances. Either they'll have learned by then what happened to him or they'll be wondering why he hasn't turned up. In either case, they'll have information I can use, starting with his name.

I jump back on the Internet and head to the Eagles home page. They're playing the Cowboys next Sunday. The game's nearly sold out, but there are still seats available . . . in the Phlite Deck. *Phlite* is a play on Philadelphia and Miller Lite, though fans think of it as the Flight Deck because you might as well be sitting 30,000 feet from the field. It doesn't matter for my purposes; any ticket that gets me into the stadium will do. I go ahead and click Purchase. Suddenly, Sunday can't come soon enough.

It's closing in on 11 p.m., and still there are a thousand stray thoughts bouncing around my brain. I need to impose some order on them before I can even think about sleep. Quinn left behind her favorite organizational tool: a five-foot-tall half-chalk, half-cork vision board that she hung on the wall beside the fridge. She would pin recipe cards to the cork half and write out shopping lists and schedules on the chalk half. It was supposed to be romantic. We were supposed to take turns cooking for each other, choosing from the thumbtacked options. After a while, Quinn started circling the dinners I managed to show up for. My excuse was always the same: I couldn't get away. To which she'd reply, "I thought you were your own boss?" The schedule from our last week together is still there in light blue chalk: Quinn, Monday through Wednesday; Christian, Thursday and Friday. None of the days are circled.

I wipe the chalkboard clean with a damp cloth, then untack the recipes and set them on top of the fridge. I feel a quick surge of sadness. It's like I'm closing the book on a part of my life I'd hoped would never end. *If that were true,* I hear Quinn say, *then you'd have done more than hope.* I tried to convince her I could change, but I didn't have a whole lot of evidence backing me up.

I turn my attention to the task at hand. The goal is to get the elements of the case out of my head and onto the board. I start by pinning up the ticket. Then I take up a piece of chalk and draw a vertical line down the center of the blackboard so that I've created two columns. At the top of the left-hand column, I write *WHAT I KNOW SO FAR.* At the top of the center column, I write *WHAT I DON'T KNOW YET.*

There isn't a whole hell of a lot to put in the first column. I know I saw a dead man lying on the reeds by the river. I know he was an Eagles fan. I know that he attended last week's game. I know he hasn't been reported missing. I know he was there and then he was gone. My best guess is that he was dumped during low tide (@ 7 a.m.) and washed away during high tide (@ noon). For now, that's all the knowledge I can reasonably claim.

The second column is where I spend the most chalk. I have no idea how he came to be lying on those reeds. (Was he deposited there by whoever killed him—assuming someone *did* kill him—or did the river carry him to that spot after he'd been dropped somewhere else?) I can't say how or when he died. I don't know his name or age or occupation. I don't know his relationship status. I don't know who besides me is looking for him, and I don't know who it is that doesn't want him found. There are plenty of other things I don't know, but these seem like the most urgent.

I stand back and look at the two columns side by side. Despite myself, I'm smiling. I've seen a hundred different actors play this role on TV. Detectives in sordid little squad rooms staring with tired eyes at a board where the facts of the case are laid out in words and pictures. I've been investigating for less than a day, and already I'm a stereotype.

All right, Christian, I tell myself. *Time to call it quits for the night.*

What I need is a bedtime buffer, a gentle transition to sleep mode. I refill my glass and carry it into the living room. I've slept in here more than once since Quinn moved out. There's something soothing about the blue glow of the television when the lights are switched off. I set my wine on the coffee table, then put my feet up and sink deep into the couch cushions. Peacock is replaying the first-ever season of *Law & Order*. I've seen it maybe a thousand times, but none of them in the last decade. Hard to believe the show originally aired more than thirty years ago. Chris Noth looks like he's twelve. I'd forgotten that George Dzundza preceded Jerry Orbach in the original cast.

I catch myself drifting in and out of the plot. There's something more pressing on my mind. An image I've been fighting off all day. It surfaces now that I've settled in for the night. I'm seeing him. I'm seeing Jon, lying on his back on the pavement with one arm twisted up around his head. Exactly like the body in the Eagles jersey.

CHAPTER
FIVE

1991

Our friendship began with Jon passing out in a back room of the reptile wing at the Brandywine Zoo. He'd just turned nine, and I was about to. It was a blazing August on the East Coast. The reptiles were stored in a hothouse. Our camp counselors, all grad students in zoology, had us gathered around a green-and-white python's terrarium. Without warning, Jon tipped over backward like a felled tree. A short while later, the paramedics came and carted him away.

I was half jealous; I'd always wanted to ride in the back of an ambulance. The glamour of it wasn't lost on Jon. He showed up the next morning with his story prepared. By the time the paramedics wheeled him out to the parking lot, he said, he was feeling fine. So fine that they let him sit up front and work the siren. On the way to the hospital ("They had to take me—it's a legal thing," he said), another call came in. A stabbing victim, just a few blocks away. The paramedics looked at each other.

"Guess it's career day," the driver said.

They found the victim slumped against the wall in front of a corner bodega. He'd taken off his T-shirt and was holding it in a blood-soaked ball against the hole in his lower abdomen. The whites of his eyes had turned yellow, and he could hardly breathe. There was blood all over the pavement around him.

"Five dollars," he said. "They gutted me for five dollars."

The paramedics removed the T-shirt and applied a real bandage. Jon was graphic about the way blood spread through the gauze. "Like a paper towel soaking up a puddle of fruit juice," he said.

As they loaded the victim into the ambulance, the cops drove up—"late as always"—and some of the shadier onlookers started to slip away. Jon climbed into the back and held the wounded man's hand all the way to the ER.

"I kept telling him, 'You're gonna be okay, sir. Just hang in there.'"

Jon knew how to spin a tale. It came naturally to him. Effortlessly. He made up voices for his characters. He imitated the static from walkie-talkies and the whirring blades of the news chopper circling overhead. He described every face in detail and quoted some colorful dialogue. He made it all easy to picture and impossible to believe.

When he was done, I said, "Man, you've got to teach me to lie like that."

I was smiling when I said it, and Jon smiled back. He had my attention because I knew he wasn't all the way lying. Of course, it wasn't even remotely possible that the paramedics had stopped to pick up a stabbing victim with a nine-year-old kid sitting in their cab. But you had to wonder if Jon really had worked a siren or ridden in the front of an ambulance or seen "a scrawny, grandpa-aged guy with snow-white chest hair" bleeding out on the pavement, because the details he gave went beyond anything he might have picked up from TV. He wasn't *just* inventing. He was borrowing. Embellishing. Mixing and matching. And I'm sure part of what drew me to Jon was the challenge of figuring out what was real and what was made up—what he'd witnessed and what he'd pulled out of thin air.

———

Jon had been to my house maybe a half dozen times before he invited me to his. The invitation felt like an event. I'd been curious about where he lived for what felt like forever. And Jon was uncharacteristically tight-lipped about his home life. He'd told me his mother was "cool" and his room was "bad-ass." That was it. Nothing about his family having relocated to Wilmington via witness protection. No pet panther prowling the basement. No moonroof above his bed. No tricked-out Maserati in the garage. All I knew for sure was that he had no siblings, and his father was dead.

I thought maybe his reluctance to share had to do with the fact that he lived on what locals called "the other side of the tracks." I grew up in the Triangle, a solidly working-class neighborhood not far from downtown. Small, manicured yards. Mature trees. Clean, well-lit streets. Jon's neighborhood was just a ten-minute bike ride away, but a world apart. Boarded-up windows. Broken streetlamps. Graffiti on the sides of private homes. I couldn't have put it into words at the time, but I was sure that Jon's imagination grew out of his environment—that the stories he told originated on the streets he went home to every day after school. If I wanted to find the nuggets of truth buried in his make believe, then that was where I had to look.

When we stepped off the school bus in front of his house, I felt instantly let down. At first glance, his block didn't seem all that different from mine. It was just another long string of sturdy-looking two-story brick row houses with classic gable roofs. True, the front yards were concrete slabs and some of the facades could have used a facelift, but that didn't seem like any big deal. What really bothered me was the lack of people. I'd expected a hub of activity. Kids playing stickball. Adults gossiping on their stoops. Music pouring through windows. I'd expected energy. Jon's energy writ large. Somewhere—probably the movies—I'd gotten the idea that a close-knit community was the upside of being poor. But this place was just as sleepy as where I lived.

I found the inside of Jon's house equally disappointing. The rooms were long and narrow and smelled like cinnamon. The decor was typical fare. Framed photos of family members. A fern in one corner of the living room. A calendar and a cuckoo clock hanging in the kitchen. It wasn't until I'd been there a while that I started to notice the blemishes. Peeling linoleum. Panels missing from a drop ceiling. Faulty plumbing. (It sounded like there was a coffeemaker brewing in one of the kitchen walls.) A dead mouse in the cat's litter box. But I couldn't link any of that back to a single detail in any of the fantasies Jon had spun for me. As far as I could see, his home had nothing to do with his storytelling.

But his mother did.

Looking back now, I think she might have been my first crush. At the very least, she made one hell of a first impression. Jon and I were sitting at a folding table in the kitchen, eating peanut butter straight from the jar. I heard her before I saw her. She was singing her way through the house. A bright, up-tempo show tune. Whenever she forgot the lyrics, she'd whistle. I looked across at Jon. He was grinning. If it had been my mother, I'd have been gritting my teeth and praying for her to stop. When she stepped through the kitchen doorway, my first thought was that she looked just like the song she'd been singing: cheerful, good-natured, maybe a little mischievous. She seemed to float rather than walk. Instead of introducing herself, she tousled my hair like we were old pals.

"You want some crackers to go with that?" she asked.

I tried to answer, but my tongue stuck to the roof of my mouth and my lips were glued to my gums. Jon found that hilarious. He filled his mouth with peanut butter and started mumbling along with me. Rather than telling us to knock it off and quit wasting food, his mother got a spoon and pulled up a chair.

"We might need to open a second jar," she said.

As the three of us sat there eating, Jon told a whopper about a short-lived standoff with a pair of Dobermans in the park. The dogs set out to chase him up a tree, but in no time Jon had them lying on their backs, begging for belly rubs. He tamed their owner too—a hulking Hells Angels type with so many tats you couldn't guess his age or race. At the end of their encounter, the man slipped Jon fifty bucks and asked if he'd come back to the park at the same time tomorrow for another training session. Jon said his schedule was booked.

"Bikers aren't my thing," he told us.

Instead of reining him in, his mother egged him on. She laughed at the parts that were supposed to be funny. She asked for descriptions of the dog owner's tattoos. She said if she ever ran into him, she'd slap his face for letting his hounds roam around loose. She was her son's biggest fan.

When story time was over, she made tall glasses of chocolate milk and sat with us while we drank them. Then she stood, pushed her chair back in and said, "All right, kids. Time for me to go to work."

I thought *work* was a euphemism. Maybe she had a hobby. Maybe she was heading upstairs to practice the cello. But no, she was talking about her shift at the local Wawa. It was the first I'd heard of people earning their living after dark.

"You work at night?" I asked.

"Night *and* day. Day and night. Working for the man isn't enough for me. I've got to work for two men."

I didn't know what she meant, but I thought it made her sound important.

"There's lasagna in the fridge," she told Jon. "Heat it at 350. Just make sure to shut the oven off after. Christian, there's plenty for you if you're hungry."

Before she could leave, Jon jumped up and gave her a hug. That wasn't something kids our age did. Not in front of other kids.

"I'll blow you a kiss when I'm back," she said. "You'll feel it in your dreams."

I watched her walk down the hallway and out the front door. Then I turned to Jon. "When will she get home?"

"Late," he said.

"Is someone coming to stay with you?"

"What do you mean, someone?"

I didn't want to use the word *babysitter*. "I don't know. Like your aunt, or your grandma."

Jon shook his head.

"Your mom lets you stay home at night by yourself?" I asked.

"Yeah," he said. "She lets me."

I thought that was the coolest thing ever. But for the first time since I'd known him, Jon looked embarrassed. And maybe a little sad.

CHAPTER SIX

I check the crime blotters and the missing persons reports every morning, noon, and night. I've given myself a PhD-level independent study on the idiosyncrasies of currents and tides. I've spent hours staring at my vision board, hoping the lists of facts and questions will set me on some new and fruitful path. But I'm stymied. Until I know who I saw lying on those reeds, there's nothing more I can do. The Eagles game is still four long days away. Technically, I'm on vacation. I need a distraction. Something to keep me occupied until Sunday at 4 p.m.

I decide to reclaim some of the responsibilities I'd passed on to Claire while I was supposed to be away, starting with the bimonthly meeting of the board for Wilmington's Downtown Development Project. The DDP represents the future of both my business and my hometown, but I dread these meetings because Dax Morelli runs them. Dax is Wilmington's most successful developer of hotel properties and new-construction communities. He's done well for himself, and he isn't shy about flaunting his money. Brioni suits, Gucci loafers, rotating Audemars Piguet watches. Dax cares about appearances—and not much else. Lately, though, there have been some questions about whether appearance matches reality. An article in a local paper accused Morelli Capital of using crowdfunding to disguise a large loan from a disreputable, if not shady, source. The source went unnamed, and the paper printed a retraction the following week, but the damage had already been done. Rumors started circulating about longtime investors jumping ship. For Dax, the DDP is a first step toward repairing his company's image.

Still, even with his reputation on the line, Dax just can't resist the finer things. That's why we're meeting at Hotel Pont Neuf when a Morelli Capital conference room would do just as well. Pont Neuf is an old-school luxury establishment, meaning that everywhere you turn, there's either dark wood or black leather. Carved oak wainscoting, stained mahogany coffee tables, overstuffed armchairs. It feels like a rich guy's man cave. The second I step inside, I want to head back out into the light.

Gloria Callaway is waiting for me in one of the lobby's arm-chairs. Gloria's a founding member of the DDP. She also happens to be the mayor of Wilmington. We've known each other since kindergarten. A quarter of a century ago, near the tail end of middle school, and then again during the first semester of our junior year at Virginia Tech, we flirted with something more than friendship. Any romance between us was ill-fated, but we've remained close and enduring friends.

She's waiting for me in the lobby because she knows I hate to enter a viper's den alone.

"Boy, you really like to stick it to him, don't you?" she says, grinning.

She's talking about my attire: polo shirt, jeans, and canvas sneakers. Dax thinks anyone he honors with his presence ought to dress for the occasion. I think my outfit suits the occasion just fine.

"This from a woman who wore a tube top to her uncle's wedding," I say.

"Those days are long gone."

True enough. Grown-up Gloria dresses like a politician—solid-color pantsuits, an emerald brooch pinned to her lapel, shoulder-length blond hair that looks as though she's come straight from the stylist's chair. But anyone who knows her can see past the uniform. Mayor Callaway is a rare breed. She's more concerned with improving people's lives than securing their votes. She wants low-income families to live comfortably. She wants to give kids from every economic sphere access to the arts. She wants to generate jobs and wealth for the city of Wilmington. Hence the DDP.

"Aren't you supposed to be in Miami?" she asks.

"Long story."

"Then we'll have to get drinks later."

"Deal," I say.

She stands and checks her watch. "Well, we're only going to be fashionably late. You do like to push that man's buttons."

"Every chance I get."

The Pont Neuf feels less like a luxury hotel once you enter the conference room. Yes, there's state-of-the-art audio and video equipment, but the faded yellow carpet would be equally at home on the floor of a Motel 6, and the furniture—swivel chairs with mesh backs and a steel-framed table with a fake-wood top—is straight out of a Wayfair catalog. Not that there's anything wrong with that; it just doesn't fit with an establishment where rooms during the offseason start at $400 per night.

Dax is sitting at the head of the table, holding court with the half dozen attendees who managed to arrive on time.

"Grab a coffee and a Danish," he says. "Ashley's Bakery makes the best in Delaware."

A quick dig at me, since Big Ocean Hospitality does all its own baking. I notice there's no Danish on the table in front of Dax. His fat-free physique screams personal trainer/personal chef.

"How's Quinn?" he asks.

Gloria flinches. It would be easy enough for me to make this ugly. Dax plays the devoted husband in public, but behind the scenes, he keeps a filing cabinet full of NDAs. I flash him a smile that says, *I know things too.*

This week's meeting is all show-and-tell. I'm here as a board member, a spectator with a vote. Besides Dax, Gloria, and me, two other board members are present: Robert and Olivia Langley. At the ripe old age of eighty-four, Robert Langley is everything Dax aspires to be: cunning, refined, self-assured, self-made, and—most enviable for Dax—the richest person in Delaware, with a net worth hovering just above $850 million. People call him the Warren Buffett of Wilmington. Unlike Dax, Robert Langley doesn't feel the need to flaunt anything. There's plenty of wealth on display in his impeccably tailored custom suits and imported Italian shoes, but whereas Dax is all flash and no elegance, Langley is all elegance and no flash. There's no gel slathered into his still-full head of hair, no vapor trails left behind by his cologne. He drives—or is driven around in—a sleek but staid Rolls-Royce, while Dax cruises town in a bright orange McLaren. And, as I've come to learn through these DDP meetings, Langley plays his cards close to his vest. He sits with an idea before he proposes it. Dax, on the other hand, feels compelled to share every thought in his head, sometimes out of genuine excitement, but more often because he views conversation as competition, and the only way he can win is by refusing to let anyone else speak.

Olivia Langley, seated between Dax and her father, is a riddle I still haven't solved. She's classically beautiful in a way befitting a tycoon's daughter, but it's hard to know exactly what her beauty is masking. Like her old man, she's a master of understatement. She dresses in solid-colored pantsuits and speaks in a whisper, but it would be a mistake to call her meek. Her resting expression is a kind of wry smile that suggests she's three steps ahead of the next-smartest person in the room. But is there genuine intelligence behind that smile, or is it just a well-practiced game face? That question will be answered once her father passes on. As Robert Langley's only child, Olivia stands to inherit every acre and dime. For now, nobody has the slightest idea what she'll do with the family fortune. She might fund cancer research and build state-of-the-art orphanages around the globe. Or she might buy a private island somewhere on the Aegean and never be heard from again.

Today's lineup of presenters is impressive. As I sit and listen, I feel myself growing more and more excited about Wilmington's prospects. The CEO of the energy company we've hired—a young, wiry MIT grad with Andy Warhol hair and fat round glasses—explains how much money we'll save in the long term by going solar.

"Our buildings won't only be affordable," he says, "they'll become the worldwide model for public housing."

The head of the Fine Arts Department at Delaware College of Art and Design gives a slideshow of work by artists she hopes to recruit. My personal favorites include a mural in the style of Basquiat, a galvanized-steel sculpture that doubles as a children's slide, a sidewalk covered in black-and-white headshots of downtown business owners.

After a quick recess (Dax needs to make a call), the architect in charge of our performing arts complex shares mock-ups of three possible designs. The first is a simple blocklike structure with grass growing vertically down its walls. The second features enormous sail-shaped swaths of silvery-blue fabric fluttering high above its roof. The third, with its sharp metallic edges and skinny windows, looks like a futuristic battleship. I'm not sure how any of these structures will blend with the general aesthetic of Downtown Wilmington, but I guess that's the point. It's time for a change.

"Before we adjourn," Dax says, "there's an issue I have to raise."

He's looking straight at me. I brace myself.

"What's that, Dax?"

"We've had to reallot some of the square footage we'd hoped to give you."

I shake my head. "We agreed on five thousand, Dax. It's in writing."

I have major plans for the convention center space. Banquets and benefits. Jazz bands and wine tastings. Wilmington's biggest New Year's bash. I already put the deposit on an ash wood bar with elephant head rail holders. This is supposed to be Big Ocean's flagship restaurant—a jobs provider for downtown and an advertisement for out-of-state franchising.

"The Delaware Historical Society has made a sizable donation," Dax says. "They want an exhibition room. There isn't any place else to put it."

"So what am I left with?"

"Two thousand two hundred."

"Less than half? That isn't going to work, Dax. It's a convention center. I'm sure we can find a spare room for the Historical Society."

I look to the Langleys for support, but as usual, father and daughter aren't about to take sides on the spur of the moment. Or maybe ever. For Robert Langley, the DDP represents his legacy; what matters is that he be remembered as one of Delaware's great philanthropists. It's hard to know why or if the DDP matters to

Olivia. She might see it as her life's work, or it might be just another tedious hurdle to jump over on the way to her inheritance.

Dax's grin tells me he's loving this. I try to remember when things turned personal between us, but there wasn't a specific moment or event. The truth is, I took an instant dislike to Dax, and I wasn't shy about letting him feel it. Bad business on my part.

"I'm sorry, Christian. It's just a matter of priorities. We can come back to this later, but for now I don't see another solution."

Part of me—the largest part—wants to tell Dax what I think of him in the plainest possible language. Gloria senses it in me. She rests a hand on my forearm.

"We'll sort it out later, Christian," she whispers. "You'll get your five thousand feet. For now, play nice."

Of course, she's right. This isn't the time or place, not with the scientist, the artist, and the architect as innocent bystanders. Not with the Langleys sitting in silent judgment.

"Okay," I tell Dax. "Let's revisit this another time."

I'm doing my best to be diplomatic, but the words come out sounding like daggers.

CHAPTER SEVEN

"I promise you, Christian," Gloria says. "It will all work out. Let me handle Dax."

We're sitting in the Oyster House, in a private booth near the back. It took us a good twenty minutes to make our way across the restaurant. People like to be photographed with their mayor. They also like to lodge complaints. Uncollected trash, undelivered mail, a neighbor's smoke alarm going off at all hours. Gloria jots down names and numbers. Knowing her, she'll probably follow up in person. The citizens of Wilmington are her flock, and she's a tireless shepherd. Gloria's always rated high on empathy. She was all of twelve years old when Jon died, but even then she acted as my confidant and consoler. It was her hand I held at Jon's funeral. Afterward, we sat for hours in her parents' backyard, retelling some of Jon's wilder stories.

"Order whatever you like," she says, closing her menu. "My treat."

"Very funny."

Oyster House is a Big Ocean restaurant, the first I launched in Wilmington. I wanted an open, breezy vibe. Tall windows, ceiling fans, long picnic-style tables. The feel of a beachfront restaurant here in the city. More than a decade later, the dining room is still packed on a nightly basis.

"I bet I can guess what you're having," I say.

It's always the same: Virginia fried oysters and a glass of Bogle Sauvignon Blanc. Gloria is an oyster lover. She'd order oyster omelets for breakfast if she could find a place that made them.

Our college-aged server introduces himself as Stuart, then stammers through the specials. I haven't met him before—managers hire front of house staff—but somebody clearly told him I'm the owner. He's a six-foot bundle of nerves with a pimple on his chin that must feel to him like the center of the universe. I reach up and give him a pat on the shoulder.

"Welcome to the family, Stuart," I say.

He looks down at me like an actor who's stepped into the spotlight and forgotten his lines. Once he's out of earshot, Gloria says, "Never fun waiting on the boss."

"Especially when he's dining with the mayor."

"Poor kid."

"I graduated from busing tables to waiting on them when I was about his age. Remember what it's like to be that young? You think the world is yours, but at the same time you're running scared."

"Sounds a lot like being mayor," Gloria says.

Stuart's back in a heartbeat with our Famous Fish Dip and crackers. Gloria watches him fill her glass, then leans forward like she's ready for the real conversation to begin.

"So," she says, "what happened with Quinn?"

"Same as always—work got in the way."

"Really? I thought the two of you were on the same page. Devoted professionals, both happy to find someone who doesn't want them home for supper."

"We were. But Quinn wanted me home at least every once in a while."

"And her move to Chicago is permanent?"

"It looks that way."

"Well, you can't give what you don't have, Christian."

There's a pause while we sample the dip and take our first sips of wine. I glance around the restaurant. The dinner hour is in full swing. Families, friends, couples, all enjoying each other's company over good food and drink. This is exactly what I pictured when I opened the place, but something feels off. Not with the restaurant— with me. It's like I'm looking at a painting that's been hanging in my house for decades: I know it so well that I can't really see it anymore.

"Have I lost you?" Gloria asks.

"Sorry," I say.

"What's wrong?"

"I wish I could say. My mind's been somewhere else lately. I've been distracted. Making sloppy mistakes."

"Anything in particular distracting you?" she asks.

I see myself gazing out the window from seat 3A. I didn't realize until now just how badly I've wanted to talk to someone about what I saw. But I know how it would look. I need more information before I can share. At the very least, I need a name.

"No," I tell her. "Not really."

She's about to call me a liar when Stuart arrives with our food. He's visibly relieved once our plates hit the table and the bulk of his job is done.

"Would you like anything else?"

"Another glass?" I ask Gloria.

She shakes her head. "I better not. I have an early meeting with the chief of police."

Stuart turns and trots back toward the kitchen. Gloria bites into her first oyster, then lets out a little moan.

I'm thinking, *Chief of police.*

I don't know why it didn't occur to me earlier. Gloria has an entire police force at her disposal. A stable of experts. People who process fingerprints and DNA. People with access to national databases. People who take their orders from her.

Go ahead, I tell myself. *Test the waters.*

"I have a hypothetical question," I say. "Suppose you, as mayor, have reason to believe a crime has been committed, but—"

"I thought we were talking about you and Quinn?"

"This is just a quick sidebar."

"All right, then. Ask me."

"Say you're walking along a deserted beach at night, and you stumble across a dead body. A man who's been shot or stabbed to death. Your phone has no signal, so you drive a few miles down the road to call it in. But then, by the time you drive back, the body's gone. Without a trace. No evidence of a crime. What would you do?"

Gloria smiles. "You're writing a script, aren't you? Your obsession with *Law & Order* is finally paying dividends."

"I have an idea I'm toying with. So, what would you do? As mayor, wouldn't you have—"

"You're not making me a character in this thing, are you?"

She's jumped to the perfect conclusion. I decide to run with it.

"I'm not sure it *is* a thing. There are some plot points I need to work out. Like, would a mayor have resources at her disposal? Even if the murder didn't exactly happen in her jurisdiction?"

"So now I've stumbled on a corpse somewhere outside of Wilmington?"

"Let's say a little farther down the coast. The location doesn't really matter. The important thing is that you're sure of what you saw. A man was murdered, and nobody's investigating. You've checked the crime blotters and missing persons boards. It's eating away at you. So, a few days later, you return to the scene. You start investigating on your own. You find some small piece of evidence in the sand. A cuff link or a money clip. Maybe there are initials emblazoned on the back. You'd have people who'd help, wouldn't you? People who'd run tests. Search databases. On the q.t., though, since officially there's no case to solve."

"You mean loyal minions?"

"Exactly."

She thinks it over while she's refilling our water glasses. "They'd have to be people I *really* trusted. People willing to put in overtime without the pay. Our budget is stretched razor thin as is, and the crime rate hasn't exactly plummeted on my watch. If word got out that I sent so much as a lab tech on a wild goose chase, then I might as well sit out the next election."

"Do you? Have people you trust?"

"Maybe one or two."

"So the scenario's plausible? A mayor using her resources to investigate a murder?"

Gloria nods. "Unlikely, but plausible. I think you should write it. It'll be therapeutic for you. I've always believed your obsession with murder mysteries ties back to Jon. Maybe now, all these years later, you can make peace. Just be sure I'm unrecognizable."

I cover my grin with a sip of wine. I've scored a major victory: Gloria and her handpicked "minions" will be there when I need them.

We order a slice of key lime cheesecake and wind down the evening with chatter about the Eagles, my brother, our hopes for the DDP. Gloria glances at her watch.

"I really should go," she says. "I need to prep for tomorrow's meetings, and maybe even get some sleep. You aren't driving back to Rehoboth, I hope?"

"Nah, I'll get a hotel."

"Smart boy."

I walk her outside, then linger for a while in the kitchen, catching up with Mikey, a chef who's been with me since the beginning. When the staff starts cleaning up for the night, I reserve a last-minute room at the Hyatt, where I stay so often they've granted me platinum status. I spend the Uber ride staring out the window, watching the streets of Wilmington rush by. I'm thinking of Jon. I'm trying to figure out what about this city has changed in the decades since my best friend was murdered.

CHAPTER
EIGHT

1994

It was early summer, our last week of sixth grade. Next stop: middle school. Jon and I both made the honors program, which meant we'd be side by side from homeroom through the final bell. Inseparable—that's what people had been calling us for three years now.

We were walking back toward my house from the basketball courts. It was nearing dinnertime, with roughly an hour of daylight left. They appeared out of nowhere. Or at least that's how I remember it. No darting from between bushes or parked cars. They just materialized on the sidewalk in front of us. Kids I'd never seen before. A year or two older than us. The looks on their faces were all the warning we needed; we turned and ran.

I was slower by a stride. A hand grabbed hold of my T-shirt and pulled. I landed hard on my back against the cement. Their leader ripped the basketball from my arms and bounced it off my head. Then they were kicking me. Stomping me. With no hope of getting to my feet, I rolled onto my side with my knees to my chest and my head buried between my elbows. I could hear them shouting to each other. *Kill him. Fuck him up.* I don't remember feeling any pain. That came later. In the moment, I was too afraid. I was waiting for it—anticipating the blow that would break my spine or crack my skull wide open.

But the kill shot never came. Soon enough, they were the ones running. Running and laughing, like they'd just had the time of their lives. I looked up and saw who they were running from. A short, stocky guy in a pin-striped softball uniform. He was brandishing an aluminum bat. He chased after them for half a block, then gave up and came jogging back. I was still splayed out on the pavement, too dazed to move.

"Hey, are you all right?" the man asked.

I didn't say anything. He reached down and pulled me to my feet. I saw my basketball lying near the bushes. It seemed like a miracle they hadn't stolen it.

"Are you hurt?" he asked again. "You want me to call your parents?"

I shook my head. I couldn't make myself look him in the eyes. The fact that he'd saved me meant I'd needed saving. I felt weak. Small. I'd have given anything to just disappear.

"How about I walk you guys home?"

Guys, plural. I turned and saw Jon standing there. I hadn't noticed him before.

"I'm fine," I said.

It was true—or almost true. My palms were scraped raw and bruises were forming up and down my body, but otherwise everything was in working order. I'd managed to protect my face, which was a small victory. It meant my parents wouldn't have to know. No one would know but Jon.

"You sure?" the man asked.

"Yeah," I said. "I just live on the next block."

That was a lie. I was a good ten minutes from home.

"Okay," he said. "But be careful."

I tried to thank him but couldn't find the words. Once he was gone, Jon put a hand on my shoulder. His pity was the last thing I wanted. Something in me snapped. I spun around and punched him square in the chest.

"You ran," I shouted. "You fucking ran."

"Hey, I found that guy. You'd be dead if it wasn't—"

I shoved him so hard that he went reeling into a parked car.

"You left me alone," I said.

He held up his hands like he was surrendering.

"Quit it," he said.

"You're a coward."

I picked up my ball, then turned my back on him and started for home.

"Christian, come on, man," he said. "They had the numbers. Nothing we could do. If I catch one of them without his friends, I'll—"

"You won't do shit. But that won't stop you from running your mouth. You'll tell everyone how you evened the score for me, took them all out one by one, left them lying on the pavement, crying for their mommies. You're worse than a coward—you're a liar."

"Like you would have stuck around if it was me they caught."

"I wouldn't have split. I wouldn't have left you alone."

"Yeah, right. Who's lying now?"

I stopped short. I was burning up inside. I wanted to hurt him. I wanted *him* to feel weak and small.

"Watch it, Jon, or I might go and tell everyone the truth about you."

"What truth?"

"All of it. How your dad the big-shot pilot didn't die in some rescue mission—he ran off because he didn't want any part of you.

And your mom's no ER nurse—she cleans toilets in a gas station. All those stories you tell. You're so full of shit, Jon. Face it. You're nothing. You're nobody."

I started walking. I thought he'd come back at me. I thought he'd say, *You're just pissed 'cause you got your ass kicked* or *I should have kept my mouth shut and let them finish you.* I was raring for a fight. A fight I thought I could win. But Jon, who spoke more words per minute than anyone I knew, didn't say a thing. He went stone quiet.

"What's the matter, you—"

I stopped mid-sentence. Somehow, I sensed he was gone. When I looked over my shoulder, I saw that I was right. There was no one on the street but me.

———

By the time I got home, I'd almost forgotten about the attack. My mind was on Jon. I couldn't stop replaying what I'd said to him. I kept hearing myself the way he must have heard me, like I hated his guts and wanted him dead. I was desperate to apologize. The phone wouldn't cut it. I had to look him in the eyes and know we were okay.

My brother was sitting on the porch with his head buried in a comic book. I knew from the smell of roast chicken that we'd be called to the table any minute. The penalty for being late was a night with no TV. I was willing to pay that price. I tapped Michael on the shoulder.

"Tell Mom I dropped my library card at the park and had to go back for it," I said.

He shrugged. Michael was a year and a half older than me, which made him a newly minted teenager. His answer to everything was a shrug.

My silver three-speed Schwinn was standing just inside the front door. I carried it down to the street, then jumped on and started pedaling as fast as my feet would go. The most direct route to Jon's house took me past a drive-through liquor store and an adult movie theater. For once, I didn't slow down to ogle the posters. My brain was running on two tracks: rehearsing what I'd say to Jon, and keeping a lookout for the kids who'd jumped us.

I heard the sirens but didn't think anything of them until I ran up against an intersection the cops had blocked off. People were gathering outside the barriers with their backs to me. I couldn't see past them, but I knew their attention was pointing toward the vacant lot where not long ago a small apartment building had been demolished. Jon liked to cut through that lot on his way home. Sometimes he'd find what he called "buried treasure." A single stiletto-heeled shoe. A knife handle with no blade. A small glass pipe burned black at one end. Stuff he could weave into his stories. Not the stories he told, but the ones he'd started writing down. His mom had pushed him into it. She was right; he had talent. His first effort landed on the front page of our school's magazine.

I thought I could navigate around the lot, but there were more barricades at the next intersection. The sirens seemed to be multiplying. There was a helicopter hovering above the lot, low enough for me to make out the Wilmington PD logo on its side. My mind flooded with worst-case scenarios. The most likely was that those kids had caught Jon alone. Maybe one of them had a gun. It wasn't unheard of.

The block between the barricades featured a long row of attached single-story garages. Jon and I had climbed onto the roof before. Not for any good reason—just because we could. I checked to make sure nobody was watching, then balanced my bike against one of the rolling doors, climbed its frame like a stepladder, and hoisted myself up. From there, I crawled across on all fours and peered out at the lot.

What I saw looked like a scene from a movie, or maybe the nightly news. Two uniformed officers standing vigil over a pair of bodies near the center of the rubble. One body belonged to a man, the other to a boy. The man was taller than six feet with broad shoulders and hair down to his waist. His right fist still clung to a revolver. The boy was Jon. His arms were twisted up over his face, but I knew him by the red high-top Converse and the blue-and-white-checked T-shirt. I wanted to jump down and run to him, but my body wouldn't budge. I felt like a little kid who'd made it to the end of the diving board and lost his nerve. I couldn't fathom moving in any direction, so I just lay there and watched.

Before long, a trio of men in white jumpsuits came strutting out onto the lot. One was wearing a backpack, and another carried what looked like a thick stainless-steel suitcase. They seemed to be taking extra-long strides, careful to step over and around the debris, as though they were afraid of twisting an ankle or smudging their suits. I turned all my rage on them. Why weren't they running? Why weren't they moving heaven and earth to get to Jon's side? It was like some part of me held out hope that he wasn't dead—that these men could save his life if only they reached him in time.

They were just starting to unpack their steel case when I heard her voice. I pushed up higher on my elbows and spun my head. She'd fought her way to the front of what was by now a sizable crowd. A barrel-chested cop was struggling to hold her back. She looked ready to claw the world to shreds.

"My son," she screamed. "That's my son."

Then her body went limp, and she let loose with a wail I thought would never end. That was when it became real for me. There wouldn't be any do-overs. No chance to say sorry. No way to take back those final words: *You're nothing. You're nobody.*

CHAPTER
NINE

My ticket for the Phlite Deck gets me into the stadium. I'm wearing a baggy Eagles sweatshirt and cap that I bought just for today. I've never been an Eagles fan. Or a fan of Eagles fans. Especially the ones from Wilmington. I've never understood why people support the team one town over just because they don't have a team of their own. Whenever I'm at Lincoln Financial Field, I quietly root for the opposition. *Quietly* because Eagles fans are rabid. I've seen people dressed in out-of-town jerseys get peppered with food and drink on their way into the stadium. I've seen them assaulted in the parking lot after an Eagles loss. I'm not the type to risk bodily harm over a game.

I'm champing at the bit to find John Doe's seat, but I want the surrounding season ticket holders settled in before I show up and start asking questions. If I'm lucky, JD came to these games with friends, coworkers, close acquaintances—people who will miss him and wonder out loud why I'm here in his place. Since I have a ticket, I figure I might as well kill some time in the Phlite Deck. On my way there, I feel like I'm being carried along by a stampede. The energy in the stadium is dialed to ten. Today's opposition isn't just any old rival; it's the Dallas Cowboys. There's no team Eagles fans love to hate more. Most of the people around me started drinking hours ago. The cries of "Go birds!" are ear-splitting. The concrete floor is already littered with empty food wrappers and plastic cups.

I ride the escalator up to the cheap seats. The Phlite Deck is so crowded that I'd have to fight my way to the front just to get a glimpse of the pregame. Lucky for me, I don't care what happens on the field. I head over to the beer line hoping a drink might calm my nerves. Fifteen minutes later, a fiftysomething woman behind the counter barks, "What'll it be?"

She's wearing a vintage Eagles winter hat and sporting a gold Italian horn necklace. A *real* local.

"Coors Light," I say.

Coors Light, aka CL Smooth. My beverage of choice at Lincoln Financial—and the only thing the stadium offers that I actually enjoy.

I take my beer and find a lone high-top table by the exit. I'm sipping and gathering my thoughts when I feel a vibration shoot up through the soles of my feet. People rush to their seats. I wonder what the hell is going on. Then it hits me. This is a *flyover* game. For certain high-profile games, the air force races three fighter jets over the field right before kickoff. As the planes rip through the sky, every pillar in the stadium shakes, and then 65,000 fans start screaming in unison, "E-A-G-L-E-S, EAGLES." Before they've gone quiet, the opening riffs to "Welcome to the Jungle" blare through the PA system.

I let all the fanfare motivate me for my own game. I finish my beer, then head back down the escalator to ground level. I pull out John Doe's pass to check the section number: 124. I look to my right and see SECTION 106 painted high up on the concrete wall. *Unbelievable*, I think. I'm at the dead opposite end of the stadium.

The walk gives me plenty of time to prep for the inevitable question: *What are you doing in our friend's seat?* The best answer

I can come up with is that I bought the ticket on StubHub and know nothing about the seller. Simple and concise. Nothing to deny. No details to keep straight. It may seem odd that I'm at the game alone, but odd is okay. Odd makes people curious. It starts them talking.

When I finally get to Section 124, I'm confronted with a more pressing obstacle: a muscular, middle-aged usher wearing a neon-yellow security jacket. He looks like the type who never smiles or bends the rules. An ex-cop, maybe. I stand out of his line of vision and wait. Sooner or later, there's bound to be a distraction, something that will force him to look away long enough for me to sneak by. The man's outnumbered by at least a thousand to one.

But the longer I stand there, the less the numbers seem to matter. This guy has mastered the art of multitasking. He carries on conversations and checks tickets and keeps an eye on the game all without missing a beat. When he stops a young mother and her toddler son to double-check their tickets, I realize I need a plan B. I dig a $100 bill out of my wallet and stick it in my front pocket. "A hundred bucks will get you into the White House, son," my father used to say.

Here goes nothing.

"Let's see your stub," the man says. His name tag reads NICK.

I reach into my back pocket, then put on a face like my gut just sank. Nick's expression tells me not to bother; no one gets the benefit of the doubt on his watch. *All right*, I think. *So how about a little graft?* My fingers are closing in around the $100 bill when the stadium erupts. I look over at the scoreboard. *Touchdown!*

"Go birds," I shout.

My team spirit doesn't score any points with Nick.

"Ticket," he says.

But then a minor miracle happens: Nick gets a call on his radio. Through the crackle, I hear the words "Altercation . . . Two adult males . . ." Suddenly, I'm the least of his worries. He turns and runs toward the trouble. I've watched enough true crime to know that every investigation needs a few strokes of luck to help it along. I figure this is my first stroke.

I start down the concrete steps. Seat 1, Row 9. There it is, on the aisle. No need to maneuver across a row of drunken Eagles fans. People in the section are still standing, high-fiving each other. I slip into the spot where my John Doe would be standing. The young woman one seat over doesn't notice me. I lean into her space.

"How did they score?" I ask. "I missed it."

I'm thinking, *Blend in, Christian. Blend in.*

"Sixty yards to AJ Brown!" she screams.

Her long blond ponytail hangs out the back of an Eagles ball cap. She gives me a second look, then turns and whispers into the ear of the guy beside her. He cranes his neck until we're making eye contact.

"How do you know Nolan?" he asks, his voice booming with alcohol.

Nolan. I feel a quick rush of adrenaline. My John Doe now has a first name.

"I don't," I say. "Just got the ticket online."

He shrugs.

"Don't worry," he tells the woman sitting between us. "Nolan's probably holed up at a poker table in AC. It wouldn't be the first time."

A long, awkward silence follows. Awkward for me—I'm not sure my seatmates notice. Are these his coworkers? Could the woman next to me be his girlfriend? Would it be weird to ask? I'm struggling to come up with an icebreaker when she reaches down for her beer. There's a tattoo on the inside of her left wrist: the digits 3-0-2 scrawled in Gothic font. It's the only Wilmington area code.

"Hey, are you from Wilmington?" I ask, pointing to my own wrist.

"I am. How about you?"

"Born and raised. I live out in Rehoboth now, but I still do a lot of work in Wilmington."

"Really? What kind of work?"

"I own a few restaurants there," I tell her, trying to sound nonchalant.

Saying you own a restaurant is like a magic conversation starter. For some reason, people always want to know more.

"No shit," she says. "Which ones?"

"Big Fish, Mikimotos, Oyster Hou—"

She cuts me off before I can finish. "You're kidding! Nolan used to work at Mikimotos. We do happy hour at the bar all the time— love the California Dream!"

"Nolan . . . ?" I cock my head like I'm trying to place the name.

"Styer. Tall, brown hair, early twenties. Talks a mile a minute."

Nolan Styer. For a second, I feel winded. Restaurants are a high-turnover business. Plenty of new hires don't last a week. She might have hit on a hundred different names that meant nothing to me. But I remember Nolan.

"This guy owns Mikimotos," she tells her friends.

"No way! We love it there, dude," one of them shouts drunkenly across the two seats separating us. "We go there all the time."

"Great stuff," I say. "Listen, I've got to run to the bathroom."

The young woman nods, her focus already back on the game. Maybe I should stick around and keep asking questions, but I'm half dazed, and I've already learned more than I could have hoped for. The victim, if that's what he turns out to be, is someone who used to work for me.

I take the concrete steps two at a time, then stride past Nick without so much as a glance in his direction. *Nolan Styer.* He worked for me over two summers—one in the kitchen, one behind the bar. Always smiling. Always telling stories. I remember because he reminded me of Jon. Could it really have been Nolan I saw lying on those reeds? Could the world be that small? A young man is murdered and his former employer spots his body through a plane window? Part of me can't make it real, while another part—the larger part—knows that nothing else will matter until I've found out how and why Nolan died.

Outside, I run to my car, climb in behind the wheel, and call Claire.

"Yeah," she says, "I remember Nolan. A real sweetheart. Troubled, but sweet."

"Listen, I need his info. Can you send me his human resources file ASAP?"

She goes quiet for a second. "Has something happened? Why are you asking for an ex-employee's—"

"Just send me the file, okay?"

Shit. I didn't mean to snap at her.

"Are you all right?" she asks.

"Sorry, Claire. I've got a lot going on. I'll explain later."

The ten minutes it takes her to forward the file feel like an eternity. I scroll down to Nolan's address. A note says he lives with his mother. I wonder if that's still true—or still would have been true. I remember Mrs. Styer. She celebrated her fiftieth birthday at Mikimotos. She was the life of her own party, joking and laughing, getting up and moving around the large table to hold one-on-one conversations with each of her friends. Nolan served her an espresso martini while we all sang "Happy Birthday." Instead of blushing, Mrs. Styer stood and raised her arms like she was conducting a choir.

"Which one's the boss?" she asked when we were done.

Nolan pointed to me.

"Stop lying," she said. "He's barely old enough to drive."

I pull out of the Lincoln Field lot and start back toward Wilmington. I have what I came for. I have a name. But this isn't the victory I'd hoped for. Like Jon, Nolan had his whole life ahead of him. He was brimming with raw energy and potential. People liked him. They were drawn to him. Now his mother will be left wondering who he might have been.

CHAPTER TEN

I pull up in front of a brick row house in Downtown Wilmington, then double-check the address Claire gave me. The Styer residence has seen better days. The paint around the ground-floor windows is peeling badly, and the stoop's railing has turned to rust. The entire block of houses seems lopsided, like it's tilting downhill. I take a minute to gather my thoughts, then get out of the car, cross the sidewalk, and ring the bell.

I spent the drive from Philly deciding what I should and shouldn't say. I won't tell Mrs. Styer that I spotted her son's corpse lying in a patch of reeds on the Schuylkill. The evidence is mounting, but I didn't see a face, and I couldn't find the body. So I've come up with an alternate scenario to explain my visit. I'm launching a new location and want Nolan behind the bar. Customers love him, and no one makes a better martini. We were supposed to talk about it over lunch on Thursday, but he didn't show up. I tried calling him, but his voicemail was full. (That much is true; I dialed the number in the file Claire forwarded and was greeted by an automated message.) Then some friends of his stopped in for Mikimotos's happy hour and mentioned they couldn't get ahold of him. I thought I'd come by just to make sure everything was okay.

It's drizzling now, with thick gray clouds threatening a real downpour. Someone's home—I can hear a television blaring inside—but nobody's answering the bell. I'm about to try knocking when the door swings open. One look at me, and Mrs. Styer's face falls. It's clear she was hoping for somebody else. It's also clear that she doesn't recognize me. In her mind, I'm a stranger, and strangers only bring bad news.

"Yes?" she asks.

She's dressed like she's about to go out—short hair neatly coiffed, rouge and lipstick applied, black sneakers laced up—but the TV is still on and there's a smell of freshly brewed coffee. She must be keeping herself ready to leave at a moment's notice. In case the police call. Or the ER.

"Mrs. Styer," I say, "I'm Christian Stone, Nolan's former—"

"Oh, of course. I know you. God, where are my manners? Please, come in. And call me Evelyn. Can I get you anything? Coffee? I have a tin of shortbread someplace."

"I'm fine," I say. "I ate a late lunch."

She forces a smile, but as soon as the door's shut behind us, her expression turns to panic.

"Something's happened, hasn't it?" she asks. "To Nolan?"

I shrink the speech I'd prepared down to a few core essentials. "I don't know. That's why I'm here. We were supposed to meet for a drink last week, but he didn't show up. Later, some friends of his told me they couldn't get in touch with him."

She nods, then turns and walks into the living room. She sits in an old, afghan-covered recliner, gestures for me to take the love seat. The TV is tuned to a local newscast. There are two phones—one cordless, one mobile—at the ready on an end table beside the recliner.

"I haven't seen Nolan," she says, tugging at a pill in her sweater, "or heard from him since last Sunday. We had breakfast together before he left for the game."

"Is that unusual? For him to go a week without calling?"

"Usually, he doesn't have to call. He lives here. Well, downstairs, in the basement apartment. He pays rent. He's good about that, even if his work isn't always steady."

The television jumps in volume as the news switches to commercials. The noise startles her. She picks up a remote and hits the power button.

"You know," she says, "you're the second person to tell me Nolan missed an appointment this week."

"Who was the first?"

"Somebody calling himself a 'rounder.' I didn't know the term. Apparently, it means he plays poker professionally. Nolan is part of a Wednesday night game. That was the first I'd heard of it. I always thought Nolan was working on Wednesday nights."

A weekly poker game with a pro gambler sounds like a potential lead. Unpaid debts. Unhappy backers. Accusations of cheating. Tempers flare when the stakes are high. There's no shortage of possible motives.

"Did this rounder give you his name?"

"Just a first name. I think it was Bill. Or Will. Some shorthand for William."

"How did he get in touch with you?"

I tried looking up Mrs. Styer on my way over here. I couldn't find her number listed anywhere. I doubt Nolan was in the habit of giving it out to his poker pals.

"He called me on my work cell. Styer Studios."

She nods toward a framed black-and-white photo hanging above the television set. It's a picture of a young girl in a summer dress running through the spray from an open fire hydrant.

"I'm a photographer. Family portraits, weddings. When I was young, I saw myself traveling the world for *National Geographic*. I guess nothing ever turns out the way you planned it."

I have a feeling she's thinking about Nolan when she says this. I have a feeling it's been a while since she's thought about anything but Nolan.

"Geez," she says, "I'm just opening right up, saying anything that comes into my head. I'm sorry. I'm not myself lately. Are you sure I can't get you anything?"

"I'm fine, really. The truth is, I'm worried about Nolan too."

This seems to give her some small comfort.

"At least that makes two of us," she says. "Nolan's friends told me the same thing they told you. They can't get ahold of him. One of them tried to console me by saying he was probably just on a bender. She didn't use that word, but she might as well have. And the police want no part of Nolan. Or of me."

"You filed a missing person report?"

"I tried—on Thursday, after the poker player called. I went down to the station. A bored-looking detective with dandruff all over his blazer asked me a bunch of questions. He looked Nolan up in their 'system' and shook his head. I'm not going to lie: Nolan's been in trouble before. Nothing big. No felonies or anything. Just petty this and petty that. Small quantities of drugs—*personal use*, they call it. Some shoplifting. One disorderly conduct. But whenever he crosses the line, I'm the one he calls to come bail him out. The fact that he hasn't called this time . . . I'm scared. I'm really scared. He's my only child. His father's been dead almost twenty years. I don't know what I'd do if . . ."

She pulls a handkerchief out of her pocket and dabs her eyes. I reach across and touch her arm. I'm feeling guilty as hell. The body in the Eagles jersey, the ticket, the fact that no one's heard from Nolan in a week—coincidences don't come that big. I have no doubt her son is dead. But nothing has changed: I didn't see a face; I didn't find the body. I can't claim to know for sure. The best I can do for Evelyn is to find out what happened to her son.

"I want to help you," I say.

She locks eyes with me. Her look says, *I'm going to hold you to that.*

"How?"

"There are people I can talk to."

She nods. "Nolan told me. He said lots of big shots came by the restaurant. People he recognized from the local news."

"I don't know how much sway I hold, but I'll do what I can."

Evelyn isn't convinced. She's been on the wrong end of vague promises before. What she wants now is action. She holds out the cordless phone. "You can call from here," she says.

I shake my head. "I need more information first."

"What kind of information?"

This is the opening I've been waiting for since she first mentioned the mother-in-law suite.

"Would you mind showing me Nolan's apartment?" I ask.

Evelyn doesn't need to think it over. I'm the closest thing she's had to hope since her son went missing.

"Just wait here," she says. "I'll get the key."

CHAPTER
ELEVEN

Nolan's basement apartment is more man cave than mother-in-law unit. Faux-wood paneling, blue shag carpet, pipes running up into the main house. A single half window near the ceiling lets in a sliver of natural light. For furniture, there's just a dresser and a convertible sofa with the bed open and unmade. A television meant for a much larger space hangs on one wall, a framed Eagles program with a cover photo of Donovan McNabb and his mother sharing a bowl of Campbell's soup on another. The kitchen area consists of a microwave and a dorm-sized fridge stacked beside the sink. A mousetrap lies near a hole in the baseboards, sprung but empty.

"This is Nolan's little world," Evelyn says. "I try never to come down here."

I assume she's apologizing for the knee-high heap of clothes on the floor and the crushed beer cans scattered across the room.

"So it's all right if I poke around a bit?" I ask.

"Please," she says. "Just pretend I'm not here."

I step over to the dresser. The top is cluttered with toiletries. Nolan placed a lot of importance on how he smelled. There's English Leather aftershave, Prada cologne, a refillable Swagger by Old Spice. His collection of hair gels could stock a shelf at CVS.

I open the first drawer. To my surprise, its contents are neatly ordered—socks folded in matching pairs on the left-hand side, impeccably ironed black T-shirts on the right side. I pull out one of the shirts and shake it open, then do a double take when I see the logo printed across the chest: SCOTCHED UP. Scotched Up is a high-end bar owned by none other than Morelli Capital, aka Dax Morelli.

"I had no idea Nolan was working at Scotched Up," I say.

Evelyn, who remains standing in the doorway as though she's afraid of crossing into her son's lair, lets out a long sigh.

"He told me he had three shifts there a week," she says. "But apparently on Wednesdays, he was off gambling."

"He was tending bar?"

She nods.

"When did he start?"

"Around the time he started paying me rent. Maybe four months ago?"

"Was it going well?"

She nods. "Especially the last six weeks or so. He met a girl there. Ashley, a fellow bartender. He brought her home once—just for a few minutes, but I liked her. You can tell she's good with people. Easy to talk to, and you get the feeling she listens. Cute too. Short brown hair, bright blue eyes. A kind of devilish grin. I was hoping she might be a good influence on Nolan, but then something happened between them. He came home really upset after his shift. I don't know if they broke up or just had a fight. He wouldn't tell me."

"But you're sure he was upset about Ashley?"

"Yes. That much was clear."

"When was this?"

"A day or two before he left for Atlantic City."

"Any chance they patched things up?"

"I really couldn't say."

But Ashley could. I'll have to make a fact-finding trip to Scotched Up, overpriced drinks and pretentious hors d'oeuvres be damned. For now, I try to set aside my deep distrust of Dax Morelli. The fact that his name has surfaced is most likely a coincidence. And not even a very big coincidence. There are only so many bars in Wilmington, and Morelli Capital owns more than its fair share.

In the next drawer, I discover a robust library dedicated to a single subject: poker. *Mastering Poker Math*, *Practical Poker*, *Tournament Poker: A Comprehensive Guide*. There must be twenty or thirty slim paperbacks, all with creased spines and dog-eared pages. I take one up at random and flip through. The margins are crammed with notes written in tiny cursive. The concerned call from the rounder makes sense now. Nolan had a passion. Or maybe an addiction.

The third and final drawer houses two stacks of collectible luxury-car magazines. I pull one out and thumb through the cellophane-wrapped issues. *Motor Life*, *Jaguar*, *The Motorcar*—none more recent than the early seventies. A 1957 issue of *Custom Rodder* features an illustration of a regal-looking two-tone Chevy on the cover. The lead story is titled "Do Your Own Professional Pin-Striping for $2."

I turn back to Evelyn.

"He's got some real classics here," I say.

"Nolan calls it his 'side hustle.' He buys and sells on eBay."

"He must know a thing or two about cars. What kind does he drive?"

Evelyn laughs. "The public bus," she says. "Uber, in a pinch. Same as me."

I take that for good news. I have one less place to search, one less thread to keep track of.

I cross the room and open the closet door. It's narrow and not very deep, but two items of interest jump out at me. The first is a shiny new pair of Dolce & Gabbana sneakers. The second is a leopard-print shirt, also by D&G. I'm no fashion expert, but I know the brand's reputation. Either business was booming at Scotched Up or Nolan's poker studies were paying dividends.

A side of Nolan is emerging, one I didn't notice when he worked at Mikimotos. He was attracted to the finer things. Or at least the flashier things. He lived in his mom's basement but had an appetite for vintage cars, fancy clothes, and high-stakes poker. Who he was and who he wanted to be were miles apart. Maybe the gambling was supposed to bridge the gap. Maybe he saw himself as the next Phil Hellmuth, a college dropout who walked away from the World Series of Poker a millionaire. When you're young, you expect a big life. You spend time deciding who should play you in the movie. It's a phase Nolan will never get the chance to outgrow.

The leopard-print shirt looks crumpled, like it's been worn and is waiting for a trip to the dry cleaners. I reach inside the breast pocket and feel some kind of plastic card wrapped in a thin sheet of paper. I pull out the paper and plastic and step back into the light. I'm holding a Borgata player's card and a receipt from the Old Homestead. I've been to the Borgata. It's a casino in Atlantic City. I stayed in its hotel and ate in its steak house, the Old Homestead. Casinos don't come any swanker. A dozen gourmet restaurants to choose from. Indoor and outdoor pools. A two-story spa. A barbershop that charges by the minute. A fitness center that looks like something out of *Blade Runner*. And a poker room that hosts some of the world's premier tournaments.

I scan the receipt and see that Nolan dropped $70 on a rib steak and $100 more on drinks. I take another look around his basement dwelling. Shabby doesn't begin to cover it. The Borgata must have felt like a secret life for Nolan. *The Talented Mr. Styer*. I read the date on the receipt. It's just ten days old.

"Did Nolan go to Atlantic City often?" I ask.

She rolls her eyes. "Far more often than I would have liked."

"According to this receipt, he was down there just before he went missing."

"He came back late Saturday. If it hadn't been for the Eagles game, I'm sure he would have stayed through the weekend."

"Why do you say that?"

"He seemed preoccupied, like his mind was still at the tables. I don't know if he has a harder time tearing himself away when he's winning or losing."

"So it's fair to say he has a problem?"

"God, yes. Just like his father. I tried everything imaginable. With both of them. I guess addiction really is in the blood, because Nolan was a baby when Paul died."

"Does Nolan have any other addictions?"

She shuffles her feet, keeps her eyes on the floor.

"I told you he'd been arrested," she says. "But the last time was more than a year ago. It's not like with gambling. He dabbles. Sometimes he binges. But he can go for long stretches without touching the stuff."

"Pills?"

She shakes her head. "Worse."

I'm guessing she means heroin, but I don't want to press.

"I'm sorry," I say. "I had to ask. It doesn't change anything. For me, I mean."

I'm on the verge of wrapping up my search when I spot a power cord sticking out from under a blanket on the bed. I pull the blanket back and find a MacBook Air with an Eagles decal covering the Apple logo. My heart rate ticks up a notch. Emails, credit cards, bank accounts, calendars, social media. Most people lay their souls bare on their laptops without even realizing it. I flip the lid open and am greeted by a full-screen photo of a royal flush. In the foreground, a pop-up window demands either a fingerprint or a password. I glance back at Evelyn.

"Do you have any idea what his password might be?"

She shrugs. "All I can say for sure is that he'd pick something I'd never guess. He's caught me snooping. More than once."

Computers aren't my strong suit, but Big Ocean has an IT wizard on the payroll. Doug Spooner, aka Spooner. Self-taught, without a diploma to his name. If Spooner's ambition matched his ability, he'd be king of Silicon Valley by now.

"Would you mind if I took this with me?" I ask. "I know someone who can—"

She cuts me off with a shake of her head. "I don't think that's a good idea. What if Nolan comes home and it isn't here? Showing you around his room is one thing, but letting you take his property? He might forgive me, but he'd never forget."

I feel a dizzying rush of guilt. Nolan won't be coming home; I'm as close to certain as I can be. But I didn't see his face. I didn't find his body. My only option is to say nothing until I have proof. I won't tell Evelyn what I saw from seat 3A, but I won't pretend to believe that Nolan is alive either. That's the deal I make with myself.

"I understand," I say. "But there's bound to be information on his computer that will help us. Some hint about where he went after the game. Who he was with. Once I have that information, I can convince other people to get involved. People with resources."

She looks at me like she's trying to decide once and for all whether I can be trusted. There are tears gathering in the corners of her eyes.

"Take it," she says. "You might learn some things Nolan would rather no one knew. Things I'd rather not know. But he's in trouble. I feel it."

I wish I had some comfort to offer her.

"I can get you into his hard drive," Spooner says. "No problem. It's just a question of plugging in the right software."

We're sitting in his office, on opposite sides of the drafting table he uses for a desk. Spooner's been with Big Ocean for five years now, and there isn't a single personal item anywhere in sight. Not a photo, or a trophy, or a poster, or a plant. Not even a bank calendar. Spooner's a big believer in the simple life: The less you have, the less you stand to lose.

"What about email accounts? Bank accounts? Credit cards? I want access to anything that requires a password."

"That would take a little longer."

"How long?"

"I'm about to head over to Oyster House to update their—"

"Updates can wait. This is the only priority right now."

He shrugs. One task is as good as another for Spooner.

"In that case, twenty-four hours, give or take. But can I ask what this is about?"

I settle on a version of the truth. "Nolan's mother is a friend of mine. She's worried. No one's seen or heard from him in over a week. The cops think he's probably out on a bender. Nolan has a bit of a history."

"And you're searching for some clue as to where he might be?"

I nod.

"Sounds like a good cause," Spooner says. "But you know this isn't exactly legal, right? What if the kid turns up and—"

"Your name will never be mentioned. I promise."

He leans back and runs a hand over his shaved scalp while he weighs the pros and cons.

"Yeah, all right," he says. "Better let me get to it."

———

I pull into the parking garage across the street from Scotched Up at a little after 4 p.m. I know from Evelyn that Ashley works nights. Post lunch and pre–happy hour, I doubt I'll have much trouble getting in a few private words with the bartender. Not to mention that this is the Monday after an Eagles-Cowboys game, and Wilmington's nursing a collective hangover.

Whoever Dax hired to design Scotched Up did a first-rate job. As you step inside, you feel like you're leaving Wilmington and entering a 1940s film set. Slate-gray walls, tessellated floor, a single candle flickering at the center of every table. A vintage player piano taps out Jazz Age ballads in a far corner of the room. It's high class from top to bottom, the kind of establishment where patrons talk in whispers even after their fourth round.

As anticipated, it's empty at this hour. Ashley's standing alone behind the bar, wearing the standard-issue black T-shirt and scrolling on her phone. She looks exactly as Evelyn described her: light brown pixie-style hair, crystalline blue eyes, a resting grin that suggests she's thinking something she'd rather not share. I take a stool and drum my fingers against the bar. Ashley glances up, startled, then slips her phone into the small pocket of her apron alongside a packet of cigarettes. She clearly wasn't expecting company for a while yet.

"What can I get for you, sir?" she asks.

I'm guessing the *sir* is mandated by Dax.

"Just a glass of house white."

"Coming right up."

She flashes a warm smile, but I can't help feeling self-conscious. If I were her, I'd be thinking something along the lines of *What's this guy in jeans and a windbreaker doing alone in an upscale whiskey bar at four in the afternoon?* It's a good question. I could cut to the chase and tell her what I told Spooner: *Nolan's missing; I'm helping his mother look for him.* But Nolan isn't just missing—he's dead. According to Evelyn, he was a user. For all I know, Ashley was using with him. Maybe he OD'd. Maybe Ashley's afraid of implicating herself. I need to start slow, feel her out.

"Here you are," she says, setting my drink on a coaster in front of me. I recognize her expression from my own time tending bar. She's sizing me up, gauging whether I want to talk or sit quietly with my thoughts. I help her along by making the first move.

"Nolan Styer works here, doesn't he?"

"You know Nolan?" she asks.

"From his days at Mikimotos. I'm the owner."

"Oh, nice. Nolan loved it there. He says it has a really fun vibe."

"We try. But Nolan brings his own fun. Does he still talk the customers' ears off?"

She laughs. If the subject of her recent ex bothers her, she isn't giving any sign.

"When he finds one who will listen," she says. "The clientele in this place can be a little . . ."

"A little what?"

She bites her lip.

"Believe me," I tell her. "I've heard it all."

She hesitates a beat longer.

"Well, they're corporate types," she says. "We're the help, you know? It's like we only exist when we get something wrong."

I take this as a good omen. She's already determined that I'm not the *corporate type*. Dax, on the other hand . . . I figure her boss is one more shared acquaintance for us to bond over.

"They say the vibe starts at the top."

She looks at me like she doesn't follow.

"I can't imagine Dax Morelli being very generous with *the help*," I say.

She shrugs. "I wouldn't know—he's almost never here. And when he does come in, it's more like he's using the place as an office. He and his lawyer take the four-seater by the piano and sit there with a stack of documents between them."

"His lawyer?"

Morelli Capital has an army of legal aid. If Dax is meeting with a lawyer off-site, it's for personal reasons. Maybe his wife has finally had enough?

"I think she's his lawyer. Nolan isn't so sure."

"Why not?"

She starts to answer, then reverses course like she's wary of saying too much. "It's stupid. You know Nolan. He's a gossip hound. He likes to tell stories."

Yes, I think. *But this time it's probably a true story.*

"Let me guess: Nolan thinks the documents are a ruse. He thinks happily married Dax is having an affair."

"How'd you know?"

I shrug. "I'd probably have my suspicions too."

"It's true they never seem to be looking at the documents," Ashley says. "What's strange, though, is that it bothers Nolan so much. He gets all quiet whenever they show up. It's like he takes it personally—like he thinks Dax is cheating on *him*."

I'm not sure what to make of that. "Do they come in often? Dax and his maybe-lawyer?"

"Not really. At least not when I'm working."

"When was the last time you saw them?"

"Maybe two weeks ago? It had to have been a Friday because Nolan was with me behind the bar."

If nothing else, my curiosity is piqued. Could there be a connection? Is the world that small? I doubt it, but Wilmington might be. Still, Dax stepping out on his wife isn't exactly news, and Nolan did have a penchant for gossip. For now, I file it away under "interesting, but probably irrelevant."

I take a sip of wine and glance around the bar. Apart from a young man folding napkins at a table in the corner, Ashley and I still have the place to ourselves. But happy hour is just around the corner. Soon, the room will start to fill up. It's time to press on. I agree with Evelyn—Ashley seems like good people. Everything she's said about Nolan has been in the present tense. She doesn't know he's dead. If I had to guess, I'd say she's thinking of whatever happened between them as a speed bump rather than a permanent state of affairs. I lean forward and lower my voice.

"Listen," I say. "I'm friends with Evelyn, Nolan's mom. I don't want to scare you, but she's worried. She hasn't heard from Nolan in over a week, and he isn't answering his phone. I told her I'd ask around. Do you have any idea where he might be?"

I expect Ashley's next words to be *Atlantic City*. Instead, she goes silent. The color drains from her face, and she grabs on to the edge of the bar for support.

"What's wrong?" I ask.

"Oh my God," she says.

"What? What is it?"

"I'm such an asshole."

"What do you mean?"

"I shouldn't have listened to him. I should have gone straight to the police."

"About what?"

She tries to answer, but she's on the verge of hyperventilating.

"Easy," I say. "Deep breaths."

Her arms are trembling. Her hand goes instinctively to the pack of cigarettes in her apron.

"Why don't we get some air?" I say. "Is there someone here who can cover for you?"

She gestures to the young man folding napkins. He drops what he's doing and comes trotting over.

"Sorry to bother you, Frank," she says, "but would you mind covering for a minute? I'm feeling kind of queasy."

Frank looks around at the empty room as if to say nothing in the world could be easier. I follow Ashley outside. My own breathing is shaky, and my heart's skipping beats. I have a strong feeling that I'm about to learn exactly how Nolan came to be lying in a bed of reeds by the Schuylkill.

THIRTEEN

"**B**y the time we'd finished cleaning and restocking the bar, it was three in the morning. Maybe a little later," Ashley says.

She pauses to take a drag off her cigarette. We're leaning against a brick wall in the alley beside Scotched Up, sheltered from a strong fall breeze. Ashley looks paler in daylight. The circles under her eyes look a shade darker. Maybe it isn't the change in lighting so much as the change in mood. She's afraid now. Afraid for Nolan—and afraid that whatever happened to him is her fault.

"He walked me to my car," she continues. "I was going to give him a lift home. He wanted to stay at my place."

She glances over at me.

"It isn't . . . he wasn't being inappropriate. We were together. Not for long, but I guess because we knew each other from work, it started to feel serious right away."

I nod. I don't say that I knew they were dating. I want Ashley to tell her story. The less I interrupt, the more naturally it will flow, almost like I'm not here.

"Anyway, I always park in the garage across the street. That afternoon, it was nearly full. I had to take a space on the roof. I hate that, because by the time my shift ends, it's empty. There isn't even an attendant after midnight. That's kind of how Nolan and I got together. He used to walk me to my car even before we were a thing. Sometimes we'd sit there talking—not about anything in particular, just chatting. One night, before either of us realized it, the sun was up. Afterward, we didn't have to say it out loud—we just knew. We were a couple."

I get the feeling she's stalling. Whatever happened on the night in question, Ashley isn't anxious to relive it. She takes another puff from her cigarette, then holds it out and looks at it like she's seeing it for the first time.

"It's funny," she says. "Nolan's always trying to get me to quit, but he has his own bad habits. At least smoking is legal. I can walk into a pharmacy and buy a pack of menthols. I don't have to look over my shoulder and wonder who's . . ."

Her voice trails off as though the thought is too ugly to finish.

"What happened that night, Ashley?" I ask.

She takes a minute—not for dramatic effect, but more like she's trying to work through the timeline in her head.

"We'd just gotten to my car. Like I said, it was up on the roof of the garage. I don't know where the guy came from. The place seemed totally empty. I remember our voices echoing as we walked up through the levels. But then, as soon as I turned the key in the ignition, I heard this screeching sound, and when I looked in my rearview mirror, there was a black sedan boxing us in. I thought we were being carjacked. I started to hit the horn—I read that you should make as much noise as possible—but Nolan grabbed my hand. He was like, 'Just stay calm, and I'll take care of it.' He said it would be over in a minute. Before I could ask what 'it' was, he got out of the car.

"I turned around in my seat and watched. There was only the driver in the sedan. He got out too. He was smaller than Nolan, but when you looked at the two of them, you could tell that didn't matter. Nolan was scared. He couldn't hold still. He kept gesturing and talking a mile a minute like he was trying to convince the guy that really they were pals. But the guy wasn't buying it. He was the picture of calm. I don't think he said a word. He just stood there, waiting. Nolan's hands were shaking so hard that he had trouble pulling out his wallet. When he did, the guy snatched it from him. He took the cash from the billfold—we made about three hundred apiece that night—then tossed the wallet on the ground and grabbed Nolan by the throat. He must have hit some kind of pressure point because Nolan went straight to his knees. This time I did hit the horn. I dug in with the heel of my palm and didn't let up. The guy took his hand off Nolan's throat and turned to look at me. He held a finger to his lips. Then he walked around to my side of the car. By the time I'd made sure the doors were locked, he was standing right there, staring down at me.

"I thought he was after my money. I was waiting for him to smash out the window and grab me by the hair. Instead, he held up his phone and took my picture. He did it so quick I didn't have time to turn my head away. Then he walked very casually back to his car, got behind the wheel, and sped off. At first, I felt relieved that he was gone, but then I realized how freaky the picture thing was. I mean, why would he do that unless he was planning to track me down later?

"I wanted to run to Nolan, but when I looked, I saw he was already on his feet. He kind of staggered back to his door and started pulling on the handle. I was so jittery that I couldn't find the passenger-side lock. I was pressing every button in sight. Windows were going up and down. There were clicking noises all over the car. When Nolan finally got inside, he just sat there massaging his throat. I asked if he was okay. He told me to start driving. I told him we weren't going anywhere until I knew who that guy was and what he wanted. But Nolan wouldn't answer me.

"'Fine,' I told him. 'Have it your way.'

"I took out my phone. He grabbed it from my hands before I could start dialing. That's when I lost it. I began wailing on him with both fists and screaming at the top of my lungs, 'Who was that? What the fuck is going on?' Nolan grabbed hold of my wrists. In this really quiet voice, he said, 'Look, I did something stupid. I owe money. But I'm dealing with it. That's all I can say for now. I don't want you involved.'

"That was more than I could take. I was like, 'You don't want me involved? He took my picture, Nolan. What is that supposed to mean? If you don't pay him, he's going to come kill me? I think I'm pretty fucking involved.'

"Then Nolan did something he never does—he went silent. A total shutdown, like he wasn't even there. Like he'd gone dead inside. I freaked. I told him I didn't care what he said, I *had* to call the police. He snapped out of it then.

"'Do that,' he said, 'and it's me they'll lock up.'

"I kept asking him, 'Why? What's going on? Just tell me what's happening.' But he wouldn't even look at me. I got so angry that I could actually feel my blood heating up.

"'Fine,' I told him. 'I won't call the cops. I won't ask any more questions. Now get out of my car.'

"I said whatever he was mixed up in, I didn't want any part of it. I said I never wanted to see him again. But I didn't think he'd actually get out. I was trying to push him. Make him talk. But . . ."

"He got out?"

She nods. The tears she's been holding back are starting to spill from the corners of her eyes.

"And I haven't seen him since," she says. "Not even at work. For all I know, that psychopath was waiting outside the garage. If I had just given Nolan a ride . . ."

At least I can put her mind at ease about that much.

"You said this was two weeks ago?" I ask.

"Yes."

"Nolan made it home safe that night. I know for a fact that he went to the Eagles game the following Sunday. Whatever happened, it's not your fault."

She wipes her eyes with the heel of one palm.

"Okay," she says. "Thank you."

I give her a second to gather herself, then ask, "Do you think you could describe the man?"

She shakes her head. "His face was mostly in shadow, and he was wearing a hat—one of those 1920s caps like they wear in *Peaky Blinders*. Plus, I was scared out of my mind."

"What about his height? Build?"

"Maybe five nine? Definitely stocky. And square. Everything about him was square. His head, his shoulders. The way he carried himself."

"And his car? Did anything stand out? A dent, maybe? Or a busted taillight?"

"I caught a glimpse of the license plate as he was driving away. I didn't get the number, but I could tell it was out of state."

"You're sure?"

"It was a light color. White, or maybe beige."

New Jersey? I'm thinking of Atlantic City, Nolan's home away from home. I have a feeling I'll be visiting the Borgata in the very near future.

"I should tell all of this to the police, shouldn't I?" Ashley asks. "Now that I know Nolan's missing."

I shrug. I doubt she'd get a better reception at the precinct than Evelyn did, but then I have nothing but doubts when it comes to the Wilmington PD.

"That's up to you," I say.

She hesitates as though she's embarrassed to ask her next question. "Do you think I'm in danger?"

I can put her mind at ease on that front too.

"No," I say. "Whoever that man was, he just wanted to intimidate you. His business is with Nolan."

And it's concluded, I think.

She starts to light another cigarette, then stops herself.

"I need to get back," she says. "Frank's a sweetheart, but he can't handle anything more complicated than a rum and Coke."

I walk her around to the front. We swap phone numbers and promise to call each other if we learn anything. As the door swings shut behind her, I feel a fresh wave of guilt. Lying by omission is still lying. Like Evelyn, Ashley deserves the truth.

And you'll give them the truth, I tell myself. *Just as soon as you have all of it.*

CHAPTER

FOURTEEN

After I leave Ashley, I head across the street to the parking garage. A quick walk around the roof reveals no shortage of cameras. If the incident itself wasn't caught on video, then the black sedan must have been. Not that I'm expecting the footage to yield much. The guy Ashley described sounds like a pro. Chances are either those out-of-state tags were fake or the car was stolen.

I find the attendant reading a paperback in his kiosk. When he slides the window open, a gust of hot air smacks me in the face. I glance down and spot one of those old-fashioned space heaters with flaming-red coils. The man's made his own little sauna, probably to keep his blood circulating while he's trapped in a five-by-five box.

"Can I help you?" he asks, holding one finger tucked inside his paperback.

I make up a story. I say I left my car with a friend while I was out of town. He parked it here on a Friday night. When he came back, he found the rear bumper hanging by a thread. A hit and run. This was two weeks ago. Any chance the garage might still have the footage?

"Sorry," he says. "The tape records over itself every ten days."

Of course, I think. *That would have been too easy.*

The window slides shut before I can tell him to stay warm.

I'm halfway back to Rehoboth when the first drops start to fall.

Before long, it's like the wind is lifting up the ocean and dumping it on the highway. I lean out over the steering wheel and keep my eyes glued to the taillights of the car in front of me. Then my phone rings. A robotic female voice tells me it's Spooner calling. I reach up and tap the hands-free button on my mirror.

"Any luck?" I ask.

"All done," he says.

"Already?"

"The software did all the work. And it didn't have to work all that hard. Your boy used the same password for everything."

"Let me guess," I say. "Styer123?"

"No, NF0les4133. The *o* is a zero."

Nick Foles—the backup quarterback who led the Eagles to a surprise Super Bowl victory over the New England Patriots. Forty-one to thirty-three is the score they won by. Given enough time, I might have guessed it.

"You're my hero," I say. "Any chance I can pick the computer up tonight?"

"Mind swinging by my place?"

"See you in an hour."

He greets me at the door to his studio apartment with Nolan's laptop tucked under one arm. He's wrapped it in bubble wrap to protect it from the rain.

"I'd invite you in," he says, "but all I've got to drink is tap water and soy milk."

I tell him I'm happy braving the last of the storm.

———

As soon as I walk through my front door, something feels off. There's a glaring bare spot on the dining room wall. A picture is missing. A silver-framed painting of Rehoboth Beach at sunrise. At first, I think there's been a break-in. Then I remember that Quinn is gone, and she took the painting with her. We bought it together at the Rehoboth Beach Arts Festival to celebrate her moving-in day. Now it's hanging somewhere in her Chicago apartment.

I change into dry clothes, then microwave a slice of lasagna, pour myself a glass of wine, and settle down at the kitchen counter with my dinner and Nolan's laptop. My hands are a little unsteady as I tear off Spooner's bubble wrap. It's the kind of nervousness you feel when you're watching someone who doesn't know they're being watched. There's a thrill in thinking that you're about to discover their secret self, the part of them they keep hidden from the world. But it's also scary, because whatever that person's secret is—good or bad—you can never unknow it. And in this case, I'm searching for Nolan's darkest, ugliest secret. A secret dark enough and ugly enough to get him killed.

I open the lid, hit the space bar, then type in *NF0les4133*. His desktop is a welter of blue folders set against an idyllic picture of sand dunes and clear sky—the factory-issued, default background. A few of the folders have typical titles—Job Apps, Tax docs, Photos: Las Vegas, Photos: NY. The rest give me reason to suspect that Nolan's gambling addiction was worse than either Evelyn or Ashley knew. NASCAR, OTB, Boxing, MMA, MLB, NBA, NFL. If you can bet on it, Nolan kept files on it.

Because I have to start somewhere, I open the folder labeled MLB. It contains subfolders for all thirty teams. I click on Phillies. Nolan created a document for every player on the roster. I choose one at random, a reliever whose name I don't recognize. The document is a spreadsheet. The sheer number of columns and rows is dizzying. Nolan logged the pitcher's stats against every active player in both leagues. Not just hits, walks, and outs, but also the percentage of curveballs, fastballs, and sliders thrown—at night, during the day, at home, away—to the starting and backup catchers.

At the bottom of the screen, the columns and rows give way to boxes of text. One box is titled Injuries, another Intangibles, another Temperament. This particular pitcher is prone to bone spurs. His pace slows with runners in scoring position. He has a DUI. He was involved in an altercation in a Chicago bar. He performs best in small-market venues, where nightlife is minimal.

I go back to the desktop and open Poker: Online. Nolan created a spreadsheet for each of the last five years. I select the most recent. At first glance, it looks like an HR payroll form. The columns from left to right are labeled Date/Hours/Buy In/Profit/Hourly Rate. There's a separate spreadsheet for each quarter of the year. In the first quarter alone, Nolan spent nearly six hundred hours playing online poker. His final hourly rate was in the black at $3.15/hr. Not enough to quit his bartending gig, but I'm sure he thought he would get there. He was determined to beat chance with science, and no one can say he didn't put the work in. I wonder how he might have done if he'd focused his appetite for risk on the stock market.

I navigate over to Safari. Nolan's bookmarks track closely with the contents of his dresser and his desktop. Poker tutorials; online poker sites; off-track betting; eBay: Collectible Vehicle Magazines; the Borgata. I click on the Gmail bookmark, and his account opens right up. He has two weeks' worth of unread messages and three years' worth of undeleted messages. Most are bait-and-switch offers from betting sites he'd subscribed to. A few are from Ashley. For now, I don't see any point in reading them.

After hours of searching, I arrive where I probably should have started—the trash bin. No one ever remembers to empty their trash bin. The title Do NOT Ignore catches my eye. I click on it, and a Word document fills the screen. The text comprises two brief sentences. Each letter is a different color, different size, different font.

HAVE 100K CASH ReADY FOR ME WITHIN 48 HOURS OR I gO PUBLIC. I'LL BE IN TOUCH WITH TIME AND LOCATION.

I think, *Holy shit.*

I read the words over until I have them memorized. Then I comb Nolan's hard drive for the second note, the one with the time and location. It's nowhere to be found. Which leaves me with a very important question: Was Nolan the sender or receiver? The blackmailer or the blackmailed? Was the thug from the parking lot demanding $100,000, or was Nolan demanding the cash he needed to pay the thug off? The second option makes more sense. The man in the *Peaky Blinders* cap wasn't worried about remaining anonymous, and based on Ashley's retelling, he was threatening something much worse than "going public."

Easy, Christian, I tell myself. *For all you know, this could be some kind of prank.*

But given where Nolan ended up, that seems unlikely. I click on File, then select Properties from the drop-down menu. I learn that the note was created on November 3 and modified the next day. My flight to Miami was on the fifth.

Holy shit.

No way this was a joke—coincidences don't come that big. I click on the Summary tab in the Properties box, but I'm out of luck. The line marked Author is blank. I still don't know for sure if Nolan downloaded the document or created it. Maybe there's another, more tech-savvy way to find out. My first call in the morning will be to Spooner.

I walk over to my vision board and take up a piece of chalk. Under the *WHAT I KNOW SO FAR* column I write: *Ransom note demanding 100K created two days before Nolan's body spotted from plane.* Under the *WHAT I DON'T KNOW YET* column I write: *Who sent/received note.* I'm about to write *Go public with what?* when my phone rings. I check the number. It's Evelyn. At a quarter to midnight. My first thought is *They've found him.* I can't answer fast enough.

"I'm sorry to be calling so late," she says. "I figured if you were asleep, you wouldn't—"

"It's fine, Evelyn. Is everything all right?"

"Yes, yes. I was just wondering if you had anything to report. And I guess I wanted to hear a sympathetic voice. So far, you're the only person who believes Nolan's in danger. My so-called friends say he'll be home once his money runs out. They don't phrase it like that, but that's what they mean."

I try to hide my disappointment; it's clear she doesn't have any news of her own to deliver. I tell her I stopped by Scotched Up. I give her a soft version of what Ashley told me.

"She said a guy came by the bar looking to collect a debt. Nolan was able to pay him some, but not all. Nolan wouldn't tell her who the guy was or how much he owed."

"Why in the world didn't he ask me for help?"

"Maybe he was embarrassed."

"Nolan? That would be a first."

We go quiet for a beat. I hear her TV playing in the background, still tuned to the news.

"Evelyn," I say, "just how much do you know about Nolan's gambling?"

"He's like his father. He tries to hide it from me. Until he can't. Why? What have you found out?"

I tell her about the spreadsheets—the endless, meticulous research. The hours he logged playing poker. For now, I don't mention the ransom note. I don't want to hurt her. But I don't want to give her false hope either. I already know how this ends. Evelyn has an inkling too.

"It's bad, isn't it?" she says. "It's very, very bad."

I wish I could disagree.

We talk a while longer before saying good night. An hour later, I'm lying under the covers with my eyes shut and Evelyn's voice still buzzing in my head. Except that it isn't quite her voice. It's a little too deep, a little too self-assured. Eventually, it dawns on me: I'm hearing Jon's mother, a woman I haven't seen or spoken to in twenty-five years. She tells me I'm lucky—I've been gifted a second chance.

You're a man now, she says. *No excuses.*

FIFTEEN

2000

I'd just turned eighteen. In a week's time, I'd be unpacking my things in a Virginia Tech dorm room. It was the moment I'd been waiting for since high school's opening bell. The moment I thought would never come. But now that it was here, I couldn't get rid of the nagging sensation that I had unfinished business in Wilmington. There was someone I had to see. A confession I had to make before I could leave home behind.

It was my first time walking to Jon's house in six years. After the shooting, my parents forbid me to set foot in *that neighborhood*. As though it were the neighborhood—and not the cops—that killed Jon. *Cops*, plural. The one who pulled the trigger, and the rest who covered it up. According to the official reports, Jon aided and abetted a man named Seth Herron in the robbery and murder of a liquor store owner, then opted to die by gun rather than face prison. He was allegedly brandishing a palm-sized 9mm. They had to say "brandishing" because ballistics would have shown the weapon hadn't been fired. It was all bullshit. Jon didn't know any Seth Herron, and he'd never touched a gun in his life. Which means that one of Wilmington's finest knelt beside his body, placed the 9mm in his hand, and wrapped his fingers around the handle.

I turned a corner and did a double take when I saw that the abandoned lot was now a communal garden. There were flower beds and vegetable patches and even a small pond dotted with lily pads. Jon wouldn't have approved. He liked the old lot—the one that looked like a film still from every postapocalypse movie ever made. Rubble and ash. Gutted appliances. Rats scurrying to and fro. Small clearings where the homeless made fires at night. It used to creep me out. I always tried to hurry us across to the other side, but there was no rushing Jon. He'd lift up bricks and burned-out tires and search underneath like we were on a treasure hunt. One time he found a syringe, another time a busted pocket watch. You could tell he was taking mental notes. Where I saw danger and destruction, he saw characters and plotlines.

I lingered for a while in the shade of a ginkgo tree and watched an elderly couple cull their tomato patch. It was a stifling late-August day, and I was happy to take my time. The thing about confessing is that you might not be forgiven. I didn't know if I could handle that.

The last time I saw Ms. Evans, Jon's mother, was at our house. It was early in the morning, more than a week after Jon died. I answered the door in my pajamas. I remember her looking as though she'd been caught in a downpour, though it wasn't raining out. Her skin, her hair, her clothes—everything about her seemed to be drowning under some invisible weight. It was clear she hadn't slept. I doubt she'd stopped crying. My mother heard her voice and came charging in from the kitchen. She told me to go to my room. When I started to protest, she shouted at me. She was scared. She was looking at Ms. Evans and imagining how easily their roles might have been reversed.

I retreated to the top of the stairs, then stood there listening. At first, Ms. Evans did all the talking. Then I heard my mother say, "How can he be a witness when he wasn't there?"

"A character witness. He knew Jon. They were together that afternoon."

I willed myself to head back downstairs. Part of me wanted so badly to confess. *You're nothing. You're nobody.* In my mind, it was those words—my words—that killed Jon. I owed it to him to come clean. But my mother wasn't the only one who was scared. My heart was pounding so hard that I could feel the reverberations everywhere in my body. When I tried to take a step, my legs wouldn't budge.

"That's not who my boy was," Ms. Evans said.

"I'm sorry," my mother said. "I'm so, so sorry. But I don't see how Christian can help."

She couldn't see because I'd barely spoken a word since Jon died, not to anyone but Gloria. I hadn't told my mother about being jumped. I hadn't told her about seeing Jon's body. By the time I made it home, my parents already knew he was dead. My father had gone looking for me. My mother was waiting by the door. She had her arms around me before I could say a thing. After that, I kept quiet. All night long, I let Mom and Dad do the talking.

Over the following days and weeks, Ms. Evans became just one more mother screaming that her son had been a good boy. A single mother who worked nights. Journalists and news anchors called Jon a "latchkey kid." They painted a picture of neglect. They made Jon's violent death seem inevitable. Meanwhile, the cops who killed him were put on desk duty until the internal investigation was finished. It took all of a week. One local paper ran the headline "Righteous Shooting" above a photo of two grinning boys in blue.

———

As I climbed the stoop, I noticed that the downstairs windows had no shades. I peered into the living room and saw Ms. Evans in overalls, a bandanna wrapped around her head and a paintbrush in one hand. The floor was covered in a canvas tarp, and the furniture was gone. When I rang the bell, she looked up to the heavens as if to say *What now?* But when she opened the door and saw me standing there, all of her stress seemed to melt away.

"My God," she said. "Christian? Look at you. You're all grown up."

She started to hug me, then pulled back.

"I'm covered in paint," she said. "But come in, come in."

Her bandanna was sweated through, and her face was glistening, but she still had that instant charisma I'd fallen for as a preteen, the smile that made you feel like everything would be okay as long as she was in the room. After Jon's death, I'd heard more than one adult say that a parent never recovers from the loss of a child, and I took them at their word. I had visions of a skeletal Ms. Evans sitting in a rocking chair with an afghan pulled over her knees and a vacant expression on her face. But if anything, she seemed younger now, probably because the last time I'd seen her she was a foot taller than me.

As soon as I stepped inside, it became clear she wasn't just renovating. The front hallway was crowded with columns of boxes. I could see more at the top of the stairs and in the dining room. The cinnamon smell I remembered was masked by paint, and the framed photos were all packed away.

"You're moving?" I asked.

"Yeah, it's time. It's past time."

I followed her into the kitchen.

"Have a seat," she said. "The landlord was good enough to leave me these folding chairs. He moved out the rest of the furniture so I could paint. I don't know if you remember, but I went a little color happy. Blue in the living room, yellow in the dining room. He wants everything white again before I leave."

"When's that?"

"Day after tomorrow. You want something to drink? I've got iced tea. The powdered kind."

Jon's favorite.

"I'd love a glass."

I unfolded two chairs while she poured, and then we sat across from each other, both of us wondering where to begin—both of us, I'm sure, feeling Jon's absence. Ms. Evans broke the ice.

"You must be college bound," she said.

"Virginia Tech."

"Excited?"

"I don't think it's sunk in yet."

"I know the feeling," she said. "It's funny—you're off to college, and I just finished. Library science. I'm going to be a children's librarian. Who'd have thought, huh?"

"It makes sense," I said. "No one loved stories and books more than Jon."

That first mention of his name changed the atmosphere in the room. It was like the air around us became suddenly easier to breathe.

"Thanks, Christian. That's a sweet thought."

I nodded at a stack of boxes beside the stove.

"Where are you going?" I asked.

"Chicago. My sister's there. And I've got a job lined up at the library right in her neighborhood. Now that school's done, I have no more reason to stay in Wilmington. It's still hard being here, you know? Half the block thinks of me as the lady whose son was gunned down by the cops. The other half thinks of me as the lady whose son was a murderer. That isn't going to change."

I didn't know what to say, so I just sipped my tea. Ms. Evans smiled.

"What is it, Christian?" she asked. "Don't get me wrong—I couldn't be happier to see you. But I'm guessing you're here for a reason."

I'd already decided to swallow my confession. No mother would want to know that the last words her son heard from anyone who cared about him were said in anger. I understood that the second I saw her through the living room window. But I had something else to apologize for—something I was sure she had every right to hate me for.

"I should have gone with you," I said. "To the press. The lawyers. Whoever it was that could have set things straight. Jon and I were together up until just before it happened. He was acting totally normal. Not that he ever would have done what they said he did. I should have helped you. I should have been your character witness."

She reached across and took my hand.

"Oh, honey," she said, "you were a child. Your parents were right to protect you. And I was wrong to ask. But I'm so glad you came today. Sometimes it feels like Jon is my secret. Like nobody noticed he was here but me."

"People noticed," I said. "You couldn't help but notice Jon."

She smiled, then took my chin in her free hand and held her face close to mine.

"You aren't a child anymore," she said. "And Jon won't be the last person you see wronged. You understand?"

I nodded.

"I do," I said.

She leaned back in her chair and stretched her arms over her head. "Lord help me, I still have half a house to paint."

"Got an extra brush?" I asked.

SIXTEEN

I've been to the Borgata countless times, but the sheer scale of the place always catches me off guard. Walking into the lobby, you feel like you're boarding a stationary cruise ship. The blown-glass sculpture hanging from the ceiling seems comet-sized, while the main hallway's receding arches give the impression that you could walk for days without reversing direction. So much territory to explore, all of it dedicated to separating you from your money. And I'm not just talking about gambling. You could spend a week here and never eat in the same restaurant twice. The boutique shops would fill most malls in America. And then there are the spas, the gaming rooms, the theaters. Whether you stay for a night or a month, there's no need to leave the building—or even step foot on the casino floor. This is the closest thing to a Vegas-style experience on the East Coast.

I check in, then head up to my room. My Borgata Black Label card earned me an upgrade to a suite one floor below the penthouse. There are two queen beds, a sauna, a lounge area with a full bar, and a view of the Atlantic Ocean. I'd be overjoyed if I were here on vacation, but I have work to do. I drop my overnight bag on the nearest bed, splash some water on my face, and rush right back out. I spend the ride down in the elevator scrolling through the alerts on my phone. I have a half dozen missed calls from Claire. She knows where I am; she just doesn't know why. I'll touch base with her later. Right now, I'm anxious to hit the tables. I have dealers, pit bosses, and card sharks to interview. With any luck, they'll be able to paint a picture of Nolan's mood and movements in the hours before he disappeared.

I pause on the edge of the casino floor and pretend for a moment that I'm Nolan Styer. What would Nolan be feeling as the blackjack tables and roulette wheels come into view? What would he be thinking? Probably a more intense version of what everyone thinks: *There has to be a way.* A way to conquer the house. Put yourself in front of the right slot machine, the right dealer, and the Borgata will grant you a new life. No more giving your best years to a boss you can't stand. No more dread in your gut as the first of the month approaches. A casino hands you a dream, then crushes it over a period of hours. I'm one of the lucky ones; I can set limits and stick to them. Once I lose X amount of money, I'm off for a stroll along the boardwalk. But what keeps people like Nolan—the hardcore gamblers, the addicts—coming back? Is it the dopamine high? Or is there something more?

I roam around for a bit while my ears adjust to the constant electronic clatter of the slot machines. It's two in the afternoon, a time when I usually feel a slight dip in energy, but not today—not here. At the Borgata, every inhale gives me a quick boost. That's because casinos continuously pump fresh oxygen into the room. They want their customers feeling extra alive. They want the hours to float by without you noticing the change from day to night or night to day. And how would you notice when there are no windows? The games might be governed by chance, but the atmosphere is choreographed to the last detail.

I take a seat at a blackjack table where there's just one player holding down the fort. I recognize the dealer. The tag pinned to her vest reminds me that her name is Kristen. I went on an hour-long win streak at her table when Gloria and I came here to celebrate my thirty-fifth birthday. At first, Gloria was "repulsed" by the place. "Look at all these people with their bloodshot eyes," she'd said, "so starved for a win that they've pinned their hopes on blind chance." By the end of the weekend, I was the one who had to pull *her* away from the blackjack tables.

"Welcome back, Mr. Stone," Kristen says.

I smile. Thousands of people pass through here every day. Either Kristen has a photographic memory or I'm more of a standout player than I thought.

I hand her my player's card. The pit boss walks over and takes down the number. My fellow player—a rail-thin man with a salt-and-pepper five-o'clock shadow—doesn't seem overly thrilled to have company. I smile at him and get nothing back.

"I'm Christian," I tell him.

"Ray-Ray," he says.

End of conversation. Judging by the red in Ray-Ray's eyes, I'm guessing he's been glued to that chair since this time yesterday.

I win the first hand with an eighteen, the second with blackjack. The third hand is less cut-and-dried. Kristen deals me an eight. I stay. She flips over a king of spades and is forced to take another card, a seven of hearts. Bust!

"Nice move, Christian," she says, grinning to herself.

Ray-Ray curses into his beer.

My luck holds over the next few hands. Twenty minutes in, I'm ahead by a thousand bucks. It feels like a good omen. Maybe all this winning means I'll get the answers I came for. Eventually, Ray-Ray skulks off in disgust. I look up at Kristen, slide her a $100 chip. She thanks me with a bow of her head.

"Mind if I ask you a question?" I say.

I see her getting her rebuff lines ready.

"It's about my cousin," I tell her.

She relaxes. I reach into my wallet and pull out a small, glossy photo given to me by Evelyn. It was taken for Nolan's senior yearbook, but apart from filling out a little, he hasn't changed much. Same dimples. Same sculpted hair he wore during his tenure at Mikimotos.

"He's a regular here," I say. "Do you recognize him?"

She glances down at the picture, then does a double take. Her professional facade falls away. You'd think I'd handed her a photo of Mick Jagger.

"Nolan's your cousin?" she asks.

"I'll take that as a yes."

"Sorry, it's just—he's a bit of a celebrity. At least among the staff."

"Big tipper?"

"One of the biggest. Did something happen?"

I'm wondering how a guy who lives in his mom's basement becomes one of the Borgata's biggest tippers, but I doubt that's a question Kristen can answer.

"We think he came here two Sundays ago," I say. "The thing is, no one has seen or heard from him since. Personally, I'm not worried. Nolan's gone off-grid before. But I promised my aunt I'd ask around."

"I wish I could help," she says, "but I don't work Sundays."

"Any chance the pit boss can check his player's card?"

She shakes her head. "Sorry."

I pass her another black $100 chip. She hesitates, then calls the pit boss over.

"Matty," she says, "this is Nolan Styer's cousin."

She says it like I'm de facto royalty. Matty seems appropriately impressed. Kristen summarizes my story: The last anyone heard from Nolan, he was on his way here. That was two Sundays ago. Then she asks Matty if he'll take a look at Nolan's player's card.

"That's not something I'd normally do," Matty says.

The "normally" seems to leave a window open. I palm another black chip, then stand and shake Matty's hand like we're being formally introduced. When I pull my hand away, the chip is gone. Matty looks thankful and apprehensive at the same time. He walks over to his computer, types in some information, then comes back a few moments later.

"Yeah, he was here Sunday night. At least as late as two a.m. Looks like he spent most of his time playing poker."

I thank them both, then hurry past the craps and roulette tables on my way to the poker room—a large, open space with inset lighting and floral-pattern carpeting. I stand in the doorway and look around while I wait for the greeter to return from seating the newest player. If it weren't for the cards and the poker chips, you'd think this was a banquet hall. None of the tables are crowded, but they aren't empty either. At first glance, the players look to me like regulars. Their faces are legit poker faces, which doesn't mean they're expressionless; it means their expressions have nothing to do with the cards they've been dealt. Some are joking, smiling, making small talk. Others seem lost in their own little world. These are seasoned gamblers. They know that any high or low is likely to be undone by the next hand.

The greeter leads me to a table in the center of the room, then sets me up with a stack of chips and wishes me luck. I silently prepare to part with my money; poker has never been my game. True to form, I bet frivolously with lousy cards for four straight hands, losing $100 in a span of fifteen minutes. The player to my left is a twentysomething who wears his baseball cap backward; the older gentleman to my right holds an unlit cigar in his mouth. Neither seems like the chatty type, and neither seems likely to leave me alone with the dealer anytime soon. Fifteen minutes is long enough to wait, so I go ahead and ask my question.

"Do any of you happen to know Nolan Styer?"

The dealer gives me his blankest stare. The kid in the cap ignores me. The older gentleman takes the cigar out of his mouth.

"What about him?" he asks.

I repeat my cover story.

"I don't know about Sunday night," the man says. "You might have better luck in the high rollers' room."

"High rollers' room?"

"Sure. It's nothing for Nolan to blow five grand on a bet."

Could there be two Nolan Styers? Bartending is a cash business, and I'm sure Nolan did all right . . . but five grand? On a single hand of poker? Nolan wouldn't have been able to fund that kind of habit if he *owned* Scotched Up.

I move on to another table, then another. In the high rollers' room, I lose all of the money I won playing blackjack, then keep on losing. I talk to the dealers. I talk to the players. Lots of people know Nolan, but nobody seems to know him well. They give me sound bites. Sound bites that don't make any sense.

"He might have been born with a silver spoon, but at least he shares the wealth," one player says. "Especially when he's on a roll. I've seen him order rounds of Scotch for the table. And not the cheap stuff."

"He's pissing away his fortune," another player says.

"Are you kidding?" a silver-haired woman asks in response. "The kid's mother is a Wyeth. That kind of money never runs out. All he has to do is auction another painting."

She turns to me.

"You should know," she says. "You're his cousin, right?"

I nod. I'm too stunned to use my words. The Wyeths are art-world aristocracy with strong ties to Delaware. Andrew Wyeth's paintings are on display in museums around the globe. Prints of his paintings hang in millions of homes from coast to coast. Everybody's seen the young woman in the pink dress crawling across the grass, even if they don't know the artist's name.

Nolan had an alter ego. Being Evelyn Styer's son wasn't enough for him. He wanted generational wealth. He wanted prestige. If he were alive, I'd take him by the shoulders and shake him.

Now there are two more questions I need to answer. Who was it I saw lying on those reeds—Nolan Styer or Nolan Styer-Wyeth? And where did the money come from? I don't know exactly how much a Wyeth original goes for, but I'm sure even a miniature would cover a few months' worth of Scotch and $5,000 bets. That's a pricey game of pretend. Did Nolan sink himself too deep in a lie? Is that what got him killed? And if he was able to raise enough money to pass himself off as a Wyeth, even for a short while, then why *was* he living in his mother's basement?

I feel unsteady on my feet as I exit the poker room. I'm down fifteen hundred bucks. I'm baffled and cranky and more than a little hungry. I need answers. I need food. A drink wouldn't hurt either.

Fortunately, I know which of the Borgata's many restaurants Nolan favored.

SEVENTEEN

The "old" in "Old Homestead" feels like a misnomer. If anything, the restaurant's inset lighting and clean lines give it a contemporary look. I take a seat at the small, intimate bar and scan the backlit bottles of top-shelf liquor. As with my visit to Scotched Up, I'm here ahead of dinner and well after lunch, meaning I have the place mostly to myself. I nod to the bartender, ask for a glass of Goldeneye Pinot Noir and a menu, though I already know what I'm going to order: the rib eye steak, the dish I found listed on the receipt in Nolan's bedroom.

The bartender is wearing a standard-issue white collared shirt and black vest. He's in his early twenties, tall and lean with wavy dark hair and unmistakable matinee-idol looks. His smile says he's sure of himself but also personable, two essential qualities when you're serving liquor to the public. Once he's filled my glass and taken my order, I start easing into a conversation.

"I know it's early for dinner," I say, "but losing money works up an appetite."

"Rough session?"

"Brutal."

From there, it doesn't take long to learn the basic facts of his life. His name is Gabe. He grew up in Vermont. He trained in classical piano at the Eastman School of Music but wound up here because Leigh, his fiancée, is a member of the Atlantic City Ballet.

"I didn't realize Atlantic City had a ballet," I tell him.

"Oh yeah. They're first-rate. The dancers come from all over the world."

"I'll have to check it out."

"Wait until December. Leigh's playing the Sugar Plum Fairy in *The Nutcracker*."

I'm thinking Gabe is just the kind of cultured and artistic young man a real Wyeth might invite to a dinner party. I use a lull in our small talk as an opportunity to pull out Nolan's photo.

"Any chance you know my cousin?" I ask.

He looks down at the photo. "Nolan's your cousin?"

Unlike other people I've spoken to, he seems more amused than awed. I'm guessing he saw through at least some of Nolan's wilder claims. His next question confirms it.

"Is it true that he rescued Lady Gaga when she fell overboard on a yacht at the Venice Film Festival?"

I grin.

"It's true that he dove in after her," I say. "But it was the captain who wound up saving both of them."

Gabe nods as if to say, *I knew it*.

"The thing is," I tell him, "Nolan's gone missing."

"Missing?"

I repeat the same story I've told maybe a dozen times by now. Unlike anyone else I've talked to at the Borgata, Gabe seems genuinely upset.

"I hope he didn't get himself into trouble," he says.

"Why do you say that?"

"The stories he tells me. Even if they aren't all the way true,

Nolan takes some risks. Life in the fast lane, you know what I mean?"

He means drugs. It occurs to me that maybe Gabe's concerned because he was Nolan's Atlantic City connection. I grasp around for a polite way to ask the question. The best I come up with is "Did you ever party with him?"

"Nah, that's not my scene. I know him as a customer. I mean, we're friendly. I'm always glad to see him. But I keep my work-life and my life-life separate."

I believe him. He has the right look—a high-society wannabe like Nolan wouldn't hesitate to score off him—but his resume is all wrong. A classical musician who follows the woman he loves to a dump like Atlantic City isn't the type to peddle dime bags on the side. Maybe I'm being naive, but I don't think so.

"You said Nolan went missing two Sundays ago, right?" he asks.

I nod. "I know that he came here, but I don't know how long he stayed or who he left with."

Gabe thinks it over.

"I'll tell you what," he says. "Leigh, my fiancée, works the front desk mornings. Early mornings—like, starting at four a.m."

Gabe and Leigh—not a pairing of names you hear every day.

"I thought she was a ballerina," I say.

"She moonlights here. We're saving for a condo."

"Smart."

It seems like everyone in Nolan's orbit is leading a temporary life while they wait for the life they actually want to take shape. Then again, that's the hospitality business.

"I don't know what kind of hours you keep," Gabe says, "but if you catch Leigh near the beginning of her shift, she might be able to help you."

"Help me how?"

He lowers his voice, leans over the bar. "There's hardly any traffic at that hour. As long as you're discreet about it, she can probably tell you when Nolan checked out. She might even be able to access security footage."

My jaw nearly hits the bar. Gabe's offering me more than I could have hoped for when I set out for Atlantic City. I almost feel bad for having doubled down on Nolan's lies.

"That would be fantastic," I say. "Better than fantastic."

He pulls out his phone, starts typing with his thumbs.

"I'll let her know you're coming," he says.

I see a very big tip in Gabe's future—and Leigh's too.

———

There's a lot of time to kill between now and 4 a.m., but then what is a casino for if not killing time? When I get back to the floor, I see that the afternoon staff has given way to the evening staff. I have a fresh set of dealers to interview—and a new crop of gamblers too. Not that I expect to learn much more than I already know. Nolan came here to live a lie. He fed the same basic story to everyone at the Borgata. Only the embellishments changed.

Still, there's no harm in asking my questions. A middle-aged woman wearing a pin-striped sweatsuit tells me that Nolan followed in his grandfather's (or is it great-grandfather's?) footsteps, became a painter in the same tradition and of the same caliber.

"He showed me photos," she says. "Seascapes, mostly. Kind of dark and gloomy. Ghost story stuff. He said he painted them in Ireland. That's where he goes for his inspiration."

I think, *Nolan was inspired, all right.* I wonder whose paintings he's appropriating. There must be corners of his hard drive I haven't discovered yet.

An older, wizened-looking man with patches on the elbows of his flannel shirt tells me that Nolan drove a vintage Mercedes and lived in a Victorian mansion in West Chester, Pennsylvania.

"Now, what are the chances?" the man asks. "I worked as a mechanic in the West Chester Mercedes dealership for forty years. And I'll tell you—Nolan knows his cars. I couldn't stump him, and believe me, I tried. Most of your blue bloods wouldn't know how to pop open a hood. They're afraid of getting a little grease on their fingers. Not Nolan. You'd never guess he came from money. He's the easiest kid to get along with I ever met."

What's becoming abundantly clear about Nolan is that he knew how to work a room. What remains abundantly unclear—what I still desperately want to know—is where his money came from. I'm feeling more and more certain that his death and the bankroll for his Borgata sprees are linked.

I lose another $500 in the poker room, recoup about a hundred at the blackjack tables, then call it a night. It's not quite 11 p.m. My plan is to catch a few hours of sleep before it's time to meet Gabe's better half. But on the ride up in the elevator, I flash on an idea I'm sure will keep me awake for a while yet. A small TV screen above the control panel is playing CNN. The story of the day involves a bank robbery in Paris. The safe deposit boxes were emptied. People lost original documents, family heirlooms, precious jewels. The anchor calls it a "heist." My mind starts playing word association. A *heist* is a kind of robbery. So is blackmail. I remember that note on Nolan's computer: *Have 100K cash ready for me within 48 hours or I go public.* It wasn't a prank or a joke. And Nolan wasn't the victim;

he was the blackmailer. Someone paid him enough to play Wyeth at the Borgata. It's the only thing that makes sense. The only thing that feels right.

I curse myself for leaving Nolan's computer back in Rehoboth. There must be evidence on his hard drive, a trail for me to follow. I found the ransom note in the trash bin, which means he was careful—or at least he meant to be careful. But he was also obsessive. He logged and tallied every dime, every hour. He kept every scrap of research. Hidden among all those sprawling spreadsheets must be an exact account of who, when, why, and how much. It will be titled so that it blends in with the other documents. The name of an athlete, a boxer, a horse. The contents might even be coded. But I'll recognize it when I see it. And any code can be deciphered.

I know I should sleep, but my mind is racing. I do what I can to calm myself down. I spend some time in the Jacuzzi. I pour myself a shot of Jameson from the bar. I do some light stretching before I get into bed and turn out the lights. Still, I'm nowhere near switching off for the night.

I turn the lights back on, step out onto the balcony, and listen to the faint sound of waves breaking thirty-seven stories below. It would be relaxing if the air weren't so damn cold. Back inside, I flip through hundreds of cable stations. No *Law & Order*, but there is a *First 48*. It's set in New Orleans. A woman was found dead in her bedroom. It was her grown son who found her. According to the coroner, she died more than a week ago. Like Nolan, her son lives at home. So why did he wait so long to report his mother's death? And who's been using her credit cards these past few days?

Little by little, the details of this case supplant my questions about Nolan Styer "Wyeth": Blackmailer. My mind quiets down just enough for me to drift off. When the alarm starts buzzing at 3:45, I wake to find the television running a commercial for the Borgata Hotel Casino and Spa.

EIGHTEEN

G abe was right: There aren't any guests roaming the lobby at four in the morning. There's nobody stirring at all except for a young woman behind the front desk who I assume is Leigh. She smiles at me as though she's both wide awake and genuinely happy to be greeting a perfect stranger at this ungodly hour. Like her fiancé, she's tall, attractive, and unmistakably confident—a natural fit for the hospitality game, and probably the ballet too.

"My name's Christian," I tell her. "Gabe said you might be willing to help me."

Her smile loses a bit of its shine.

"Of course," she says. "You're looking for your brother?"

"Cousin."

"Right."

The paranoid part of my brain wonders if I'm being tested—if maybe Leigh senses a hole in my cover story. Somehow, she strikes me as more world-weary than Gabe. Still, she waves me around to her side of the desk, then sets an old-fashioned call bell on the counter.

"This way," she says.

I follow her into a small side room equipped with three state-of-the-art computer stations.

"My boss isn't scheduled to be here for another half hour, but sometimes he shows up early, so we need to be quick."

"I understand," I say. "And thank you. I really appreciate your help."

She sits in front of one of the outsized monitors and logs into the Borgata system. "What do you want to know?"

"For starters, when Nolan checked in, and when he checked out."

She types *Nolan Styer* into a dialogue box, then hits Return. A little scrolling, and she has an answer for me.

"That's odd," she says.

"What is?"

"He got here around seven p.m. that Sunday. He paid for a suite, but then he checked out at one in the morning."

It's the kind of information that only raises more questions. Did something, or someone, compel Nolan to leave prematurely? Was he eccentric enough to rent a room just for show? Or was he allowing someone else to use his room while he spent the evening gambling? And if so, then for what purpose?

"Can you check his player's card?" I ask. "See how he did at the tables?"

She looks up at me with a renewed sense of suspicion.

"I'm wondering why he left in such a rush," I say. "Nolan's impulsive. If he won big, then he might have wanted to keep the party going somewhere else. If he lost big, then he probably just wanted to put the Borgata behind him."

It sounds vague as I say it, but Leigh's satisfied enough to switch screens. For a quick beat, her professional facade drops away.

"Wow. Your cousin had quite a night."

I look over her shoulder.

"Wow is right," I say.

The casino paid Nolan forty grand and change, all blackjack winnings. Those books in his dresser drawer must have taught him well. I might want to read them myself. Leigh shuts the screen, pushes back in her office chair.

"Is there anything else?" she asks.

She's clearly hoping I'll say no, and I don't blame her. Giving me access to a customer's data is a fireable offense. Leigh doesn't have any personal investment in Nolan—or in me. But the man she's agreed to spend the rest of her life with called in a favor. He put her in a tough spot. I feel bad for taking advantage, but I won't get another opportunity like this one.

"Actually, Gabe said you might be able to let me look at the security footage?"

She whips her head in my direction. "Did he?"

I nod. My instinct is to slip her money, but I have a feeling she'd balk. The best I can do is make my pitch.

"Look, I'll be honest," I say. "I think Nolan's in real trouble. His mother's worried. We tried getting the police involved, but Nolan has a history. It isn't unlike him to drop out of circulation for a while. But this time feels different. Always before, he's given us some sign that he's okay. A text. A post on social media. This time, nothing. His voicemail is full, and no one's heard a peep from him."

If you take away the premise that Nolan and I are members of the Wyeth clan, then I actually am being honest. I tell myself I'm like a true crime author, changing details but keeping the essence of the story.

Leigh drops her head, lets out a long sigh, then says, "Does it matter that the footage is in black-and-white and there's no sound?"

"Not at all. I'm more interested in who he was talking to than what he was saying."

She sets up screens for me in two different tabs. Screen one is frozen on a blackjack table; screen two is frozen on the entrance to the Borgata.

"Just use the commands at the bottom of the screen," she says. "You'll have to scroll. But I really need you gone before my boss gets here."

"Understood."

She takes a phone out of her pocket.

"What's your number?" she asks.

I recite it for her, and she taps in the digits.

"I'll keep an eye on the parking lot from my computer out front," she says. "If you get a blank text, it means my boss is pulling in. You need to shut everything down and exit through the side door."

"I owe you," I say. "Just name your price."

"Let's wait and see if I lose my job."

She heads back to the lobby, and I take her place. I set my phone on the desk beside the keyboard, then open the blackjack tab. The time stamp reads 7:15; the camera is positioned behind the dealer. I spot Nolan right away. He's sitting at the center of the table, wearing a blazer and a bolo tie. There are two players to his left and two more to his right—one woman and three men, ranging in age from midthirties to early seventies. I do as Leigh instructed and hold down the fast-forward icon. The players look suddenly more caffeinated. It's like watching an early Charlie Chaplin film, with the actors flailing their arms around and gathering their chips at double the normal rate of speed.

At first, nothing spectacular seems to be happening. Nolan wins. Nolan loses. Nolan orders a drink. But then his luck starts to hold.

He's on a run, impressive enough for a small crowd to gather behind him. As he keeps on winning, the crowd gets bigger. I lift my finger off the mouse, let the tape run at normal speed. Nolan appears to be taking his success in stride. He smiles at the dealer each time his pile of chips grows, but of all the faces on the screen, his is the least animated. He's playing a part: the Zen card shark. It has to be a performance because this isn't the Nolan I knew at Mikimotos. *That* Nolan was all fast talk and big gestures. All eyes on him at all times. Here, it's as if he's wearing someone else's body language. I wonder if he changed his voice too—slowed the cadence, lowered the pitch, adopted a high-tone accent.

A server brings him another drink, and he sets what looks like a $100 chip on her tray. Out in the lobby, Leigh's talking to another early riser. I check the time. I have a maximum of twelve minutes left. I push the fast-forward to its quickest pace. As best I can tell, there's nothing to see but more of the same. Nolan amasses an ever-larger pile of chips. The crowd around him swells and ebbs. The server brings fresh drinks and carts empty glasses away. Not once does Nolan pump his fist or jump out of his seat. Why would he? Forty grand is nothing to a Wyeth.

But he does get up from the table one time. He gestures that he'll be right back, then holds his phone to his ear as he walks off camera. I check the time stamp when he leaves and the time stamp when he returns. He's gone from 11:09 to 11:24, a total of fifteen minutes. I record a voice memo on my own phone noting the times. It's rare for somebody on a streak like Nolan's to take even a bladder break. I'm guessing he *had* to answer that call. The question is, How can I get hold of his phone records?

I switch over to the other tab, find a still shot of the area beneath the golden portico where Ubers and buses and limos drop off customers. Leigh paused the footage at 1 a.m. I only have to scroll forward a few minutes before Nolan appears. Already I notice what feels like a big clue: He's changed his clothes. He's wearing an oversized Eagles jersey and faded jeans. The outfit I spotted him in from the plane. The outfit he died in. He must have used his $200 suite as a dressing stall. He looks left, then right, then sets a small gym bag on the sidewalk in front of him. I wonder what's in the bag besides a blazer, a bolo tie, and forty grand.

He's on his phone again now, this time typing with both thumbs. Five minutes later, a car pulls up to the curb. Nolan slings his bag over one shoulder and starts forward, then stops short when the driver gets out to greet him. The footage is shot from an overhead angle. I can't see the expressions on either of their faces. The man holds up both hands in an I-come-in-peace gesture. He isn't wearing a *Peaky Blinders* cap; that would have been too easy. But I can see he is shorter than Nolan, and the car is a dark-colored sedan. Then again, most people are shorter than Nolan, and there's countless dark-colored sedans in the Uber fleet.

The man walks around and shakes Nolan's hand. Nolan does all the talking—nodding and gesturing nonstop, exactly as Ashley described. The man turns and opens the back passenger seat. Nolan hesitates, then gets in. I squint at the license plate as the car drives away. It's a light color, but I can't make out the numbers. I wish Spooner was here to blow it up for me.

My phone dings. I look down at a blank text. *Shit.* I hope Leigh's boss is a slow walker. I rewind the tape to the moment when the driver gets out of his car. Then I lift up my phone and start recording. The entire sequence lasts a little less than five minutes. By the time I'm watching the car pull away for a second time, I hear a deep male voice chatting with Leigh.

I can tell by her tone that she's asking him questions, drawing out a story, stalling in case I'm not gone. I shove my phone in my pocket, shut down both tabs, and bolt for the exit. I make a silent promise to come back for the opening of *The Nutcracker*. It will be me leading the standing ovation. And Leigh will get the biggest bouquet any dancer has ever seen.

Meanwhile, I'm feeling a little shaken. I've just attended a private screening of Nolan's final hours. And I'm pretty sure I've seen the man who killed him.

NINETEEN

I sleep for a few hours, then switch on the lights and call to order breakfast off the room service menu. A staffer with a friendly voice tells me my omelet will arrive in twenty minutes max. I pass the time by studying my video of the surveillance footage. I rotate the screen in every possible direction, hold my phone at every conceivable angle. The license plate never comes into focus, but I do notice a few things about the driver.

First, he keeps his chin tucked down like he knows where the cameras are and is keen to avoid them. At no point can I see his face, but as he walks toward Nolan, I do get a clear view of his build: short, stocky, and square—a perfect match with Ashley's description of the thug from the parking lot. Which doesn't mean this is the same guy, only that he *could* be the same guy.

Second, in the frame where he's holding out his hands as though to calm Nolan down, the left sleeve of his jacket slides back, exposing what looks to me like a stainless-steel Rolex watch. It could be a knockoff—there's no way to tell given the quality of the film and the size of the screen—but if it's legit, then it's worth a cool twenty grand.

After I've eaten, showered, and consumed a full pot of coffee, I head down to the business center to do a little research. I start with my standard scan of the day's police blotter. Still no mention of a body matching Nolan's description. Next, I search for *blackmail, Wilmington DE*. Most of what comes up is cyber-related. Sextortion stuff. Demands for cryptocurrency. But the note on Nolan's computer talked about a physical drop-off. Something I've come to appreciate about Nolan: He was fundamentally old-fashioned. Fine art, vintage cars, bolo ties, and games that have been around for a few centuries. He reminds me of a character in an Elmore Leonard novel.

Back in my room, I decide to do a little delegating. I text Spooner my video of the security footage with the message *Need clear image of driver and license plate. Possible?* I give him the time stamps, which by now I have memorized. Seconds later, I get a reply: a thumbs-up and a thumbs-down emoji, which I guess means *maybe*. I write *Do your best*. Then I call Evelyn. I'm hoping she and Nolan were on the same phone plan. It's a shot in the dark, but it pays off; mother and son signed up for a family discount. I ask if she can access his records for the last billing cycle. She asks me why I need them. I don't want to say, *Because I think he might have called his murderer from the floor of the Borgata*, so I give her an answer straight out of *Law & Order*.

"If the police were doing their job, they'd be interviewing the last people Nolan talked to. I figured I might give it a try."

"Geez," she says. "Why in the world didn't I think of that myself?"

She promises to get me the records ASAP.

I look over at the clock on the nightstand. It's going on 10 a.m. Time to bring my Borgata excursion to an end. It may have cost a small fortune, but I've discovered a side of Nolan I never would have known existed otherwise. Which means I'm miles closer than I was two days ago.

———

I'm a few exits from Wilmington when my phone pings. It's Gloria. *Lunch. 20 minutes. Mikimotos.* It reads like an order. Gloria's texts are usually wordier, with a fair number of *pleases* and *thank yous* thrown in. This is an invitation to a scolding. I search my brain for anything I could have done wrong. Then it hits me. There was a meeting of the Downtown Development Project committee this morning. I was so wrapped up in the rise and fall of Nolan Styer-Wyeth that I completely forgot. *Shit.* Gloria might be my best friend, but I'm in no mood for an unscheduled stop, especially not one where I'm sure to get dressed down.

By the time I arrive, she's already seated at a table near the back. She flashes the kind of smile she might give an opponent in a debate.

"I'm sorry," I say, taking my seat. "I just now remembered."

"That's your excuse? You forgot?"

I shrug. "It's the truth."

"Well, Dax sure was pissed."

"And that's bad news?"

She reaches across the table and pinches my arm. "You need him on your side, Christian."

I've barely sat down when our waiter arrives. Instead of taking our order, he delivers two grilled chicken teriyaki bento boxes and two Cokes. I look at Gloria.

"I took the liberty of ordering for us," she says. "I'm in a rush, but I felt we needed to talk."

"You mean I needed a talking-to?"

"It's not just the meeting, Christian. Claire tells me you're more checked out than ever. You aren't returning phone calls. Your one-week vacation has stretched into two weeks, and you haven't even gone anywhere. So tell me: What's happening? What has you behaving so un-Christian-like?"

Is it time to let someone in? I've already enlisted Spooner's help, but that's different. It's not like I confided in him. And he isn't the mayor of Wilmington. Then again, it's probably a good idea to have the mayor on my side. I remember our conversation at the Oyster House. Gloria said she had "one or two loyal minions" she'd trust with an off-books murder investigation. But I wasn't ready to involve her then. I'd only glimpsed a body from a plane and found an Eagles ticket in a trash heap. That was it. Now, I know who was lying in those reeds. I know when he was last seen alive. I know he led a double life, and I know there are people who had a motive to kill him.

Still, I can only let Gloria in so far. I can't tell her that I'm sure Nolan's dead. Not until Evelyn knows. Not until the body resurfaces.

"A former employee of mine has gone missing," I say. "I'm friendly with his mother. She's understandably distraught. I'm trying to help."

"So you've become emotionally involved?"

I shake my head. "It's more than that. I'm going to find him, Gloria. Whatever happened. Whatever it takes."

She sets her chopsticks down with a piece of chicken still stuck between them.

"This isn't a screenplay, Christian," she says. "We have professionals who handle these things."

"Except they won't. Nolan, the kid who's disappeared, has a record. Personal use. His mother reported him missing once before. It turned out he was on a bender. The police aren't interested in looking for him a second time."

"Maybe they're right. What makes you think he isn't on a bender now?"

Because I saw him lying dead on a bed of reeds beside the Schuylkill.

"Like I said, I've been investigating."

"Investigating? You're an investigator now?"

I pretend not to notice the sarcasm.

"This kid was into stuff, Gloria. The kind of stuff that gets people killed. He went around claiming he was heir to a fortune when really he lived in his mom's basement. He gambled. He owed money. I don't know how much, but a lot. And I'm pretty sure he covered his debts with a blackmail scheme. If I can just find out *who* he was blackmailing, then—"

"And how are you supposed to do that?"

I think, *You've let her in this far.*

"I have his laptop," I say. "Nolan's a compulsive note taker. He keeps a spreadsheet for everything. The information has to be hidden somewhere on his hard drive."

"What information?"

"The names of his victims. How much he was paid. How often. It's probably in code, but—"

"You know there are police who do that sort of thing for a living. Highly trained experts. Even in Wilmington."

"I have my own experts."

She smirks at me between bites.

"You sound like a child," she says.

"The police don't solve crimes, Gloria. They cover their own asses."

"You're thinking of Jon?"

I nod.

"A few bad apples thirty years ago—"

"It's more than that, and you know it."

She shrugs. "Cops are human. Humans are designed to cover

their own asses. But it's ridiculous to think that you, Christian Stone, can do the job of a digital forensics examiner."

"What I'm looking for isn't that complicated. It's just a game of hide-and-seek."

"Has it occurred to you that you're committing a crime?"

"What crime?"

"Withholding evidence?"

"I won't know for sure that there is evidence until I find it."

She gives me her most disapproving glare.

"Listen to yourself," she says. "Suppose this kid got on the wrong side of some dangerous people. Suppose they killed him. Wouldn't they kill you just as quickly? This isn't your field, Christian. I know you're bored. You're more successful than you ever could have dreamed you'd be, and now you're wondering, *Is this all there is?* It's called a plateau. It happens to the best of us, but trust me—reinventing yourself as a crime fighter isn't the way."

"But I'm close, Gloria."

She reaches back over our plates, rests her hand on my forearm. "Then I have all the more reason to worry. You're a dear friend, Christian. I don't want anything to happen to you."

"I'll be careful," I tell her. "But you're wrong. This isn't about boredom. Maybe it started that way, but it's become something much bigger. Nolan had his faults, but he deserved better. And his mother reminds me of . . ."

"Jon's mother?"

I nod.

"Well," Gloria says, "if I can't stop you, then I guess I have to help, if only to protect you from yourself. I know you have fantasies of a vigilante mayor, and that might work for a screenplay, but in reality there's only so much I can do. I don't assign cases. Mostly, I yell about the crime rate. But I do have friends. So what is it you need? Tell me, and I'll make some calls. But once I get other people involved, you'll have to share. Everything. No exceptions."

A reasonable person would jump at the offer, so why don't I hear myself saying yes? Is my deep-seated suspicion of the police holding me back? Or am I just determined to solve Nolan's murder on my own?

"Give me a couple of days," I tell her.

"And then?"

"Everything I have is yours. I promise."

CHAPTER TWENTY

L ater that afternoon, I hunker down in my kitchen with Nolan's laptop. My theory that he hid the details of his blackmail scheme in one or more of his gambling spreadsheets makes for tedious work. I learn the heights, weights, and off-field habits of so many athletes that my eyes start to gloss over. At the Borgata, I felt like I was making discoveries by the minute. I even allowed myself to believe that I was closing in on Nolan's killer—that I was just one clue away. Now, it's like everything is moving in slow motion.

At 5 p.m., I get an email from Spooner. The subject line reads *Blowups of security footage*. I can't click fast enough. At first, I feel deflated. The license plate is just an outsized blur, and a larger image of the driver only reveals a comb-over—no clear shot of his face. But then, as I look more closely, I think maybe there's enough. Maybe, if you'd seen him before, you'd recognize him from this photo. He's wearing a bomber jacket and black, zipped-up boots. His ears jut out to the sides. His hands are visible, and you can just glimpse the tip of what must be a very long nose.

Yes, I think, *if I knew him, I'd recognize him.*

I phone Scotched Up to see if Ashley's working. No luck. A polite male voice informs me she won't be in again for a while. I'd rather show her the driver's photo in person, but I have no choice. I find her name in my contacts and press Call. She answers after the first ring.

"Christian?"

She sounds hopeful, like she thinks I must be calling with good news.

I hate to disappoint her.

"I was wondering if you'd take a look at something for me," I say. "A photo of a man who may or may not be the guy from the parking lot. The quality isn't great, and you can't see much of his face, but—"

"Send it," she says.

I do. Seconds later, I hear her draw in a deep breath.

"It's him," she says.

"You're sure?"

"Same build. Same jacket. He's even standing in front of the same car."

Her voice sounds like it's on the brink of shattering.

"How did you find him?" she asks.

"I didn't. I just found this footage."

"Where?"

If I say the Borgata, she'll know he came for Nolan. I'm not ready for that. I repeat the promise I made to myself outside Scotched Up. *I'll give her the truth—just as soon as I have all of it.*

"A gas station," I say. "Not far from the parking garage."

She doesn't ask for more details. I give her a moment before I launch back in.

"Have you remembered anything else from that night, Ashley?"

"I keep going over it in my mind. I don't think there's anything else to remember."

"And you have no idea what this guy wanted from Nolan?"

There's a pause while I hear her light a cigarette, then inhale.

"Well, he obviously wanted money. If I had to guess, I'd say he was some kind of bookie. Nolan bet on everything. He could have been a dealer too, but I doubt it. Nolan only used once in a while, which is weird because he was addicted to just about everything else."

"What about the guy? Now that more time has passed, does anything stick out about him?"

She takes a long drag off her cigarette, then says, almost matter-of-factly, "He's dead, isn't he? Nolan's dead."

It's like she's asking me to make something real for her.

"We still can't be sure."

Which is technically true. The line goes quiet. I start to say something, then realize that Ashley has hung up. I can't help but feel like all I've done is inflame an open wound.

Except that now you know, I think.

I know that the man who picked Nolan up outside the Borgata is the man from the parking garage. Still, it's hardly a breakthrough—more like confirmation of something I'd already accepted as fact.

I step over to my vision board. After a short trip to the Borgata, the *WHAT I KNOW SO FAR* column is pulling even in length with the WHAT *I DON'T KNOW YET* column. Under the former, I add: *Man who threatened Nolan in parking garage = man who picked him up at Borgata (last established sighting of Nolan)*. But then I have to add three more questions to the "don't know" list. *Who is this man? What did he want with Nolan? Who does he work for?* The three-to-one ratio is disheartening. How am I supposed to find this guy without a name, a clear photograph, a license plate, or an obvious connection to Nolan?

It's the blackmail, I tell myself. *It has to be the blackmail.*

I settle back down at Nolan's laptop and resume poring over his spreadsheets. A half hour later, I get a text alert; Evelyn's sent the phone records. It doesn't take me long to identify the call Nolan made during his blackjack run. It's a Massachusetts number, which may be a clue in itself. I tap in the digits and get an automated message telling me the line is no longer in service. A burner phone. Also a clue, but not one I can do much with.

I turn back to the laptop. Over the next few hours, I make just one minor discovery. In a subfolder labeled *Portfolio*, I stumble on a trove of paintings—mostly seascapes and high-tone nudes. It takes me a minute to work out that these aren't reproductions lifted from the Internet but rather photos of the original canvases, which makes sense given that Nolan was posing as the artist. He must have spent a long time gallery hopping before he found a Wyeth-like painter who was (a) clearly talented and (b) largely unknown. I admire his effort, but solving this small piece of the mystery doesn't bring me any closer to IDing his killer.

By midnight, I'm starting to feel overcome with futility. That ransom note in the trash bin must have been a rare oversight. Nolan was obviously careful about getting rid of anything that might incriminate him. I Google *Is there a way to recover deleted files from a Mac?* and find myself scrolling through advertisements for various brands of "data recovery software."

Sounds like another job for Spooner . . . I'm not sure how much more I can ask him to do without paying him overtime. I pick up my phone, then remember that Spooner's an early-to-bed type. The call can wait until morning.

I should go to bed myself given how little I've slept, but I hate to end a day without having made any real progress. Still, my eyes need a break from the spreadsheets. Driving back from Atlantic City, I had an idea. It didn't seem like much of an idea at the time, but now I think it's worth a shot.

I go into the home office I've quit using since Quinn left and pull a foldout map of the tristate area (DE, PA, NJ) from my desk drawer. Back in the kitchen, I spread the map open and pin it to the cork portion of my vision board. I circle the approximate location of the Schuylkill Marina in red marker, then take a small spiral notebook from the kitchen junk drawer and start jotting down the names of every town and subdivision I can find within a ten-mile radius. I'm no fan of Nextdoor, but maybe a neighbor out for a late-night stroll saw or overheard something I can use. What that something might be I don't know, but I figure I'll recognize it when it's in front of me.

Soon enough, it feels like I've swapped one needle in a haystack for another. Most of the posts on the app are typical Nextdoor fare. Ring-camera evidence of a neighbor leaving his Great Dane's mess for someone else to pick up. Heated debates over propositions on local ballots. A plea for people to turn off their car alarms more promptly. A warning about rude staff at the local coffee shop. An endless barrage of complaints, some thinly veiled, some downright aggressive. It's mind-numbing stuff, but as with most social media, the dopamine rush sucks you in. There's always a chance that the next post will make all your scrolling worthwhile.

It's roughly 2 a.m., and I've reached the last neighborhood on my list, a suburb of Mantua Township in New Jersey. At first it's more of the same—yard sales and missing pets and summaries of PTA meetings. But then I spot this:

FOUND: ROLEX WATCH.

On the afternoon of November 7th, my son was riding his bike home from school along the Mantua Creek path (between 5th and 6th streets) when he found this watch in the mud. I wiped it down, polished it, and filed a police report. There are initials engraved on the back, so no false claims, please!!!

There's a photo of the watch. It looks identical to the one Nolan's driver was wearing.

I jump off my stool and run to the map. The area described in the post is almost directly across from the Schuylkill Marina. I allow myself a triple-fist-pump and a loud "Yes!" The day's been a long slog, but I've finally hit the jackpot. The question now is, What next? I don't know the initials, and the watch is forensically useless now that she's cleaned and polished it. Besides, the chances that Nolan's killer has been in touch are nil. I know *I* wouldn't risk claiming an object that tied me to a murder, not even a Rolex worth twenty grand.

What's of real interest here is *how* that watch came to be lying in the mud across-river from the Schuylkill Marina. Was there a struggle? Did this woman's son unwittingly locate the actual crime scene? Fortunately, she was good enough to be very precise about where and when her son found the watch. More fortunate still, her full name appears below her avatar. I look her up on Facebook, and right there in her cover photo is a heavily freckled grade-school-aged boy riding a Schwinn.

Kids are creatures of habit. He probably follows that path home from school every day. Which means I know where I'll be tomorrow at 3 p.m. If I can get him to talk to a stranger, I'll have him show me exactly where he found that watch. If I can't, then I'll scour every inch of the Mantua Creek Trail between Fifth and Sixth Streets.

TWENTY-ONE

I have Spooner meet me in the Big Ocean parking lot. I tell him I'm in a rush. The truth is, I don't want to bump into Claire. If she expressed concern about my unofficial leave of absence to Gloria, then she won't hesitate to grill me. I'd end up spending the better part of an hour dodging questions about my love life, my diet, my sleep habits. Better to keep myself scarce.

"Any documents in particular you're hoping to recover?" Spooner asks, leaning through the passenger-side window.

There's no point in withholding when Spooner will see for himself soon enough.

"I think Nolan might have been blackmailing someone. But I don't know who or why."

Spooner's eyes get big.

"Okay," he says. "Wow. This is some little side gig you've got going."

He takes the laptop off the passenger's seat and tucks it under one arm.

"Whatever you find or don't find," I say, "this needs to stay between us."

"Of course."

"Thanks, Spooner. I owe you."

"Are you kidding? This beats the hell out of tweaking POS systems."

I watch him trot back inside, then pull out of the parking lot and start for Mantua Creek.

————

The drive takes just under two hours. The suburban area fronting the creek looks like *Anywhere, USA*—well-maintained midsize homes with pastel-colored vinyl siding and neatly trimmed lawns. It's the kind of place young families move to for the school system and the crime rate. The wide streets and mature trees scream safety. Which might be why the author of the lost-watch ad didn't think twice about laying out the details of her son's route home from school.

I park on Sixth Street and walk toward the water. A narrow trail cuts through a wooded area and leads to the paved bike path running along the creek. It's quiet here even at 2:45 in the afternoon. I Googled the most direct route from Atlantic City to Mantua Township. If traffic cooperates, it's only an hour's drive, which means that Nolan and his likely assassin could have made it here by a little after 2 a.m. At that hour, the place would be deserted. Especially on a Sunday. No witnesses, and a good thirty yards of trees between you and the nearest house—assuming this is where Nolan was killed and/ or dumped, which for the moment is a big assumption.

The sky is overcast, bordering on menacing. I hope the threat of rain didn't cause the boy who found the Rolex to opt for the school bus this morning instead. I need him to tell me where to search. And if he happens to name the initials on the back of the watch, I wouldn't mind that either.

I'm here early, so I have time to get the lay of the land. It's a pretty spot, even in late fall when the branches are bare and the flowers dormant. The sound of the creek is loud enough to drown out whatever neighborhood noises might otherwise filter through the trees. It isn't, however, loud enough to mask the roar of jets passing overhead. Roughly one hundred yards from here, Mantua Creek empties into the Delaware River; another few hundred yards north, the Delaware crosses paths with the Schuylkill. Philadelphia International Airport is nestled in the alcove where the two rivers meet.

I glance up at a passing plane and discover a treehouse perched in a towering oak. It's large and sturdy looking, a new build, with walls made of varnished planks and a well-crafted A-frame roof. I figure the treehouse must be what draws the boy to this spot. Jon and I would have loved it. We would have spent hours watching the planes. Jon would have made up stories about the people they were carrying and the places they were traveling to.

I decide to do a little searching before, hopefully, the boy arrives. I start a few yards back from the creek, then work my way closer to the water, into a marshy area dense with grass that rises above my ankles. I'm thinking maybe Nolan didn't go quietly. Maybe the watch came off in a struggle. And if there was a struggle, then there might have been other clues left behind.

I'm parting reeds with my hands when I take one step too many and plunge my right foot into icy-cold water. I jerk my leg back, but my shoe is already soaked through. The joggers and cyclists speeding by must be wondering what in the world I'm up to. I keep at it, scouring every inch of ground. My hands are wet and muddy. I'm sweating despite the temperature. A half hour later, I haven't uncovered so much as a bubblegum wrapper.

It's just after three o'clock. As if on cue, a redheaded kid on a bike comes barreling down the path. He must not be the type to linger once he's set free. I hurry to catch him before he passes me by, but it turns out he's stopping anyway. He pulls onto the grass near the treehouse, hops off his bike, then stands and stares at me like maybe I'm the stranger his parents have warned him about.

"Great treehouse," I say. "I'm thinking of building one for my son."

That seems to put him at ease. He climbs off his bike and lowers the kickstand.

"It's a lookout tower," he says. "Someone built it so they could keep an eye on the boats and planes."

"Someone?"

He shrugs. "I just found it here. It was abandoned. My dad fixed it up. I don't think anyone but us uses it."

"What do you use it for?"

"I told you—it's a lookout tower."

"Of course. You can see for miles up there."

He nods. "You can spot stuff on the ground too. In places where people don't usually walk."

I have a feeling he's leading me right where I want to go.

"What's the coolest thing you've found?" I ask.

He turns toward the creek and points. "There was a watch lying over there by those rocks. My mom is trying to find out whose it is. She says it's really expensive. At first I wanted to keep it, but now I'm hoping there's a reward. I want a phone, but my parents won't buy me one."

"It's funny," I say. "I just lost a watch last week. Somewhere along this path. It must have fallen off while I was jogging." I show him the watch I'm wearing. "I bought this as a replacement, but I don't really like it very much."

I'm suddenly ten times more interesting to him than I was a few seconds ago.

"What kind of watch?" he asks.

I parrot back the description from his mother's post.

"I shouldn't have been wearing it while I was running," I say. "That was dumb of me."

Now he's very nearly jumping out of his skin.

"What's your name?" he asks.

I think, *The engraved initials.* They won't mean anything to me now, but I might be able to put a name to them later. Guessing is risky, but what choice do I have?

"Evan," I tell him. "Evan Worley."

His dream of a reward is abruptly dashed.

"Not the same watch," he says.

"How can you be sure?"

"The one I found has an *S* and an *H* on the back."

Yes. S and *H.* As in shit happens or Stephen Hawking. Should be easy enough to remember.

"Have you found any other cool stuff?"

"Loads."

"Like what?"

He looks up at his treehouse. The strain on his face indicates that his better judgment is battling a strong impulse to say more than he should. The impulse wins.

"Wanna see?" he asks.

"Sure," I say.

"Okay. Follow me."

"Into the treehouse?"

He nods.

"You don't think I'm too big?"

"My dad climbs up all the time."

I scan the bike path. Hopefully the small trickle of passersby will assume that *I'm* the boy's father. I watch him ascend the rope ladder, then test my weight on the bottom rung. I'm pretty sure it would support a man twice my size. By the time I'm inside, the boy has pulled back a small plastic tarp and is prizing up one of the floorboards with his fingertips. The junk he lifts out and sets on the floor tells me that he hasn't shared this hidey-hole with his parents, not if they worry about things like tetanus. He's squirreled away bent and rusted nails, bottlecaps, soda cans, loose change. Stuff you'd find if you were combing the beach with a metal detector.

But there is one object that doesn't fit with the others. One object I'm sure would cost the boy his treehouse privileges: a syringe with the plunger pushed down and a brownish residue covering the base of the barrel. Parks and bike paths are notorious for attracting addicts. A stray bit of drug paraphernalia could be totally unrelated to Nolan. Then again, I could be looking at a murder weapon.

"I'm a collector," the boy says.

He sounds proud, as though practicing such a distinguished hobby elevates him above other kids his age. Maybe it does. He's curious. He has imagination. He reminds me of Jon rummaging around in that abandoned lot, searching for what he called "buried treasure."

"When did you find this?" I ask, pointing to the syringe.

"Same day I found the watch."

I try not to let my excitement show.

"You know, every good collector is also a salesman," I say.

"A salesman?"

"You want that phone, don't you?"

He rolls his eyes. "Do you even know how much phones cost?" he asks.

"You have to start somewhere, don't you?"

He thinks this over, then nods like I'm onto something. I take out my wallet.

"How much for this?" I ask, pointing again at the syringe.

He grimaces. "That's the best thing I've found. I'll never get another one of those."

I smile despite myself; the kid's a natural. "How about five bucks?"

He shakes his head like I've insulted him.

"I tell you what—throw in that silver bottlecap, and I'll give you ten."

His expression tells me that I'm in the right ballpark.

"Twelve," I say. "That's as high as I'll go."

He grins, then holds out one hand, palm up. I'm the proud new owner of a used hypodermic needle and the cap to a bottle of pilsner. I pull a handkerchief from my pocket, lift the syringe by the thumb rest, and drop it into a Ziploc bag I brought along just in case.

"A pleasure doing business," he says, a line he must have picked up from a shopkeeper or a street vendor. He's sweeping the remainder of his inventory under the floorboards as I say my goodbye and start back down the ladder.

TWENTY-TWO

I call Gloria during the drive home. To my surprise, she picks up on the first ring. I figure I must have caught her between meetings.

"Christian," she says. "It's always such a relief to look down and see a friend's name on the screen. I spend most of my day fielding calls from people who either want something from me or want to blame me for something."

"In that case, I'm not sure I'm calling as a friend."

"Oh?"

"Sorry, but I want something from you."

Her sigh echoes around the car like a gust of wind.

"Spit it out," she says.

I tell her about the syringe and how I came to find it, then ask if she'll introduce me to her favorite forensic analyst. Her response is less than encouraging.

"Are you fucking serious, Christian?"

"You said—"

"I thought I was humoring you. I'm the mayor. I can't in good conscience support your vigilante crusade. If word got out—"

"I know. Your bid for the governorship would be in serious jeopardy."

"You know, but you don't seem to care."

"I'll be discreet."

"It's more than that. You're mucking around in places you don't belong. This isn't playtime, Christian."

"I'm not playing."

"But you are. If you really believe this young man was murdered, then you need to go to the police. Get a full-fledged inquiry underway."

"You said you'd make some calls if—"

"*If* you turned over everything you've found."

"You gave me a couple of days."

"I didn't say anything about aiding and abetting you in the meantime."

I go quiet. Silence has always made Gloria uncomfortable.

"Listen," she says, "I might be able to give you a name and a number. But I have to talk to him first, make sure he'll do me an off-books favor. You're putting people's careers at—"

"I told you, I'll be—"

"Discreet, I know. But let me handle the backstory. You can't tell him you think the syringe is a murder weapon. That really could cost him his job. Let's say you found it in the trash at one of your restaurants, and you're concerned that an employee is using. You want to make a quiet intervention, but you need proof first."

"Thank you, Gloria."

"He hasn't agreed to anything yet."

"I know, but—"

"And this is the end of my unofficial involvement. After this, if you want to use police resources, then you ask the police."

"Got it."

"Good."

I'm about to launch into a more robust thank-you when I realize the line's gone dead.

I spend the rest of the two-hour drive ruminating over Gloria's "playtime" comment. Maybe she's right. Maybe I should hand this off to the pros. Maybe my role all along has been to prove that there *was* a crime, convince the police to do their job.

But have I done even that much? The evidence I've gathered is still circumstantial. A vague blackmail note. A threatening encounter in a garage. Nolan throwing money around the Borgata, pretending to be a Wyeth. Even if the syringe comes back loaded with his DNA, all I'll have is proof that a known drug user was using drugs. The police won't be convinced until Nolan's body turns up, if it ever does.

—————

That night, I'm dreaming about a treehouse by the airport when a loud thud startles me awake. I sit up and look around. The bedroom is lit by an eerie blue glow. It takes me a second to realize that I've left the television on. I figure there was some kind of glitch with the sound; one of Quinn's pet peeves is that commercials are always twice as loud as the show.

"Alexa," I say, "turn off the TV."

I settle back down and am just starting to drift off when I hear a second bang followed by what sounds like glass shattering. I have no doubt the noise is coming from inside the house. My first thought is that it's Quinn making a late-night return. I start to call her name, then think, *But what if it isn't?*

I slip out from under the covers, tiptoe into the hall. I hear a scattering of objects somewhere near the kitchen, then footsteps rushing through the house. Adrenaline kicks in. I charge down the stairs, turn toward the dining room, and am immediately bowled over by a black-clad figure in a ski mask who must have fifty pounds on me. I'm pushing myself up off the floor when a second, less substantial man in black hurdles over my body. A gym bag whacks me across the back of the head.

I get up and chase after them as far as the front door. I'm hoping to catch a license plate, or at least a make and model, but they're already halfway down the block in an SUV with its lights off. Seconds later, another unlit car speeds by. Then a third. And a fourth.

What the . . .

I shut the door and lock it, not that the locks have done me much good. Then I walk through the downstairs rooms, switching on every light. All pictures larger than a postcard have been pulled from the walls and set on the floor. The burglars must have been looking for a safe.

Ironically, one of the objects I heard drop was a print of an Andrew Wyeth watercolor called *The Lobster*. Claire bought it for me on a lark when we opened Big Fish Grill. The glass in the frame shattered and spilled all over the dining room floor.

In the kitchen, I find the cabinet doors hanging wide open. Luckily, I've never been the type for china or expensive cutlery. The robbers did, however, make off with a small roll of cash I kept in the junk drawer and used for tips whenever I ordered delivery. More importantly, I see how they got in. There's a perfectly round hole cut into the glass in one of the sliding back doors.

I check the living room next. They knocked the television over and stripped the cushions from the couch, but as far as I can tell, they didn't take anything. The home office is a different story. My personal laptop, external hard drive, and Bose speakers are gone. The wires that connected them are lying scattered across my desk.

This is the kind of thing even I call the police about. I run back upstairs and grab my cell phone off the nightstand. But before I can start dialing, I hear sirens. It's like the neighborhood is being swarmed. I stand out on the balcony while I finish the call. Pockets of flashing neon-blue light rise up from the surrounding blocks. A bored-sounding operator informs me that there are units in the area. I could have told him that much.

I get dressed, then head out onto the street. It's like a block party in the dead of night. The neighbors are milling around on their lawns, most of them wearing bathrobes and slippers. There's a sedan with a muted siren spinning on its dash parked two doors down. Norman and Shannon, a couple in their eighties, are standing at the curb, talking to a plainclothes detective who's young enough to be their great-grandson. A second detective steps out of the car and starts toward me. He's tall in a way that doesn't suit him, as though he were really a foot shorter but had been stretched to his current height. He can't be more than a year or two older than his partner. Maybe Rehoboth forces its baby cops to work the graveyard shift.

"Good evening, sir," he says, once we're in speaking range.

"It was better before I got robbed," I tell him.

"No doubt. You're Mr. Stone?"

I nod.

"I'm Detective Dennis Dunne. Mind giving me the tour? Showing me what was taken?"

I'm not sure what to make of the fact that he doesn't ask for my ID. On the one hand, who would be out here impersonating me at this hour? On the other hand, if this were a neighborhood of rusty trailers and shotgun shacks, I doubt he'd take anything for granted.

The tour is brief. He jots down notes as I show him the overturned couch cushions, the mess in the dining room, the desk where my laptop no longer resides. He asks all the predictable questions: How many were there? What were they wearing? Did I hear their voices? Did I notice anything at all that might help detectives identify them? What makes him different from other cops I've encountered is that he actually seems to listen to my answers. Maybe it's his youth or the fact that Rehoboth is a relatively gentle beat, but he doesn't strike me as jaded or cynical. I can't imagine him pocketing cash bribes in back alleys. I can't imagine him planting a gun on the eleven-year-old boy he'd just shot to death.

He takes me at my word when I say they didn't make it upstairs, then ends by telling me that crime techs will be by to dust the back door, though probably not until late tomorrow morning.

"They have their hands full," he says. "These were flash robberies. A gang breaks into as many homes in a neighborhood as possible, all at the same time. They grab what they can and get out quick. The idea is that the police will be overwhelmed, won't know who to tackle or where to start looking."

"How do they know which houses to pick?"

"They scout the area. First choice is always a house where the family's away. Second choice is the elderly. Third choice is anyone who lives alone."

"I guess I'm option number three."

He hands me his card, and I walk him to the curb as though he were an invited guest. His partner is waving to him from a lawn on the opposite side of the street.

"Hey, Buckethead," the partner calls. "Come take a look at this."

Detective Dunne breaks into a trot. He passes under a streetlamp, and I see right away how he got his nickname. The top of his head is flat and long, while the sides taper down toward a broad, equally flat chin. His shadow looks exactly like the silhouette of a man whose head has been replaced by a bucket.

I spend some time comparing notes with Norman and Shannon.

They were hit harder than me. Family photos in silver-plated frames, a Stradivarius violin worth seventy grand, an art deco vase given to them as a wedding present. Belongings that can't be replaced.

"Forty-nine years on this block and never so much as a noise complaint," Norman says. "I guess we were overdue."

I tell them to let me know if they need anything, then head back inside. I'll give the place a thorough cleaning after the techs are done. For now, I return chairs to their upright positions. I sweep broken glass into a pile. I put the cushions back on the couch.

The sun's coming up by the time I crawl into bed. My last thought of the day is *Thank God Nolan's laptop was with Spooner.*

TWENTY-THREE

I get a solid four uninterrupted hours before the lab geek arrives. First he texts me from his van. Then he rings the bell like he's tapping out a melody that's stuck in his head . . . long-short, long-short, short-short-long. Shouldn't this be a solemn occasion? I throw on a pair of jeans and a T-shirt and jog downstairs. By the time I reach the front hall, he's tapping on the bell again. I yank the door open, but as soon as I see him, my irritation is gone. Maybe it's the Ichabod Crane physique and the shaggy hair. He looks harmless—and smart in a way that probably doesn't help him socially.

"Hi, I'm Gary Rakan from the Rehoboth Beach Police Department's Division of Forensic Science," he says, holding up his laminated ID. "I'm here to dust your back door for prints."

I wave him in.

He's wearing overalls and carrying what looks like a fishing tackle box. If it weren't for the van parked out front, the neighbors might take him for a plumber or an exterminator.

"Would you like some coffee?" I ask. "I was just about to brew a pot."

"Never touch the stuff. When you're as skinny as me, just a drop gives you the jitters."

He follows me into the kitchen, then heads straight to the sliding doors, kneels down, and pulls a pair of latex gloves from his front pocket. I realize he's walked right past my vision board without giving it so much as a glance. The burglars didn't bother with it either, but then why would they have?

"Looks like a professional job," he says, nodding at the hole in the glass. "Chances are they wore gloves, but you never know. I'll dust both sides."

I start up the coffeemaker while he steps out onto the patio. Then I move over to my board. I haven't updated it since I got back from Mantua Creek. To the right of the *WHAT I DON'T KNOW YET* column, I have just enough room to squeeze in one more category: *PHYSICAL EVIDENCE*. Apart from the Eagles ticket, there hasn't been much of that so far. I start to write *syringe*, then erase the letters and opt instead for a crude drawing of a hypodermic needle.

Beneath the drawing, I write *DNA* followed by a question mark.

I'm reading over the *WHAT I DON'T KNOW* column, looking for anything I can wipe away, when Gary steps back inside. It dawns on me that I have an expert at my disposal.

"Can I ask you something?" I say.

"Sure thing."

I try the same tack I took with Gloria.

"I'm writing a crime novel," I tell him, pointing to the board like it's my outline.

"Is that so?" he asks. His tone says, *You and everyone else I meet.*

"It's just an idea I'm toying with. But suppose a syringe was found in a creek, tangled in the reeds. Is there any chance you could pull DNA from it, or would the water have washed it all away?"

"How long had the syringe been there?"

"A week. Maybe ten days."

"It depends. DNA degrades in water. Conventional wisdom says you've got twenty-four hours, give or take. On the other hand, I read about a case where DNA was recovered from clothes that had been lying at the bottom of a pond for almost a month. What was the syringe used for? In your novel?"

"Heroin."

"Well, in that case, you'd probably be in business. Chances are the needle sucked some of the victim's blood up into the barrel where the water couldn't get at it."

I nod.

"Thanks," I say. "That makes a lot of sense."

Especially if there was a struggle. Nolan's killer would have been rushed. He would have stabbed Nolan with the needle rather than simply injecting him. The execution, so to speak, would have been clumsy.

I'm filling my largest mug with coffee when my phone rings. I pull it from my pocket and see Gloria's name scrolling across the screen.

"His name is Dr. Low," she says.

No preamble. Not even a hello. It's always straight to business with Gloria.

"He's brilliant. And as honest as they come. You owe me. 200 South Adams Street. He'll be expecting you at two p.m."

"Gloria," I say. "I can't tell you how much . . ."

But I'm too late. She's already hung up.

Gary signals he's done by standing and stretching his arms toward the ceiling.

"I'll need your prints too," he says. "For elimination."

It's an obvious step in the procedure, but the idea of giving ten unique identifiers to an employee of the police department puts me on the defensive. Gary picks up on my hesitation.

"It's just for this case," he assures me. "You won't end up in our database."

I'm relieved, but also embarrassed. Now it looks like I have something to hide.

"Either way is fine," I tell him.

When he's gone, I spend a good twenty minutes scrubbing the ink from my fingers.

———

On my way to Wilmington, I stop back at the Big Ocean corporate office. Spooner meets me again in the parking lot.

"Nada," he says. "The recovery software didn't turn up any new files."

I shake my head. "That can't be right. Nolan was compulsive. He logged everything."

"I tried two different programs. There's nothing there to recover."

"Is the software foolproof?"

Spooner shrugs. "One way or the other, it's the only option."

"Yeah, all right," I say. "Sorry to keep taking up your time with this."

"Sorry I don't have better news."

Me too, I think. I was convinced I'd find the key to Nolan's blackmail scheme somewhere on that hard drive. Now it feels like I'm back at square one.

———

"I'm here to see Dr. Low," I say. "He's expecting me."

The man behind the desk is in uniform. I can't tell if he's a genuine cop or a glorified greeter; the bulletproof glass keeps me from leaning forward and checking for a gun. Either way, he looks terminally bored, like he's been bored for so long that he can't remember what it's like not to be bored. He picks up his phone and dials an extension in slow motion, then gestures for me to take a seat. There are a handful of empty folding chairs lined up against the far wall. I pick the one in the middle and sit with a brown paper bag on my lap. The syringe is inside the bag—a lazy but effective cover.

Before long, a middle-aged man with shoulder-length white hair and thick, unruly sideburns comes charging into the lobby, grinning at me like we're old friends.

"Dr. Low?" I ask.

"So good of you to bring me lunch, Mr. Stone," he says, improvising a cover story.

I don't know why we need one. Apart from the wholly uninterested guard, there's nobody within earshot. I stand and hand over the bag. I start to thank him, but he cuts me off.

"I'll let you know as soon as I have the results," he whispers.

Then he turns and walks away.

The encounter isn't what I'd imagined. I thought I'd be invited down to his basement lab and asked to wait while he ran some tests. I'd hoped for instant, or at least expedient, gratification. Instead, I'm left with a vague promise; "as soon as" could mean a few hours or a few months. I think of the opening narration to that show *The First 48*—the bit about the chances of solving a murder diminishing after forty-eight hours have passed. It's been hundreds of hours since I glimpsed Nolan's body from the plane. And I'm an amateur with limited resources. How diminished are my chances?

I need to make something happen. I need a breakthrough.

———

I get back in my car and drive into the heart of downtown. There's a large, laptop-friendly café I like called Brew Haha on Delaware Avenue, just around the corner from Hotel Pont Neuf. This time of day, I'm sure to find a seat. I'm also lucky enough to snag a parking spot right outside.

I order a latte from the heavily tattooed barista, then claim a spot at the counter lining the front window and fire up Nolan's computer. This isn't like me. I'm not the type to hole up in a café. I feel uncomfortable, out of place. But I tell myself I'm not allowed to go home until I've found something—I don't care if I have to read every narrow line of every sprawling spreadsheet.

I stay true to my word. Minutes turn into hours. The work is just as tedious as I remember. I start to imagine coded text everywhere. I wonder if a racehorse's name might be an anagram for Nolan's blackmail victim. I wonder if the jockey's winnings equal the sum Nolan demanded.

It's going on 6 p.m. when I get the stroke of luck every investigation needs to help it along. I hear the guy seated next to me say into his phone, "Just email it to yourself. It's cheaper than the cloud."

Just email it to yourself . . . A trick as old as the Internet.

I go to Bookmarks and call up Nolan's Gmail account. I've skimmed it before, but with more than 2,000 unread messages in his inbox, I decided to take the subject lines at face value. It didn't occur to me that Nolan might have been hiding his most incriminating documents in plain sight. And on a platform he could access from any device.

I click on Search, then enter Nolan's email address in both the

To and From filters. The result is a big blank. My heart sinks a little. Then I run my eyes down the list of folders on the left-hand side of the page. There are forty messages stored in Drafts. When I looked at them initially, they seemed like accidents—Gmail saving copies of messages Nolan abandoned mid-sentence. I'd opened a few and then given up the hunt. This time, though, I click on every message, including the ones titled "no subject."

Halfway down the page, I hit paydirt. At first, I think I must be hallucinating. I feel winded. Even a little dizzy. I never would have imagined the world could be that small. I'm looking at photos. Two of them. Both featuring Dax Morelli and Olivia Langley.

Olivia Langley, daughter of Robert Langley, Delaware's wealthiest man.

Olivia Langley, who's engaged to New York City's most successful developer.

Olivia Langley, who is definitely *not* Dax's wife.

In the first photo, they're kissing. Dax is pressed up against an SUV and has his hands on the small of Olivia's back. In the second photo, they've moved inside the SUV and are doing something far more intimate. I remember what Nolan's girlfriend Ashley told me about Dax's visits to Scotched Up, the bar where they both worked. Dax spent hours at a back table with a woman Ashley assumed was his lawyer, though Nolan made a different assumption.

"What's strange is that it bothers Nolan so much," Ashley told me.

Not so strange after all. It must be damn awkward to have the man you're anonymously blackmailing hunkered down at a table just across the room. Especially when that man is your boss.

TWENTY-FOUR

Two hours later, I'm back home in Rehoboth, sitting at the island in my kitchen with a glass of Goldeneye and Nolan's laptop open in front of me. I have two very educated guesses that I need to prove: First, Dax Morelli was Nolan's blackmail victim; second, Nolan was killed by the man who assaulted him in a parking garage, then picked him up at the Borgata. My working hypothesis is that Dax hired this man to make the blackmail go away. When threats didn't work, it was time to eliminate Nolan altogether. The question is, Where would Dax go to hire a professional thug/killer?

The answer is almost too obvious: the mob. There have been vague rumors about Dax building his fortune on mafia money for as long as he's been in business, but a little over a year ago, the rumors got very specific. Dax became the subject of a short-lived scandal. An article in the *Wilmington Tribune* claimed he'd joined forces with a shady New Jersey developer. Together, they were building a string of hotels along the Jersey Shore. According to the article, the project was funded by an organized crime syndicate and staffed with mob-affiliated contractors, steel fabricators, and teamsters.

The journalist who wrote the article made a convincing case. He named names. For a moment, it looked like Dax was about to plummet from grace, but the next day, the *Tribune* printed an apology and a retraction—same as when they accused him of using crowdfunding to disguise shady loans. It's like Dax has a guardian angel embedded with the fourth estate.

I can't remember the name of the Jersey developer, but the *Tribune* has an online archive. Five dollars gets me past the paywall. When I type Dax's name into the search engine, a full page of headlines pops up. The majority concern commercial properties in the Wilmington area. If nothing else, Dax is prolific. I doubt you can walk a square block without passing one of his buildings. Some people might call it a monopoly.

The most recent articles have to do with the Downtown Development Project committee. I'm probably mentioned in some of them too but only in passing. Dax is the face of the DDP. As far as the public knows, he's the one creating jobs and giving low-income families a nice place to live. He's the one giving downtown a facelift and keeping kids off the street. Never mind that he cares more about repairing his reputation than revitalizing his hometown. In Dax's eyes, Downtown Wilmington exists for one reason: to fund his mansion in Westover Hills.

The strange thing is that the *Tribune* seems to care an awful lot about Dax's reputation too. The words *philanthropist, altruist, benefactor,* and *patron* all make an appearance beside his name in the headlines.

I scroll through two years' worth of search results but don't find the article I'm looking for. I reverse direction, thinking I must have missed it. I read every title from June 2020 on up to the present. Nothing. The mob article is gone. The retraction is gone. For a moment I wonder if I have the wrong paper—but no, I'm sure it was the *Tribune*. Somebody removed those articles from the archive. Dax's guardian angel must be on the payroll. Either he bought a high-ranking member of the *Tribune*'s editorial board or else he bought the whole damn paper when I wasn't looking.

I need confirmation. I need to talk to someone who remembers the article and the retraction and that brief moment when it looked like Dax was in real trouble. Someone who might even remember the name of the Jersey developer with the mob ties. I pick my phone up off the counter and call Gloria.

As usual, she cuts straight to what she thinks is the chase.

"I haven't heard from Dr. Low yet, if that's why—"

"No, no," I say. "This is about something different."

"But it's still about *something*, isn't it? I remember when you used to call just to talk."

"I'm pretty sure that was before you became Mayor Callaway. Your time wasn't so precious then."

"Fair enough," she says. "So what is it?"

"I just got curious about something, and I thought you might be able to help. Do you remember that *Tribune* article about Dax and the Jersey developer—the one with mafia ties? I've been searching the archives, and—"

"Dax? You're calling me at nine thirty at night about Dax?"

"Since when is nine thirty out of bounds?"

"Since I became Mayor Callaway. My day planner starts at five a.m."

"Sorry. It's a quick question. I was just wondering if you remember the developer's name?"

"Why?"

I know in advance that she won't like my answer, so I keep it vague. "It ties in with the other thing."

"Other thing?"

Her tone says she won't let it go. I take a deep breath.

"Look," I say, "I've found a connection between Nolan and Dax. A potentially important one."

"What? As in, Dax is a suspect?"

"Maybe."

"Oh, for fuck's sake, Christian. Your obsession with the disappearance of a bartender you barely knew is bad enough. Now you've folded in your vendetta against Dax?"

"There's no vendetta, Gloria. I'm just—"

"Come off it. You've had it in for that man from the second you laid eyes on him. And now he's all but castrated you by cutting the size of your space at the convention center in half."

"This has nothing to do with the DDP."

"Of course it does."

"I just want to know the name—"

"I don't remember, Christian. And I'm not sure I'd indulge you if I did. Ask the reporter who wrote the goddamn article. I can't continue this charade. Just leave me out of it."

She hangs up before I can get another word in. I don't love being dressed down, but at least she's given me a lead to follow. There's barely enough staff at the *Tribune* to fill a WeWork cubicle. Tracking down the crime reporter shouldn't be all that hard.

———

The next day, I find him eating his lunch in Rodney Square. I recognize him from his byline picture. It surprised me that his photo was so readily available online. Most people wouldn't suspect this of Wilmington, but its crime rate is four times the national average, and its homicide rate is one of the highest in the country. If I were writing about the most violent people in a violent city, I'd want to keep a low profile, but Ed Motley's headshot is right at the top of every one of his articles. And whoever answers the phone at the *Tribune* was only too happy to tell me where to look for him.

He's sitting on a bench, hands wrapped around a fat hoagie. A skinny guy with a big appetite. The white in his beard seems premature; I'd guess he's early thirties. He's wearing what must be a decades-old denim jacket and faded Doc Martens. If I didn't know better, I'd have guessed activist rather than journalist.

"Mr. Motley?" I ask.

He looks up at me with a mouth full of bread and cold cuts.

"I'm sorry to bother you," I say. "I'm—"

"Christian Stone," he says, swallowing. "I know you from the DDP."

I'm not sure if his recognizing me helps or hurts my cause. Either way, it shows that he's been keeping abreast of Dax's business ventures. I take a seat beside him.

"That's right," I say. "I'm interested in an article you wrote a while ago, but I can't seem to find it anywhere. It was about Dax Morelli and a project he was codeveloping in New Jersey."

I see Ed's journalist brain kick into gear. I know what he's going to ask before he asks it.

"You mean you're doing a little background check on your fellow committee member?"

My first impulse is to smile and deny, but then I realize it's not such a bad cover story.

"Something like that," I tell him. "But unofficially. Very unofficially. I just want to make sure there's nothing that might blow up in our faces later. The DDP is the best thing to happen to Wilmington in a long time. I don't want the finished product mired in scandal."

He's nodding, but I can't tell if I've won him over or lost him.

"Sorry," he says, "but I can't give you any assurances one way or the other. That story nearly cost me my career."

"Does that mean what you wrote wasn't true?"

He shrugs. I decide to give him a little push.

"Who quashed it?" I ask.

His smile says, *Nice try*. At the same time, I have a strong impression that he shares my distaste for Dax.

"I'm not asking for assurances," I say. "Just a little information. Completely off the record."

"What kind of information?"

I want to say, *All of it. Everything you've got*. But this is a delicate dance. Ed Motley doesn't know me from Adam. He has no reason to trust that I won't share whatever he tells me with Dax, my fellow committee member.

"As I remember it, your article insinuated—maybe more than insinuated—that Dax was in bed with the mob. I want the name of his connection. Just a name. I'm not asking for proof or a backstory. I can do the legwork myself."

He slides what's left of his sandwich back into a paper bag, then turns and gives me a long, hard look.

"I can't," he says. "And when I say I can't, I mean legally. Believe me, I'd shout what I know from the rooftops if I could. I put a lot of hours in on that story. But I need this job. I have a kid depending on me. There isn't a big market for disgraced journalists."

I nod.

"I get it," I say. "I do. But can you give me anything? A hint? A direction to look in."

He stands, brushes crumbs from his jeans. I stand with him. I think he's going to turn and walk away, but instead he leans forward, whispers in my ear as if to drive home the point that this is strictly confidential.

"You'll be interested to know who Dax has drinks with every Monday evening at the BBC Tavern," he says.

His back is to me by the time I get out a "thank you."

As luck would have it, today is Sunday. Just twenty-four hours and change to wait.

TWENTY-FIVE

I'm sitting across the street from the BBC Tavern in a slate-gray rented Buick with lightly tinted windows. I went with a rental because Dax might recognize my car. I got here at five o'clock. It's six now. Ed Motley didn't happen to mention what time Dax turns up for drinks; he only said evening.

I've spent the last hour watching people enter and exit the restaurant. So far, no one fits the mafioso bill. No tracksuits. No Armani suits. No gaudy rings or overstuffed cigars. If that's even how mobsters dress outside of TV. I'm not sure I've ever seen one in real life. For all I know, Dax's connection could be an elderly woman in a muumuu.

Despite the tinted windows and the legal parking spot, I feel conspicuous as hell. This is the longest I've ever sat in a car without going anywhere. I imagine everyone who walks by knows I'm on a stakeout. I imagine them whispering to each other, wondering if I'm a Fed or just a private detective on a divorce case. It's silly, but I can't shake the notion that I'm on display. So it's almost a relief when my phone rings and I have a reason to appear busy. I look down and see Gloria's name on the screen.

"I want to apologize," she says.

"Apologize?"

"For hanging up on you. And for not being more supportive. You caught me at a bad time."

I'm slightly taken aback. For as long as I can remember, there's been an unspoken agreement between us: No apologies required. Our friendship would always outweigh any petty slights.

"What's wrong?" I ask.

"Am I that obvious?"

"Not usually."

She hesitates.

"Listen, Christian," she says. "I'm worried about you."

I feel myself bristle.

"I'm fine," I tell her.

"I don't think you are. You're not acting like your normal self. Or anyone's normal self."

"How am I abnormal?"

"For starters, you were supposed to go to Miami, but then you didn't. But you didn't go back to work either. And apparently Claire can't get ahold of you. I don't think you've ever played hooky before in your life. Even on vacation, you refuse to silence your phone."

"Claire's overreacting."

"Claire isn't the issue. She isn't the one asking me to have syringes tested for DNA."

This is more new terrain for us. Gloria's always been there when I needed her, but she's never shown preemptive concern. Then again, this is the first time I've solicited her help in an off-books homicide investigation. How much more concerned would she be if she knew the full truth? That this all started with me glimpsing a body from a plane. A body that no one else saw. A body that wasn't there when I went to look for it. She'd probably use her influence to book me a rubber room.

"Gloria," I say, "is this an intervention?"

"I'd rather call it a dinner. I have a rare evening free. Come over now and let *me* feed *you* for a change. We can talk."

"About?"

"Your case. My *minions*, as you call them. I've had some informal conversations. There are people I can put you in touch with. Professional investigators."

"Why encourage me if you think I'm teetering on the deep end?"

"That's not exactly what I said. Just come over and we'll talk. I have a very fine bottle of Chianti waiting for you, and . . ."

I miss what she says next because I'm distracted by the sight of Dax's McLaren entering the parking lot. Seconds later, I watch him saunter around to the front of the restaurant and disappear inside.

"I'd love to," I say, "but it will have to be another night."

"There won't be another night. I can't just clear my schedule at the drop of a hat. I promise you I—"

"Sorry, Gloria. I have to go."

Now there's a Porsche pulling into the BBC lot, followed closely by a Lincoln Navigator. Both mafioso-worthy cars, but then the occupants turn out to be a pair of handsy thirtysomething couples dressed to the nines. More date night than *Goodfellas*.

Fifteen minutes pass without any new traffic. The other members of Dax's party must have arrived first. I'll catch them when they leave. Until then, there's other information I can gather. I step from the rental car, cross the street, and enter the parking lot like I have every reason in the world to be there. It's dark out, but the lot is well lit. No need to call attention to myself by using a flash. I hold my phone at my hip and snap a quick picture of each license plate as I walk past the first line of cars.

I've just started on the second line when a rock-hard blow to the back of my skull sends me sprawling. I throw my arms out in front of me just in time to avoid landing on my face. My first thought is *I'm having an aneurysm.* But I know that isn't right. I roll onto my back and look up to see a man in a ski mask looming over me; after the robbery, that makes three masked assailants in as many nights. He slips what must be a blackjack into his pocket, then hurls himself on top of me and starts pummeling.

The first shot catches me on the temple, the second flush on the bridge of my nose. My vision blurs, and I can taste the blood flowing over my lips. His fists are flying too fast for me to strike back. I cover my face while he beats on my forearms and shoulders, same as when Jon and I got jumped all those years ago. *Don't lose consciousness*, I tell myself. *Whatever happens, don't lose consciousness.* Still, I keep anticipating the blow that will break me.

But soon enough, he begins to tire. His punches land with less force. I hear his breathing grow heavier. He's about to quit—I can feel it. And that's when I reach up and rip off his mask. It's some kind of reflex action—as if, in that moment, my will to know is stronger than my will to survive. The unveiling isn't a surprise. I've spent hours looking at photographs of this man. I recognize him by the thinning hair, the ears jutting out to the sides, the long, pointed nose.

I hear myself shout, "You killed Nolan."

His expression says, *And now I have to kill you.* That wasn't the plan. This was supposed to be a beating. But I've seen his face.

He gets to his feet, unzips his jacket, starts to reach inside. Before I can react, he stops cold. He's looking out at the street. I hear voices heading toward us. A large, slightly inebriated party, all of them talking at once. Nolan's murderer curses under his breath, then snatches the ski mask from my hand and runs.

The pain in my skull doubles as I push myself up. I stumble, then get my legs under me and start after him. I'm not thinking, just doing. Adrenaline has taken over. This is the man I've been hunting, and now he's getting away.

I reach the sidewalk in time to see him climbing behind the wheel of a black sedan. My head is throbbing and my chest aches as I sprint across the street to my rental. I fumble with the key fob, then cut an illegal U-turn, nearly clipping a delivery truck in the process. The driver lays on his horn and shouts out his window. I keep my attention focused on the taillights of that sedan.

He's a good six car lengths ahead of me, but there's no one between us. I push down on the gas, then almost immediately hit the brake. He's done the last thing I expected: He's stopped at a red light.

Our bumpers are inches apart. What do I do now? The adrenaline has eased up just enough for my brain to take charge. The man's an assassin. I saw him reach inside his jacket for a gun. He's taunting me. He wants me to get out of my car. He wants me to walk over to his window. I won't do it, but I won't retreat either. This is when I call the police. I'll follow him. I'll keep giving directions until the squad cars catch up with us.

I pull my phone out of my pocket, but then he does something else I don't expect: He takes off through the red light, narrowly avoiding a collision with a west-bound SUV, then another with an east-bound F-150. There's a cacophony of screeching brakes and frantic horns, and then everything goes still for a beat while the drivers take a breath, thankful they aren't crawling out of a pileup.

Meanwhile, the intersection is blocked. I've lost him. And I didn't even get his license plate. I couldn't because there wasn't one.

TWENTY-SIX

I spend the short drive back to the restaurant plotting what I'll do to Dax. I picture myself standing over his table, dripping blood into his bread basket. I imagine throwing a drink in his face. I imagine climbing up on a chair and announcing to the dinner crowd that Dax Morelli and his mob buddies had a guy work me over in the parking lot. Because I know things. Things that will land Wilmington's golden child in a maximum-security cell. I can almost hear the gasps and murmurs. It's the kind of blind-rage fantasy you play over and over while you lie in bed at night. In real life, I'll have to be more discreet. Maybe I'll ask for a private word. Maybe I'll just smile and whisper, "Nice try."

But when I pull into the tavern's lot, I see that the McLaren is already gone. I take the spot it occupied, then beat on the rental's steering wheel with both fists. Pain radiates up my forearms. Soon, I start to feel other pains. Pains I'd kept at bay by focusing on Dax and my attacker. The agony in my head comes roaring back, coupled with an ache in my chest that only lets up if I hold my breath. I'm not a doctor, but I'm guessing Dax's hired hand broke my ribs when he hurled himself on top of me.

I switch on the overhead light and take a look at my face in the rearview mirror. That blow to the nose caught me flush. My eyes are already swollen and turning colors, and it looks like I'm wearing a blood goatee. If there were a way to reach the tavern's bathroom without walking past the host and a dozen different tables, I'd do it. I don't have a handkerchief on me, and since I've only had this car for a few hours, there aren't any napkins or Kleenex lying around. All I've got to work with is a half-empty bottle of water and the sleeves of my charcoal-colored sweater. With a little effort, I'm able to wipe most of the blood away, but there's nothing I can do to cover my eyes; my sunglasses are sitting in the glove compartment of my actual car. Whoever answers the door at the Morelli estate is in for a little shock.

———

Westover Hills sits ten minutes outside of Downtown Wilmington, but it might as well be in another country. The few homes you can see from the street look like they were built for the king's entourage. The ones you can't see from the street, like Dax's, are fit for the king himself.

I've been here before, but I still manage to get turned around on the side roads. I'm about to fire up the GPS when I realize I'm passing in front of Dax's estate. I hit the brakes and back up, then curse under my breath. There's an obstacle I hadn't anticipated: a seven-foot-tall wrought-iron security gate. It must have been open for guests the night of the DDP dinner party. I doubt the intercom with the keypad will get me anywhere. No way Dax is inviting me in tonight. He probably thinks I'm on life support in a Christiana Care ICU.

I make a U-turn, then pull onto the grass on the opposite side of the street. Come hell or high water, I'm getting past those gates. But how? It's a little late in the day for solicitors, and Dax wouldn't buzz in his own mother without an appointment. I can only think of two options. First, I pull up to the fence, climb onto the roof of the rental, launch myself over, then hike the Morellis' ridiculous mile-long driveway while praying the security cameras don't spot me. The second, more serious, option involves calling Dax and telling him in my calmest, most reasonable voice that either he lets me in or I finish Nolan's blackmail job—those pictures of him with Olivia Langley go straight to the tabloids.

I have my phone in my hand when I get what feels like a stroke of luck. The gates open in slow motion, and an Xfinity van exits the property. I throw the rental into drive, hit the gas, and make it inside with maybe a second to spare. Motion-sensor lights guide me up Dax's private road. About midway, I brake to let a pair of deer saunter across en route to a pond that just misses being a lake.

I drive through another acre of forest before the Morelli McCastle comes into view—a sprawling three-story stone edifice with decorative turrets and arched windows. Why a childless couple needs a home large enough to shelter a small village is beyond me. I follow the circular drive around a Versailles-worthy fountain and discover another bit of luck. The front double doors are propped wide open. There's a truck parked near the steps with WILMINGTON FITNESS painted across its side. Two hulking men emerge from the back carrying a treadmill wrapped in a plastic tarp. The Morellis are having their gym upgraded. Xfinity was probably here to install the latest entertainment package.

I park behind the truck and walk inside. The men with the treadmill have disappeared either upstairs or down one of three vaulted corridors. The entranceway reminds me of the Borgata's lobby. There's a Tiffany chandelier the size of a Smart car dangling from the ceiling and a trio of outsized abstract paintings covering the walls. Two of the largest flowerpots ever made flank a marble staircase. The cacti growing out of them are taller than me and have foot-long purple blossoms. I don't know what they're called, but I'm sure they're not native to Delaware, and they probably aren't meant to live indoors. Dax must pay someone a small fortune just to keep them alive.

I look around and realize I have no idea which direction to turn in. The place is a labyrinth. Dax could be anywhere. Or he could be somewhere else entirely. He could be meeting Olivia Langley in one of the dozen hotels he owns. I think about calling him after all, but now that I'm here, I'd rather not ruin the element of surprise. I figure eventually someone will wander through and tell me where to find him.

I don't have to wait long. The someone who wanders through is Holly Morelli, Dax's perfectly proportioned wife. She's trailing the steroid cases down the stairs when she spots me pretending to admire the chandelier.

"Christian?" she says. Then, when I turn and make eye contact: "My God, what happened to you?"

"Your husband happened to me."

"I'm sorry?"

I shake my head. "It's a joke. I slipped in the kitchen at Miki-motos. Landed face-first."

"That's awful."

"It looks worse than it feels."

Though at the moment, that's hard to believe. My brain is trying to beat its way out of my skull, and my field of vision is shrinking as my eyes swell. Part of me wonders if maybe I should be in an ICU.

"Gentlemen, you know the way by now," Holly says to the deliverymen.

I can't tell if she's uncomfortable because I'm here or because I'm hurt or because she's afraid to leave the strangers in her home unsupervised. Holly always looks a little uncomfortable, like she's sure she's forgotten some essential detail that will haunt her down the line.

"Is Dax expecting you?" she asks.

"He is," I lie. "The gate was open, so I just drove on up. I don't think he knows I'm here yet."

"He's in his study. Let me show you."

We start down the hallway to my left, Holly in the lead. She's wearing a black Lululemon tracksuit and rainbow-colored Golden Goose sneakers. Even her casual wear costs more than the average family's wardrobe. I'll give the Morellis this, though: They'll make good use of that gym. Not an ounce of body fat between them.

We walk past a sitting room and a den and the longest galley kitchen I've ever seen. A woman in an apron quits rummaging through the refrigerator and smiles sheepishly at Holly. Holly doesn't smile back.

When we reach the end of the east wing, Holly knocks on a thick oak door, then swings it open and ushers me inside.

"You have a visitor," she announces.

Dax is sitting behind his desk, his jacket draped over the back of his chair and his tie hanging loose around his neck. The study looks more like an Ivy League library, all walnut wainscoting and built-in bookcases loaded with antique tomes.

"Christian," he says, "my God, what happened to you?"

"That's what I said," Holly tells him.

Then she turns and shuts the door behind her. And just like that, I'm alone in a room with Dax.

"Have you read all of these?" I ask, waving at the walls of books. "Or are the pages blank?"

"What are you doing here, Christian?"

His voice is flat, affectless. I move to the edge of the desk and glare down at him.

"You're a piece of shit, Dax," I say.

"I'll ask you again," he says. "What are you doing here?"

"Letting you know that your little stunt failed."

"My little stunt?"

I point to my face. "You can't scare me off, Dax. I know what I know. Your time is coming."

"My time is coming? Look, is this about your space at the convention center? I did what—"

"Fuck the convention center."

I slam my palms on his desk and lean out over him. He stands, locks eyes with me. His face is a blank slate. He'd be the picture of poise if it weren't for the slight tremble in his legs.

"I'm calling 911," he announces, reaching into his pocket. "I don't know if you're drunk or concussed, but either way, you need help. And you're trespassing."

"Perfect," I say. "Tell them to send two squad cars."

He has the phone in his hand, but he isn't dialing.

"You're talking in riddles," he says.

"Then let me be real clear: Nolan Styer sends his regards."

Everything changes once that name's in the air. Dax drops back into his seat. His posture goes slack. He tosses his phone onto the desk.

"I take it you've seen the photos," he says.

"That's the least of what I've seen," I tell him.

He sneers up at me.

"I knew it," he says.

"Knew what?"

"This is another shakedown," he says, his spine stiffening back up. "Your junkie friend wanted money. You want your five thousand square feet. I never thought much of you, Christian, but I would have hoped you were better than this."

He's talking himself into a fit of rage. He slides up to the edge of his chair, waves his arms at nothing.

"You know what?" he says. "I'm going to do what I should have done from the beginning. I'm going to tell the world myself. Starting with Holly. I'll call her in here right now. You're welcome to watch. It'll give you and Nolan something to laugh about while you're rotting in jail."

His hand moves toward the phone. He stops himself. There's something else he wants to get off his chest.

"I haven't been the most loyal husband," he says. "But Olivia isn't just another fling. I love her. You must find that hard to believe. You think I'm working a connection, angling for her old man's backing. When you travel in my circles, everyone you meet either wants something from you or has something you want. Relationships are just greed and small talk. But not with Olivia. In Olivia's case—"

"You'd love her even if she was poor?"

"Mock me all you want. It's the truth."

"What about Nolan? Was he *too* greedy? Or were you protecting your mistress?"

"Nolan got everything he asked for. I'm not giving any more. It's over, Christian."

This time when he reaches for the phone, I grab his hand. I could have interrupted him at any point, but I had to be sure. You don't get where Dax is without knowing how to put on a performance. But for once he isn't performing. I know him well enough to tell the difference. He's willing to blow everything up for Olivia Langley. And he has no idea that Nolan is dead.

"I told you," I say, "you can keep the fucking convention center. And I have zero interest in your love life. That's not why I'm here."

The blank stare is back.

"So why are you here?" he asks.

I hesitate. Crossing Dax off my list of suspects and confiding in him are two very different things. On the other hand, he could be useful. He knew Nolan was his blackmailer, which means he did a little investigating of his own—or, more accurately, paid someone to do it. He probably has information I don't. I decide to feel him out.

"You called Nolan a junkie," I say. "How did you know he has a habit?"

"People tell me things."

A sudden wave of vertigo sends me reaching for one of the room's hardbacked chairs. I lower myself down. The motion of sitting sparks a stabbing pain in my chest. Luckily, it's short-lived. Dax seems oblivious.

"What else do they tell you?" I ask.

He shakes his head. "You can't just show up at my home and start acting like some grand inquisitor. I'm the one asking questions now. So tell me what you're doing here."

I might as well take the plunge. If I'm wrong and it is Dax behind the curtain, I won't be giving him any information he doesn't already have. And if I ever need to keep him in check, I have leverage. I have Nolan's photos.

"Nolan was murdered," I say.

His surprise seems genuine. Then denial kicks in.

"Bullshit," he says. "I would have heard about it."

"Nobody's heard about it. They haven't found the body yet."

"Then how do you know he's dead?"

"He's been missing for weeks. The last anyone saw of him, he was getting into a car with the same guy who knocked me senseless in the parking lot outside the BBC Tavern tonight. While you were inside having drinks."

Dax looks like he's trying to figure out which part of my story bothers him the most. "Are you saying that you were following me?"

"More like waiting for you."

He's about to ask why when the answer dawns on him. "You think the guy who busted up your face—and *possibly* killed Nolan—was working for me?"

"Until about five minutes ago I did."

"That's ridiculous."

"No, it isn't. Just consider who you were having drinks with at the BBC Tavern."

He cocks his head, tries his best to look indignant. "What do you know about who I had drinks with?"

"Only rumors," I say. "But I'm pretty sure you just confirmed them."

Now he's agitated. He shifts his weight, moves objects around on his desk.

"What is this, Christian? It's like you're on some kind of crusade. How is whatever happened to Nolan your business?"

But I've shared all I'm going to. He doesn't get to know what I saw from seat 3A. He doesn't get to know about my friend Jon being gunned down or the promise I made to Jon's mother: *Never again. Not on my watch.*

"You didn't answer my question," I say. "Who told you Nolan had a habit?"

He sighs as though he's giving up, then opens the center drawer of his desk, fishes around for a key, and uses it to unlock the bottom drawer to his left. He pulls out a blue file folder with fancy lettering on the front.

"I give you this," he says, "and we're done. You never mention Olivia and me in the same sentence again. And you destroy whatever photos you have. Deal?"

"That depends. What's in it?"

"Information. Names and numbers. Nolan's bookie. His dealer. How much he owed to each. You'll find plenty of people had a motive to kill him. I hired a *real* private investigator when the blackmailing started. He was thorough. He gave me an arsenal to fire back with. I didn't act on any of it, mind you. I even let Nolan keep his job. I was waiting to see if he'd come at me again. If he had, I would have been prepared. But my preference was to let the whole thing die quietly."

He drops the file on the desk between us. The lettering reads FIRST STATE INVESTIGATION. A white tag at the top reads NOLAN STYER.

"Do we have a deal?" he asks.

I take up the file.

"Sure," I say. "As long as everything you've told me is true."

TWENTY-EIGHT

I stay up most of that night poring over the First State Investigation file. Dax wasn't lying: Lots of people had reason to want Nolan dead, from friends he suckered into pyramid schemes to an ex who accused him of maxing out her credit card. But his victims are all civilians with day jobs. His dealer is a senior at Goldey-Beacom College. I'm looking for someone with the means and know-how to hire a contract killer. Only one person fits the bill—Vinny Martizano. Nolan's bookie is a "made" guy who operates out of an eponymous pizza parlor on Front Street in Philly. Dax's PI snapped a black-and-white photo of Vinny pinching Nolan's cheek in a way that looks none too friendly. I'll have to ask Mr. Martizano what they were talking about. Next stop: Philadelphia, PA.

After a few hours of sleep, I wake up feeling like my head and torso have been crammed into a body cast that's four sizes too small. The ten-step walk from my bed to the bathroom is brutal. A double dose of Advil, a pot of coffee, and some gentle pacing help limber me up. By the time I leave the house, I'm nearly functional.

I pull up in front of Vinny's Pizza at 10:50 a.m. It looks like any other New York–style pizza shop in the country: an unassuming brick facade with a neon sign in the window and a ragged awning covering the entrance. The staff inside is prepping for an 11:30 start.

There's nothing to suggest that their boss has been credibly accused of everything from loitering to homicide. Accused, but—thanks to a stellar legal team and skittish witnesses—never convicted.

I spend most of the next half hour searching for a parking spot. With a few minutes left to kill before Vinny's opens, I decide to get the lay of the land. I walk around into the alley and stroll past the rear of the parlor. There's a man in an apron hosing out trash cans. Behind him, the back entrance is propped open. I peer inside, expecting to see a kitchen. Instead, I find a no-frills meeting room furnished with a large card table and fold-out chairs. Apart from a single poster featuring an Italian soccer team, the walls are bare. An old man sits alone at the table shuffling a deck of cards. I linger just long enough to see Vinny pat him on the back as he passes through on his way to the restaurant. I wonder who the old man is. I wonder what kind of decisions get made in that room.

By the time I walk back around to the front, the CLOSED sign has been flipped to OPEN. I'm the first customer of the day. It's early for lunch, but the smell of baking dough sparks my appetite. I order two sausage and olive slices and a medium Coke. The kid who serves me keeps looking at my face and then looking away. I almost forgot that I'm walking around with swollen, purple blisters for eyes.

Vinny is sitting in the booth closest to the back room, slowly turning the pages of what looks like an enormous ledger. I take the booth nearest the front and sit facing him while I eat. Apart from staff, it's just the two of us. The actual restaurant isn't any fancier than the back room—same drop ceiling, same linoleum tiling, same bare-bones decor. It has the mom-and-pop feel of Nicola's in Rehoboth Beach, and the pizza, despite a slightly thin crust, is almost as good. I'd probably be a regular if I lived nearby. Whatever misery Vinny's caused, he's at least done one good thing for the people of Philadelphia.

When I'm done eating, I toss my paper plate and cup into the trash bin, then walk toward the back like I'm heading for the restroom. I come to a sudden stop in front of Vinny's table.

"Hey, aren't you Vinny Martizano?" I ask. "The owner of this place?"

I say it like I'm a longtime fan who never dreamed I'd get to meet my idol. I'm hoping a little friendly banter will set the mood. Vinny doesn't bite. He doesn't even bother looking up. I won't be turned away so easily. I fold my arms across my chest and continue hovering until he can't ignore me a second longer.

"I'm in the middle of something here," he snaps.

This should be the part where I turn and walk away, especially after last night's beatdown. There might be age spots on the backs of Vinny's hands, but his sleeveless T-shirt reveals biceps decades in the making, and the jagged scars on his neck and arms suggest he has stories to tell. Plenty of them.

"It'll only take a minute," I say.

"Make an appointment."

"I'm here now."

That gets his attention. Vinny's used to striking fear. He looks up at me with a slight grin.

"I can tell by your face that you're a stubborn bastard," he says. "You've got thirty seconds."

I take that as an invitation to join him.

"Let me get straight to the point," I say, sliding into the booth. "My friend Nolan has gone missing. I was hoping you could help."

"Nolan? Who the hell is Nolan?"

I show him the headshot I've saved to my phone.

"This kid's a friend of yours?" he says.

"A former employee."

"No offense, but your former employee's a bum."

"A bum?"

"A deadbeat. He borrows more than he can repay. He's got no control over his own appetites."

"When was the last time you saw him?"

"I'm supposed to remember dates?"

"Roughly?"

"Atlantic City, maybe a month ago. I collected a payment from him. Most of the fighters he bets on end up looking worse than you look now."

"A large payment?"

"Not large enough. Kid still owes me thirty grand. You want the truth—I'm looking for him too. Suddenly, he's a ghost. Doesn't answer his phone. Doesn't show up at his place of employment. None of the AC crowd has seen him. He's skipped. But he'll come back. They always do. If you find him before me, tell him I'm done asking nice."

I'm getting the same feeling I had in Dax's study: This isn't the guy. Would a mobbed-up bookie kill someone who still owed him that much money? Wouldn't he be more likely to send a message via a loved one? I think of my attacker snapping that picture of Nolan's girlfriend. I think of Nolan's mother alone in her tiny row house. Are they safe? Would Vinny be more or less likely to harm them if he knew Nolan was dead?

"Suppose he couldn't pay?" I ask.

"You mean all of it? I charge a high interest rate."

"I mean none of it. Not a single dime."

"Then he better stay gone."

"But that would be the end of it? No retribution against friends or family?"

"What is this? Are you negotiating on the kid's behalf? You got him stashed somewhere?"

Vinny's short fuse is burning fast. Time to cut to the chase.

"I don't know where he is," I say. "But I know where he was last seen. And I know who he was seen talking to."

I show him a second photo, a blowup from the security footage outside the Borgata. I watch his face closely. He tries to hide it, but there's more than a glimmer of recognition.

"This could be anybody," he says.

"With those ears?"

"I've never seen the guy before."

"We both know you have. We both know what he does for a living. And we both know what that means for Nolan."

"If we both know so fucking much, then what do you need me for?"

But it's clear he answered his own question while he was asking it.

"Wait a minute," he says. "You think I hired this prick? For Nolan? I told you, the kid owes me thirty grand. I'm not gonna sink another hundred into making him disappear. Your friend with the ears is high-end. I'm not the type to drive a Lamborghini when a Cutlass will get me there just as quick. You know what I'm saying?"

"You're saying you'd have your own people handle the job."

He shrugs. "Something like that."

I tap the screen of my phone. "So then maybe you wouldn't mind telling me this guy's name?"

"I thought you knew—"

"I know what he does. I don't know who he is."

Vinny looks at me like I'm some new species of stupid.

"You could save everyone a lot of hassle and put a bullet in your own skull," he says.

"No one will ever know I talked to you."

"Why do you care? Who is this kid to you? You're no cop. I'd have smelled it by now."

I glance around at the parlor.

"I own restaurants," I tell him. "Same as you. Like I said, Nolan used to work for me."

"The guys who work in my restaurants, I don't even know their names."

"We bonded."

He shakes his head like I'm a lost cause.

"Your thirty seconds are up," he says. "One final word of warning: You could catch a lot worse than a beating just for asking the question. That is, if I was to whisper in the right ears."

The threat feels empty. I sense Vinny wants to give me that name. Maybe it's personal. Maybe he and Nolan's killer have crossed paths before. Maybe it's just that Nolan's death cost him thirty grand. All he needs is a little push. I take out my wallet, pull a $100 bill from the billfold, and set it on the table. I let him see that there are more where that came from.

"Pretend I lost a bet," I say.

He looks down at the table.

"Keep pretending," he says.

I pull out another hundred, and then another. I don't stop until the dozen bills I withdrew for this purpose are resting in a stack on Vinny's side of the table.

"Now give me your driver's license," he says.

"My driver's license?"

"You want the intel or not?"

I don't like the idea of handing a career criminal a document loaded with my unique identifiers, but I've invested too much to turn back now. I tug out my license and slide it across the table. Vinny snaps two close-ups with his iPhone, one of the front and one of the back.

"Now I should have no trouble finding you if things go bad," he says, pushing the license back toward me. "You still want that name?"

I nod. He rolls up the bills and tucks the wad into his front pocket.

"You're in the wrong city," he says. "The guy you're looking for will go wherever the money takes him, but his roots are in Boston."

"And his name?"

He pulls a pencil from the ledger, writes two words on a napkin, and passes it to me.

"Just make sure you've got your will made out," he says. "Keep poking around, and chances are you'll vanish like Nolan real soon."

TWENTY-NINE

The name on the napkin is Shaun Hadlow. *S. H.*—the initials on the Rolex found at Mantua Creek. As soon as I get home, I head straight for Nolan's laptop and type those two words into Google. An italicized query at the top of the results page asks if I meant "Shaun Harlow." I take another look at the napkin. No, that's definitely a *d*.

I scroll down. There's a handful of Sean Hadlows, a single Shawn Hadlow, and no Shaun Hadlows. The absence of a clear match takes me by surprise; Google *Christian Stone* and you get seemingly endless pages of hits. Maybe Vinny did miss a letter; I doubt he's the type to worry about spelling. I click on the first Shaun Harlow's Facebook profile. He lives in Kenya, works for the Red Cross, and looks nothing like Nolan's killer.

I wouldn't expect a hit man to maintain a heavy social media presence, but—assuming Shaun Hadlow is his real name—there has to be a trace of him somewhere. Zero visibility is impossible in this day and age. I try adding *Boston* to the search terms and am rewarded with a new crop of Seans, Shauns, and Harlows. There's also a Shaun who "had low" testosterone before being treated at a Boston clinic and another who "had low" self-esteem before starting group therapy at Massachusetts Mental Health. The names Shaun and Hadlow never show up side by side.

The longer I search, the more determined I become. I'm like a kid trying for his high score on a video game; nothing else in the world matters—not thirst or hunger or the call of nature. I won't budge from this stool until I've found my man. In a moment of true desperation, I dig out my credit card and sign up for PeopleTracker, one of those sites that promises to locate anyone anywhere in the world. Pay a little extra and PT will provide a criminal background check. It's probably a scam, but the part about the background check sucks me in. A man like Shaun Hadlow, however good he might be, must have spent some time behind bars.

Or maybe not.

It turns out I've paid PeopleTracker $14.50 to tell me that there's no Shaun Hadlow listed in the Boston area. But there is an ancillary match. A woman named Laura Hadlow (maiden name Montgomery) married S. Hadlow (no further information available) on January 1, 2000. The couple currently resides at an address in the Charlestown area of Boston. They have two sons, ages twenty and eighteen. Laura works as a pediatric oncology nurse at Mass General, a position she's held for fifteen years.

The Shaun Hadlow who attacked me would have been in his mid to late twenties when the ball dropped on the new millennium. He's the right age. But does the rest of the profile fit? Would a man whose resume is a body count be able to sustain a decades-long marriage? Would he be able to keep a secret that big for that long? How would he explain the large, tax-free infusions of cash? How would he explain the odd knife or gunshot wound? The periodic visits from law enforcement? Over the course of his career, Shaun must have had his near misses. A victim who landed a few crushing blows on his way to the afterlife. A detective with questions but no proof.

Or, then again, maybe not. I've watched my share of true crime documentaries. Plenty of serial killers have wives and children who didn't suspect a thing until the SWAT team arrived. Ted Bundy, BTK, the Green River Killer, to name a few. If anything, a stable, public-facing life is more the norm than the exception. Shaun, a serial killer by profession, must know how to compartmentalize. The danger of being discovered must be part of the allure.

I switch over to Facebook and type *Laura Hadlow Boston* into the search box. There are a few hits, but only one exact match. Her profile picture shows an attractive middle-aged woman in a sleeveless blouse flanked by two athletic-looking teenage boys. *Two sons, ages twenty and eighteen.* The picture is a few years out of date, but this has to be the Laura Hadlow I found on PeopleTracker. Now I just need confirmation that the *S* in her husband's name stands for Shaun.

Luckily, her account is public. I start clicking through photos, scanning the adult-male faces. There aren't many. Most of the pictures are from the hospital. Laura's taken countless portraits of her "favorite patients"—girls and boys sitting up in their hospital beds, wearing bandannas or baseball caps. Almost all of them are smiling. She must care deeply about these kids, many of whom are probably terminal. She wouldn't be the first saint to have cast her lot with the devil, but part of me hopes that I'm wrong—that my Shaun and her S. are two different people.

There's an album of family photos too. Graduations, holidays, and especially vacations. Laura and the boys standing in front of a geyser at Yellowstone. Laura and the boys standing on the deck of a ship with their backs to the ocean. I start to wonder if maybe she's a single mother. Then it dawns on me. It must be Shaun behind the camera. He's managed to keep a low profile by assigning himself the role of family photographer. Clever. Of course he's clever. How else would he be walking around free?

Still, he hasn't been able to erase himself entirely. After scrolling through what feels like hundreds of photos, I hit pay dirt—a picture of Nolan's killer lying on a tweed sofa with a baby asleep on his chest. He's grinning and kissing the top of the infant's head. Depending on which son he's holding, the picture is either eighteen or twenty years old. Shaun has thick, curly black hair, and his tank top reveals an athletic physique. Laura's Facebook caption reads *Found this in a shoebox in the basement.* The comments suggest that Laura and Shaun are well liked: *You could see the resemblance even then . . .* ; *The man never ages!*; *What a beautiful family.*

This is it! I've got him! I hop off my stool and start a little victory dance, then freeze up when an ache in my side reminds me that the man I'm so happy to have found beat me senseless just twenty-four hours ago. I take a second to let the pain pass, then whisper, "I'm coming for you, Shaun Hadlow."

Upstairs, I pull an empty Coach Trekker bag from my bedroom closet and start filling it with sweaters, T-shirts, jeans—whatever's easiest to grab out of my dresser. I'm leaving for Boston as soon as I'm packed. I'm not sure exactly what I'll do when I get there, but the objective is simple enough: find out who hired Shaun to kill Nolan.

I'm stuffing toiletries into a travel kit when my phone pings. It's a text from Gloria: *Spoke with Dr. Low. No usable DNA on the syringe.* An hour ago that news would have hit me hard, but now it barely registers. My focus is pointed in one direction: north. Why fret over the loss of the murder weapon when you have the murderer's home address?

It occurs to me that Shaun might not be there now. He could be out ending a life anywhere in the world. But he'll return eventually. He's a family man. What will his wife do, I wonder, when she learns the truth? Will she stick dutifully by her husband's side throughout the trial? Will she bring him care packages and write him letters? The pediatric cancer nurse who married a contract killer. The headlines write themselves.

I carry the overnight bag downstairs, then sit back down in front of Nolan's computer. Before I slide his laptop into my day bag, I need to make a hotel reservation. I hit the space bar, and the screen lights up. A message in a blue box tells me I have a Google alert for the search *body found near water Delaware Pennsylvania New Jersey*. I reset all of my alerts on Nolan's computer after mine was stolen.

There have been other hits, but the descriptions of the deceased were all wrong. So my hopes aren't high when I click the link to an article in the *Cape Gazette*.

HOMICIDE DETECTIVES INVESTIGATING AFTER BODY FOUND ON LEWES BEACH

At approximately 4:40 p.m., Delaware State Police responded to a report of a dead man "found on Lewes Beach by a couple walking their dog," according to a DSP spokesperson.

The man was pronounced dead at the scene. Police found no means of identification on his person. Once his identity has been established, family will be notified.

The Delaware State Police Homicide Unit is investigating. Information may be provided anonymously via Delaware Crime Stoppers at delawarecrimestoppers.com.

It's more of an announcement than an article. I rush over to the map on my vision board. I spotted Nolan's body lodged in a bed of reeds on the Schuylkill River. The Schuylkill flows into the Delaware. The Delaware empties into Delaware Bay, home to Lewes Beach.

The geography works. It's Nolan. It has to be. But I won't know for sure until the police make their identification. By which point Nolan's mother will have been informed. A pair of strangers with detective's shields will have knocked on her door and delivered the news in a clinical monotone. I think of Jon's mother wailing on the wrong side of the police tape while the cops held her back. I want something better for Evelyn. I want her to hear from a friend—or at least an ally.

And there might be a way. I happen to sit on the board of Beebe Healthcare, Lewes's small-town hospital. Board membership comes with an all-access badge. *All access* includes the morgue.

Boston can wait another day. Identifying Nolan is the new priority.

I'm on my way to Lewes. I called ahead and managed to casually ask—after a painful ten-minute conversation about the fairway at Baywood Greens—if the body from the beach was being stored at the Beebe Healthcare morgue. According to Nick Hertrich, Beebe's CEO and the friend who first talked me into serving on the hospital's board, the body of a homicide victim would, under normal circumstances, be sent directly to the medical examiner's office in Wilmington. This particular body, however, is in such bad shape that the crime scene unit wanted it checked for contagion before they'd transport it to a major urban center. I didn't ask Nick what he meant by "bad shape." It was enough to learn that Nolan's corpse is lying in the hospital's basement, awaiting a team of infectious disease experts. At least, I'm assuming it's Nolan's corpse. I won't know for sure until I see him with my own eyes.

I don't want it to get back to Nick—or to any of my fellow board members—that I've been creeping around the morgue, so I park in the hospital's rear lot and enter through the door reserved for coroners and funeral home staff. The attendant, a young woman with violet streaks in her blond hair, looks up from a textbook and greets me with a smile that seems a bit too cheerful for the setting. When she shuts the book, I see the title is *Forensic Pathology*, third edition. Morgue attendant might be a grim gig, but I imagine it's the perfect way for a future medical examiner to put herself through med school.

"I'm Erica," she says. "How can I help you?"

She's kind enough not to comment on the state of my face, but I can see her looking.

"My name's Christian Stone," I say, tapping the badge I've clipped to my shirt pocket. "I'm on the hospital board."

Erica pulls a folder over her textbook like she's afraid I'll scold her for studying on the job. I have zero disciplinary authority, but it's probably better for me if she doesn't know that.

"The morgue came up at the last board meeting," I say. "Just some routine budgetary issues, but I realized I've never actually been down here. I thought I should take a look."

"I'd be happy to give you the tour. Though maybe *tour* isn't the right word. There's only the one large room."

"I don't want to take you away from your post," I say. "Just point me in the right direction and I'll—"

"Are you kidding? This time of day it's . . ."

She cuts herself off. I have the impression she was about to say *dead in here.*

"You'd be doing me a favor," she says. "I need to stretch my legs."

I'd been hoping to show myself around, but it's clear Erica won't take no for an answer. Which turns out to be a good thing, because as soon as we step through the double doors and into the morgue proper, I realize I'd have no idea where to begin my search. In one sense, the room is exactly what I'd pictured based on TV-show depictions dating all the way back to *Quincy, M.E.*: walls lined with squat stainless-steel doors, spotless linoleum tiling, and a thermostat set to icebox. But it's bigger than I'd anticipated. Much bigger. I wouldn't have guessed a small town like Lewes needed more than a half dozen drawers to accommodate its dead, but there must be thirty or forty metal doors spread over three long walls. Nolan could be behind any of them. Of course, I can't come out and ask Erica to show me the Lewes Beach body. But maybe if I get her talking . . .

"So what's the basic intake procedure?" I ask.

"Most of the time, bodies are tagged by the nurses upstairs on the hospital floor, then brought down and stored here until the funeral home of the family's choice can claim them. If the cause of death is unknown, then the hospital is legally obligated to contact the coroner."

"What if the cause of death is homicide?" I ask, though I already know the answer.

"Timely question," she says. "I'm sure you've heard about the corpse that washed up on Lewes Beach. I don't know the details. I only know that the police are treating it as a homicide. Normally, the victim would be transported from the crime scene straight to the coroner's office in Wilmington. But there are some questions about contagion. Our infectious disease team is going to take a look before we ship him on."

"So he's here now?" I ask.

"Right over there," she says, pointing.

I follow her finger with my eyes. Cabinet 17, two rows from the bottom on the wall to my left. I feel my heart rate tick up a few notches. The body I spotted from a thousand or so feet in the air might be near enough for me to touch.

"Do they know who he is yet?" I ask, doing my best to sound like a local showing interest in a rare hometown scandal.

"This is kind of gruesome," Erica says, "but his face is like, you know . . . well, it's not so much a face anymore."

It's a good thing she'll be cutting up the dead instead of the living; I doubt she'd rate high on her bedside manner. The more immediate concern is, How will I recognize Nolan if his features are no longer intact?

"That's awful," I say. "I guess they'll have to ID him using DNA?"

"Yeah, the crime techs took a sample at the scene. If he's in the system, they'll find him."

Shit. Somehow I had it in my mind that the medical examiner would process Nolan's DNA as part of the autopsy. It hadn't occurred to me that the techs might get a head start. For all I know, detectives might already be on their way to Evelyn's house.

"How long will that take?" I ask.

She shrugs. "Hard to say. I'm sure it's a top priority, but they're always dealing with a backlog in Wilmington."

"And what if there isn't a match?"

"Then they'll start combing through missing persons reports looking for males with his body type. Hopefully a relative can identify him based on his clothing."

"He's still dressed?"

That takes me by surprise. On TV, the bodies in the morgue always seem to be naked under the plastic sheet. It means that I might be able to ID Nolan after all, since I know what he was wearing when he left the Borgata.

"With a potential crime victim," Erica says, "they leave the clothing untouched so as not to disturb any evidence."

"He must not have had his wallet or phone on him."

"That would have made things too easy."

What I need now is to get a look inside cabinet 17. But how? I've asked all the questions I can ask without arousing suspicion. And Erica, who's started rubbing her arms as though warding off frostbite, is clearly ready to conclude the tour.

"So, this is it, really," she says. "Not a lot to see. Just a large refrigerated space and a lot of drawers."

"Thank you," I say. "You've been very helpful."

As I'm following her out through the double doors, I yank off my badge, then crouch and slide it back toward the center of the room. We say our goodbyes, and I step over to the elevator. While I wait for it to arrive, I look down at my chest, then pretend to be searching for something in my pockets. I turn back to Erica.

"I must have dropped my access badge," I say. "Would you mind if I run back and grab it?"

"Be my guest," she says.

I have my hands on the morgue doors when I hear the elevator ding behind me. I glance over my shoulder and see a pair of nurses wheeling a body on a gurney. Two bare feet stick out from under a white sheet. Erica jumps up with a clipboard in hand. There's paperwork to fill out before the deceased is assigned a cabinet. That should give me just enough time.

I retrieve my badge off the floor, then rush over to cabinet 17. I slide the metal tray halfway out and start to unzip the body bag. The refrigeration kills any odor, but that doesn't stop me from gagging. Erica meant it when she said the face was no longer a face. The skin is bloated, bruised, and scraped beyond recognition. The gashes on the top of his head run so deep that I can see through to his skull. At some point in his journey downriver, he must have been sucked into a rapid and slammed repeatedly against the rocks.

I want to turn away. I want to stop and regroup, but there isn't time. The nurses will be bringing that body in here any minute. Summoning every bit of my resolve, I force myself to yank the zipper down until the full torso is exposed. The jersey is in shreds, but I'd recognize that shade of green anywhere. An Eagles jersey. The jersey I spotted from seat 3A. The jersey Nolan was wearing when he left the Borgata.

I feel sick and dizzy and desperately sad. At the same time, I'm glad they'll be using DNA to identify Nolan. It means Evelyn Styer will never see what I'm seeing now. How would she go on? How would a mother make it from one day to the next with an image like this lodged in her mind?

I zip up the body bag and manage to shut the cabinet door just as Erica and the nurses begin wheeling in the newest resident. I raise my badge and nod to Erica. She acknowledges me with a quick smile as she directs the nurses to a cabinet on the far wall. Once I'm through the double doors, I bolt up the stairs and out to my car. There's a reusable grocery bag lying on the back seat. I open it up and set it on my lap, just in case. After a few minutes of deep breathing, the nausea passes.

I look at the clock on the dashboard. It's only 9 p.m. Hard to believe this is the same day I ate at Vinny's Pizza and tracked down Shaun Hadlow. And it isn't over. I still have a call to make. I pull out my phone and scroll through my contacts. I let my thumb hover for a beat before I tap Evelyn's number. She picks up on the first ring.

"It's him, isn't it?" she says. "The body on Lewes Beach. It's Nolan."

"I'm so sorry, Evelyn."

"I saw a report on the news. I didn't want to believe it, but at the same time I was sure."

I remember the moment Jon's mother learned her son was dead. I remember her fighting to break through the police tape, battling a cop twice her size. I remember her scream drowning out every other sound. This is different. On some level, Evelyn already knew Nolan was gone. What I'm giving her is confirmation. It makes for a quieter anguish. Her voice is dull and muted. It's as though she's been hollowed out inside.

"Are you going to be okay?" I ask. "I'm in Lewes now, but I can come to Wilmington if you—"

"No, thank you. I need to be alone."

"Are you sure? Is there someone you can—"

Two quick beeps tell me the call has ended. I consider driving straight to Wilmington, then decide against it. Evelyn's friends filled my restaurant for her fiftieth birthday. She'll have people to lean on once the numbness wears off. What she needs from me is the truth. She needs me to find out who hired Shaun Hadlow.

THIRTY-ONE

I leave for Boston that night. There's no point in waiting until morning; it's not like I'd sleep anyway. As soon as I shut my eyes, I'd be staring into Nolan's body bag, seeing the face that's no longer a face. The long drive will give me something else to focus on. More importantly, I'll have eyes on Shaun's house at the crack of dawn. I want to know where he goes and what he does, which means I need to get there before he leaves for the day. Assuming he does leave for the day. And assuming he's in Boston. If he happens to be out of town, I'll wait. I don't care if I have to take up residence; I'm not leaving MA until I know who paid to have Nolan murdered.

I spend most of the seven hours on I-95 obsessing over a single question: *Why?* Why was Nolan killed? The most obvious answer—over gambling debts—doesn't hold water. Not if, as Vinny claimed, Shaun charges a six-figure fee. Which brings me to the second most obvious answer: Nolan was a sloppy extortionist. Solving your blackmail problem by paying the ransom to a hit man makes sense. Pay a blackmailer once, and he'll almost definitely come back for more. Pay an assassin once, and you have a permanent solution. So was I too quick to dismiss Dax? I remember the look on his face when I told him Nolan was dead. Dax is a good liar, but he isn't that good. Could Nolan have been blackmailing someone else? I didn't find any evidence that he was, and neither did Dax's PI.

If Nolan wasn't killed over gambling debts or ransom demands, then there has to be another motive, one I haven't discovered yet. I replay everything I know about his life. Yes, he had a drug habit, but I doubt his college-kid dealer travels in the same circles as Shaun Hadlow. Nolan liked to pretend he was art-world royalty, but I can't see the Wyeth Foundation hiring a hit man to dispose of an impostor. If I rule out gambling, extortion, and drugs, then what's left? Nolan's orbit wasn't that big, so what am I missing?

At just after 5 a.m., I pull into the final rest stop before Boston and buy two slices of lemon loaf and a thirty-one-ounce Americano. Adrenaline has me feeling like I've slept ten hours, but I know from past all-nighters that the fatigue could kick in anytime.

There's a sunglasses rack sitting outside the entrance to the rest stop convenience store. I realize that in my hurry to get on the road, I probably didn't think enough about the fact that Shaun will recognize me if I get too close. And if for some reason he failed to recognize me, my matching black eyes should jog his memory. I buy a pair of cheap black sunglasses, a Red Sox baseball cap, and a Harvard sweatshirt—items I normally wouldn't be caught dead in—then change in the men's room and review my outfit in the mirror. It isn't a total transformation, but as long as I keep to the background, Shaun won't give me a second look.

A half hour later, my GPS informs me that I've arrived at my destination. I roll to a stop and survey my surroundings. The Hadlows live in the Charlestown section of Boston. It isn't a neighborhood I'm familiar with, and it isn't exactly what I'd pictured for Shaun. I'd been thinking *killer in suburbia*. A luxury subdivision with sprawling lawns and block after block of newly constructed villa-esque homes. But it's clear at a glance that Charlestown has been around since before the Tea Party. The narrow streets predate cars. There are no front yards at all, and not much in the way of sidewalks. Bishop's crook lampposts accentuate the colonial feel. The skinny row houses remind me of Philadelphia—or maybe San Francisco, because the terrain is so hilly and uneven. It's a neighborhood with character. And money. The homes aren't just historic; they're well preserved. And, in the case of the Hadlows, modernized. Shaun and his wife have the only house on the block with a built-in garage at ground level and big bay windows jutting out of each of the remaining two floors.

A delivery van pulls up behind me, and the driver taps his horn. I can see how a garage would come in handy. Parking is at a premium, and double parking would mean closing the block to through traffic. I circle back around and snag a spot three doors down and across the street from the Hadlows. By the time I'm done maneuvering my car into the space, I've got about an inch of wiggle room on either side.

It's just shy of 6 a.m. The sun isn't up yet, but the sky is starting to brighten. There aren't any lights on in the Hadlow home. I figure I have some time to kill, so I take out my phone and Google the Boston Harbor Hyatt. I've got some points built up on my rewards card, and the Hyatt has the advantage of being on the other side of the water from Charlestown. I don't want to step out for a midnight snack and bump into the man who would have shot me dead if it weren't for the timely arrival of a few drunken bystanders.

I remind myself that it's only been two days since Shaun jumped me. For all I know, he still intends to finish me off. I'm a loose end, the witness he left behind. Maybe he's casing my street in Rehoboth right now. Maybe, but I doubt it. If he'd really wanted to eliminate me, he wouldn't have burned through that red light. He would have led me somewhere off the beaten path, then put a bullet in my head. He must have figured that a quick glimpse of his face wasn't enough to ID him, in which case killing me would be riskier than leaving me alive.

At roughly a quarter after six, the Hadlow residence shows its first sign of life. The bay window on the main floor lights up. I sit up straighter and lean out over the steering wheel, hoping a better angle will allow me to peek through the cracks in the oak shutters. No such luck. The most I can see is a passing shadow. Is it Shaun's shadow? His wife's? One of the boys? Now my adrenaline really kicks in. My left knee starts bouncing up and down, and I can hear my fingers drumming on the dashboard. I feel like I might implode if my target doesn't show himself soon.

A half hour later, the garage door opens, and a forest-green two-door BMW pulls out as far as the curb. I get a good look while the driver pauses to check for traffic. It's Mrs. Hadlow, dressed in scrubs with her hair pulled back in a ponytail. No surprise that the oncology nurse is the first out the door. I just wish I knew for sure that her husband would be following her soon.

By 7 a.m. the sun is up and the lampposts have switched off. There's activity on the block now, people leaving for work or walking their dogs or taking their morning jog. This isn't the kind of busy urban street where a guy sitting in his car might go unnoticed. I fall back on the camouflage strategy I adopted outside the BBC Tavern. I pretend to be talking on my phone. It seems to work; the most I get is a passing glance.

While I'm fake-listening, I notice that one of the houses near the end of the block is for sale. It hasn't been renovated like Shaun's, but it shares the same basic row house DNA. I move my phone onto my lap and hunt the listing down on Zillow. *Holy shit.* The asking price is $1,800,000 for just under 2,500 square feet. And it's a fixer-upper, with the emphasis on *fixer*. Each room is gaudier and in greater disrepair than the last. Brothel-red rugs and faux-wood paneling in one room, sagging ceilings and dingy walls in another. The kitchen's been gutted of everything but its sink, and the brass chandeliers in the bedrooms are hanging from frayed electrical wires. Shaun's place, assuming the interior matches the upgraded exterior, must be worth a cool two and a half million. I take a quick peek on Glassdoor.com and find that an oncology nurse's salary tops out at 120K. So where does Shaun pretend the money comes from? And how does he fool the IRS?

At 8:15 a.m., the garage door opens again. I hold my breath, waiting for a black sedan to emerge. Instead, Shaun the high-end hit man is sitting behind the wheel of a beige Toyota Camry. No flash for Mr. Hadlow, at least not when he's cruising the streets of his hometown. I lower the brim of my Red Sox cap and pull out after him. *Showtime*, I tell myself.

I just hope Shaun doesn't notice he has an audience.

THIRTY-TWO

Boston Shaun is cautious behind the wheel. No illegal U-turns. No burning through red lights. Not so much as a rolling stop. We wind our way across Charlestown, then launch into rush-hour traffic on the Mass Turnpike. I wonder where we're headed. I wonder if Shaun listens to music or podcasts or audiobooks while he drives. I wonder if that's tea or coffee he's drinking from his thermos. Today, I'm an unauthorized observer of Shaun Hadlow's daily grind, and my goal is to soak in every last detail.

After forty stop-and-go minutes, he exits the turnpike and I follow him down tree-lined suburban streets to what looks like the neighborhood's main drag, a six-lane boulevard lined with strip malls. At the third intersection, he pulls into the parking lot for an urgent care center. I turn into the adjacent lot, park in front of a nail salon, and sink down until I'm sure only my Red Sox cap and sunglasses are visible from outside the car. When I look over, I see Shaun rummaging around in the trunk of his Camry. He's dressed in a suit that matches his car—beige, respectable, unlikely to draw a second glance.

Urgent care . . . Already my mind is racing. Maybe Shaun's here seeking treatment for an infected stab wound or a bullet hole that won't stay closed. It would make sense that he'd use a facility in a neighborhood far from his own. He could pay out of network, leave no trace. He might even have a special arrangement with one of the doctors—a wad of cash in exchange for discretion. On TV, the bad guys always keep a veterinarian on the payroll. Urgent care would be a major upgrade.

But why would Shaun wear business attire to an off-book medical appointment? When he pulls his head out of the trunk and stands up straight, I see he's balancing two columns of small blue-and-white boxes in his arms. He carries them inside, then returns empty-handed just a few minutes later.

Our next stop is just one exit down the turnpike. Shaun double-parks in front of a circa 1970, boxlike building with a sign above the awning that reads WALTHAM MEDICAL PLAZA. I pull in beside a fire hydrant and watch his reflection in my passenger-side mirror as he assembles a fresh stack of boxes. It's clear now that my first guess was wrong. Shaun isn't wounded—he's a goddamn sales rep. I imagine those boxes filled with sample-sized vials of some newly discovered, cutting-edge vaccine. Shaun Hadlow doing his part to relieve mankind's suffering. Dr. Jekyll, meet Mr. Hyde.

By the time he's done making his delivery, the sky has shifted from overcast to menacing. We've just started driving again when the deluge begins. The rain turns out to be an asset; it's falling so hard that I can stick close to Shaun's bumper without fear of him spotting me. Over the next hour, he stops at another urgent care, another private practice, then a pharmacy. His suit darkens by a few shades as he jogs in and out of doors, but his disposition remains sunny. He's light on his feet. He whistles. He smiles at strangers, holds the door for an elderly woman, and even bends down to pat a sopping wet beagle on the head. If I hadn't seen his face outside the BBC Tavern, I'd be sure I had the wrong guy. Boston Shaun is no assassin—he's Scrooge on Christmas morning.

At noon, with the rain falling even harder, he pulls into a shopping center in Wellesley, takes a small duffel bag from the rear seat, and ducks inside a gym. I park a few rows back, just close enough to watch Shaun through the gym's plate-glass window. He's standing at the front desk, chatting with a handful of people I assume are trainers because they're all wearing the same black T-shirts. Shaun does the talking while the staff nods and laughs. The scene looks familiar. It's the kind of reception I get whenever I step into the kitchen at one of my restaurants. These tanned and toned twentysomethings are eager to stay in Shaun's good graces. He isn't their client; he's their boss. I look up at the sign above the entrance. The gym is called the Body Zone. Shaun has a sense of humor.

And he's clever. If I'm right and he owns the place, then this is his version of Walter White's car wash. A hit man raking in six figures per corpse needs to launder his money, same as a meth manufacturer. A gym makes sense. It would be easy enough to create fake accounts—and difficult to audit given that most gyms survive off the members who never show up.

Today, Shaun's also a customer. The man behind the counter hands him a towel, and he heads off to the locker room. I figure this is my chance to stretch my legs and relieve my bladder; I've been holding in thirty-one ounces of coffee for the better part of five hours. There's a Chinese restaurant at the far end of the strip. I ditch my sunglasses and grab an umbrella off the back seat. After so much driving and so many sleepless hours, my legs are less than steady. It doesn't help that the asphalt looks like it might slide out from under me in the rain.

I order kung pao chicken to go and use the restroom while I'm waiting. I catch a glimpse of myself in the mirror and understand why the woman who took my order seemed to look everywhere but at me. My shiners are in the early fading stage. The skin around my right eye has turned the color of jaundice. My left eye looks like it's peeking out from inside an exploded varicose vein. Meanwhile, my assailant is a few doors down, packing on more muscle.

I climb back into my car, stick a glob of chicken in my mouth, and call up Google on my phone. Five minutes of poking around on the Better Business Bureau's database and I have my confirmation, but with a catch. The Body Zone, a chain with four locations throughout the Boston area, is jointly owned by S. and L. Hadlow. I hadn't pictured Laura Hadlow—a nurse who spends her days caring for deathly ill children—anywhere near Shaun's business. I want to believe that her husband is duping her along with the IRS, but what if she's involved? What if she's the one who cooks the books? Ted Bundy was a suicide hotline operator. Nothing's too cynical to be true.

I watch the Body Zone members come and go while I finish off my lunch. The clientele is purely upscale. Corporate types ducking out of the boardroom for a quick afternoon sweat. I'm picturing spa-like amenities, everything from steam rooms to eucalyptus soaps. High fees must facilitate the fake bookkeeping; if Shaun were running a $10-per-month facility, he'd have to forge a small city's worth of memberships to hide his murder profits.

For once, I'm hungry enough to eat my fortune cookie. The slip of paper inside reads *All things are easy with persistence*, which is more of an affirmation than a fortune. I'd been hoping for an actual prediction, something along the lines of *The justice you seek is near at hand* or maybe *The path you're on chose you for a reason.* Some cosmic stamp of approval. Some nudge or wink to tell me that I'm not, in Gloria's words, "mucking around" where I don't belong. *I guess you'll just have to make your own fortune, Christian*, I tell myself.

At one o'clock on the dot, Shaun steps out of the Body Zone with a fresh coat of gel in his hair, and as if by magic, the rain comes to an abrupt halt. He opens his trunk, takes inventory, and then it's back on the road.

His afternoon is a mirror image of his morning. Another urgent care, another doctor's office, another pharmacy. Rinse and repeat. Through it all, I pick up only one potential whiff of a double life. At 3:25 p.m., standing outside a storefront private practice, Shaun makes a ten-minute call on one cell phone, then slips it in his jacket pocket, pulls out a second phone, and makes a five-minute call. Both times, he does most of the talking. It could be that one of those calls was to a handler or a client. Then again, maybe Shaun has one cell for his day job and another for personal use.

When he's done making his rounds, Shaun drives back to Charlestown and stops roughly a dozen blocks shy of his home, at a restaurant called the Warren Tavern. He's lucky enough to snag a spot right in front of the entrance, directly beneath a sign that reads Food and Spirits, since 1780. I circle the block and park diagonally across the street. Shaun's standing at the curb, smoking a cigarette—his first of the day—while he waits for the rest of his party to arrive. I'm hoping the cigarette marks the arrival of his sociopathic alter ego. Shaun the Pharmaceutical Rep would never let nicotine anywhere near his lungs. Shaun the Hit Man, however, sucks down unfiltered Pall Malls and drinks Wild Turkey from a flask. He speaks in grunts and would sooner slit your throat than smile at you. But he's careful. He meets his clients in crowded bars where room din eliminates the risk of being overheard. He's the first to arrive and always sits with his back to the wall.

At least, that's how they'll portray him in the movie. In real life, it turns out, Shaun's meeting Mrs. Hadlow for dinner. He sees her coming, flicks his cigarette into the gutter, and throws his arms open wide. They kiss like the newlywed stage never passed, then link arms and walk into the tavern.

I could wait around, see if they make any illicit stops before heading home. But that seems unlikely. This is date night. This is Boston Shaun living his best life. And what a life it is. Set aside the fact that he's a contract killer, and what you have is a hardworking, conscientious family man with an entrepreneurial spirit. A man who loves his wife and has done right by his children.

I put the car in drive, then shift back to park. I realize something's been on my mind almost since the day began. I take out my phone and dial Quinn. The call goes straight to voicemail.

"It's me," I say. "I was just thinking about you."

I hesitate for a beat, then add, "About us."

THIRTY-THREE

By a quarter to six the next morning, I'm back in Charlestown, parked diagonally across from the Hadlows' residence and nursing a fresh thirty-one ounces of Gracenote coffee. A half hour later, the first-floor bay window lights up. At 6:45, the garage door rolls open, and Laura's forest-green BMW pulls out. At 8:15, the garage door opens again, and out comes Shaun. I note the times in a small spiral pad. They're identical to yesterday's. The Hadlows have their morning routine mastered down to the minute.

It's a pattern that continues over the course of the day. Shaun's Thursday feels like a do-over of his Wednesday, only with different locations and slightly better weather. After a tedious hour of stop-and-go traffic, he exits the turnpike in Jamaica Plains, where he delivers more blue-and-white boxes to more pharmacies, urgent cares, and doctors' offices. He must be in the seeding phase of the sales process, handing out samples in hopes of closing the deal at a later date. I doubt it's thrilling work—certainly not as thrilling as beating up a stranger in a parking lot or chauffeuring a young man to his death—but I'll say this for Shaun: He's committed to his cover story. His resting smile never fades. The spring in his step is practically a skip. Anyone who didn't know better would think the man lives for sales.

Unless . . .

I'm parked across the street from the Dorchester Body Zone when I'm hit with a sobering thought. Maybe Shaun *has* spotted me. Maybe all the whistling while he works is a performance for my benefit. *Knock yourself out, amateur. Let me take you on the dullest ride of your life.* It's the safest of all possible measures. Confront me, and there'd be witnesses. Kill me, and he'd have another crime to cover up. So why not give me a guided tour of Boston's small-time medical facilities? Let me gather all the proof I want that Shaun Hadlow earns an honest paycheck. No wonder he's in a good mood; he's probably laughing his ass off.

Whether he's on to me or not, I have to face facts. Following him around is a slow ride to nowhere. All I'm getting—all I can hope to get—is the bare bones of his daily itinerary. Maybe one of these locations is a front. Maybe his hit man handler is a physician, a nurse, a pharmacist, a lab tech. Someone who signs for the blue-and-white boxes, then leads Shaun into a back room and gives him the why, when, and how of who dies next. The problem is, I have no way of knowing. I can't see through walls. I can't slip a listening device into Shaun's blazer pocket. And, because he got a good look at my face while he was pummeling it, I have to keep my distance. I still stand by my pledge: I'm not leaving Boston until I know who bankrolled Nolan's murder. I'll just have to find another way.

In the meantime, I stick behind Shaun as he hits three more doctors' offices and a pharmacy, then smokes his lone cigarette—his signal to himself that the workday is done—while pacing the sidewalk in front of an urgent care. Forty minutes later, he's pulling into his garage in Charlestown. And that's when it dawns on me. The proof I'm looking for must be hidden somewhere inside that house.

A little black book. A shoebox stuffed with souvenirs of his kills. Or maybe, like Nolan, Shaun keeps a coded spreadsheet. There has to be something I can trace back to his most recent employer.

Breaking into the home of a prolific assassin might seem ill-advised, but I have an idea. It involves the Hadlows' garage door. This morning, I noticed that it closes in slow motion; Mrs. Hadlow had reached the end of the block before it was fully shut. It must be a safety feature—the pediatric nurse making sure she doesn't concuss any toddlers. I time the door now as it closes behind Shaun. I count one-Mississippi, two-Mississippi . . . I'm up to eight-Mississippi when the bottom of the door hits concrete. That's more than enough Mississippis for what I have in mind.

I'd been planning to wait around in the hopes that Shaun might reemerge and give me a very different tour of Boston, but now I don't bother. Instead, I follow my GPS to the nearest Target, where I buy a hooded tracksuit and a cheap pair of running sneakers. Back at the hotel, I order room service, then fire up Nolan's laptop.

I head straight to Laura Hadlow's Facebook page. This time it isn't Shaun I'm interested in; it's his sons. I scroll back through a year's worth of posts until I find the photo of mom and her boys at Yellowstone. The caption reads *Brian, Adam, me, and Old Faithful.* I get the information I need by letting the cursor hover over the tagged boys' names. Brian, the older brother, is pursuing a master's in chemistry at Stanford. Adam is in his last year at the University of Tokyo, studying Japanese literature. A pair of grinning brainiacs who likely have no idea they're riding a body count into their dream futures. The only hint of family dysfunction is that they've both moved as far away from the nest as possible. Which is exactly what I wanted to confirm. Neither son lives at home—or near enough to stop by unannounced.

After seven solid hours of sleep, I drive back to Charlestown and park around the corner from the Hadlows. It's 6:20. That gives me twenty-five minutes before Laura leaves for the hospital. Two mornings in a row, she had the street to herself when she pulled out of the garage. By the time her husband starts his day, the block has come to life. I've seen packs of grade schoolers, corporate types climbing into their cars, retirees out for a speed walk—all potential witnesses. If I'm going to beat the crowd, I'll have to enter the home as Laura exits. I just hope I can find a place to hide until Shaun's gone.

At 6:30, I stick in a pair of earbuds and head to the bottom of the Hadlows' block. So far so good; I'm the only soul in sight. I grab on to a stop sign with one hand and begin stretching my quads. Looking down at my "sweat-wicking" heather-gray nylon tracksuit, I feel like the last clown out of the car. Jogging has never been my thing. Quinn got me to try it once, along the beach at sunrise. She said it would provide me with energy to burn throughout the day. I made it thirty yards before I broke into a leisurely stroll—back toward the house. Maybe I'll give it another chance . . . if Quinn gives *me* another chance. The fact that she hasn't returned my call doesn't worry me. I know her. She's going slow, thinking things through. When she does call back, she'll have questions. This time, I'll have answers.

After fifteen minutes of half-hearted limbering up, I spot Laura Hadlow's forest-green BMW nosing its way out onto the sidewalk. Once it's on the street and heading toward me, I start my jog. I count one-Mississippi, two-Mississippi. I keep my head pointed down. At six-Mississippi, I break stride, kneel as though tying a shoelace, then flatten myself on the sidewalk and roll under the garage door with maybe an inch to spare.

I sit up in the dark and listen—first for a voice from the street threatening to call the cops, then for any sign that Shaun's stirring. There's nothing on either front. No vigilant neighbors. No running water or creaking floorboards. No sound at all except for my own breathing. My heart's beating like a kick drum and I'm lightheaded as though I just ran a marathon for real. I've broken into the house of a contract killer *while he's home*. I've never felt so alive and terrified at the same time.

I take out my phone and switch on the flashlight. Apart from Shaun's Camry, the garage is practically bare. There are twin racing bikes mounted against one wall, a trio of fishing poles against the other. That's it. No clutter, which means no place to hide.

I find the door leading into the house, press my ear against it, and listen until I'm satisfied Shaun isn't lurking on the other side. That's the good news. The bad news is that the door is locked. My first instinct is to abort the mission and exit the way I entered. I'm in a no-witness zone. All Shaun would have to do is dump me in his trunk and drive me out to the Berkshires. Then again, there's no dead bolt barring my entry, just a simple mechanism on the door handle.

I switch off my phone's flashlight, call up YouTube, and type in *How to pick a lock*. Pages of videos appear. I click on one that looks promising, then mute the volume and call up the subtitles. A man with a horseshoe mustache starts lecturing me about key pins and driver pins, plugs and sheer lines. He claims the basic design of a simple door lock dates back to the Civil War. He drones on for a full three minutes before informing me that I'll need a lockpick set.

I return to the results page, scroll down until I spot the title *No key? Try a credit card*. The host of this video is wearing a Stetson with the brim pulled down over his eyes as though he's worried he might be incriminating himself.

"Nothing to it," he says. "Just shove the card between the door and the frame, then push and wiggle until the spring bolt pops."

His demonstration takes less time than most people need to dig their keys out of their pocket. When he's done, he holds up a mangled credit card, then makes a circa 1950s joke about the card belonging to his wife.

I take out my wallet, flip through the plastic sleeves, find a laminate rewards card to one of my own restaurants. I can't remember how or why it got there, but I'm pretty sure this is the only use I'll ever have for it. After a couple of deep breaths, I start my reenactment of the video I've just watched. My initial "pushing" and "wiggling" produce nothing but a loud rattling sound. I step back, listen for any hint that I've alerted Shaun. The only sound I hear is my own pulse throbbing in my ears.

I hold the door steady with the ball of one foot and try again. Just when I think the card will break in two if I apply any more pressure, the door pops open. I step through, pull it shut behind me, and turn the lock.

I'm standing in a small laundry room equipped with a stacked washer-dryer and a utility sink. Again, nowhere to hide. At this time of the morning, there's just enough natural light to see by. I switch off my phone. I think about taking off my sneakers but decide against it; I might have to run for my life at any moment. Walking heel to toe, I pass through the laundry room and into the kitchen.

I stop dead in my tracks when I hear what sounds like a small explosion.

THIRTY-FOUR

But it isn't an explosion. Shaun, master of stealth, snores at a sleep-apnea decibel. I hear him as soon as I step into the kitchen. It's the kind of deep, resonant cacophony that vibrates through the floorboards. As long as he's unconscious, I'll be able to gauge the distance between us, which feels to me like a major stroke of luck. Even better, it sounds like Shaun's here on the main floor. The master bedroom must be at the back of the house. All I have to do is make it up the stairs without waking him, find one of the boys' vacated rooms, and wait until I hear the garage door open and shut.

But first I have to find the staircase. The Hadlows renovated the interior of their home without updating its eighteenth-century layout. Modern touches include inset lighting, top-of-the-line appliances, decorative beams across the ceiling. What the renovation doesn't include is an open floor plan. Once I exit the kitchen, there's nothing but doors in every direction . . . all of them closed. This is a family that values privacy, which I guess shouldn't come as a surprise.

I move down a long hallway toward the rear of the house, gently opening and shutting each door as I go. I discover a dining room, a living room, a den, and two closets. That brings me to the back hallway, which is lined with six more doors. The snoring is coming from the far left. I stand still for a minute while I try to think like an architect. If the second floor is also built around two intersecting hallways, then the stairs must be behind the middle door. Otherwise, they'd lead directly into someone's bedroom. I reach out, turn the knob nice and slow. I notice I'm feeling lightheaded, then realize I've been holding my breath. I'm close enough to Shaun to wake him with a loud sneeze.

My guess was right. I've found the passageway to the second floor. I step in and silently pull the door shut behind me. Now there's a new obstacle: Either the Hadlows haven't gotten around to renovating the staircase yet or they decided this was the place to keep some old colonial charm. If the space were any narrower, I'd have to turn sideways. Halfway up, my shoulder brushes against a picture frame and sends it bouncing down the uncarpeted stairs. I freeze in place and listen. There's a quick stutter, and then the snoring resumes. I decide not to risk chasing after the picture. If Shaun stumbles across it, he'll assume it was Laura who knocked it loose. In the meantime, I need to get off these craggy stairs.

At the top of the landing, I find another hallway and more closed doors. I shouldn't have any trouble staying out of Shaun's way; this is a house built for hide-and-seek. The second door on the right features a nameplate written in Japanese characters. It must be Adam's room. I step inside and find myself surrounded by a little slice of Tokyo. A tatami mat lies beside a platform bed. Rice paper blinds cover the windows. A samurai sword with a long, curved blade hangs above a bare laptop desk. There's nothing for me to duck behind, but unless Shaun starts his day with a little meditation—which seems unlikely—I can't imagine what reason he'd have to come in here before work.

I sit cross-legged on the floor just to keep myself from pacing. I don't have long to wait. Shaun must be one hell of a deep sleeper, because when his alarm goes off, it sounds like a barrage of artillery fire. Then I realize he's set multiple alarms and placed them all around his bedroom. Maybe Shaun the Pharma Rep takes Ambien to drown out whatever conscience he has left.

The house quiets down for a moment, and then I hear something I hadn't anticipated—Shaun clambering up the stairs. My heart rate hits a new top speed, and I'm pretty sure that if I tried to scream, no sound would come out. I force myself to stand, then inch my way toward the sword and wrap one palm around the handle. It isn't just Shaun's steps I'm hearing. It sounds like he has someone on speakerphone. Or rather two people, one male and one female. There's a distant quality to their voices. I cup one ear, but I can't make out what they're saying through the static and the sound of my heart pounding in my chest.

But then, as Shaun gets closer, I begin to catch bits and pieces. I hear "Control to 221," then something garbled, then "Approaching suspect vehicle . . . suspect nowhere in sight." The laughter I hear is Shaun's. He passes in front of Adam's room, mere feet from where I'm standing. I hear the description of a car. I hear the letters and numbers of a license plate. I hear more laughing—mean-spirited, like somebody's being made a fool of and Shaun's loving it.

Then there's water running in the room next door. Shaun cranks up the volume on his police scanner. I hear him say, "You stupid ass." I have the impression he's listening as much for entertainment as to stay informed. I'd wondered what kind of radio station he tuned into while he drove around Boston; now I'm guessing this is it. Shaun has a hobby. I imagine him rooting for the bad guys to escape, then figuring out what he'd do differently once they're caught. It helps to keep his mind sharp, like crossword puzzles or sudoku.

He's out of the shower in a flash. There's the sound of a blow-dryer, and then I hear the scanner passing back in front of Adam's door and down the stairs. He carries it with him through the house. He leaves it on while he eats breakfast. He shouts at it, curses at it. Now and again he laughs hysterically, as though he's letting his madman out before the day begins.

Soon enough, I hear a muffled rumbling as the garage door rolls up, then back down. Only then do I realize I'm still gripping the hilt of the sword. I let go, remind myself to breathe. The danger is gone. I'm alone now. I can take my time.

At least within reason.

CHAPTER THIRTY-FIVE

I begin by looking for Shaun's home office. As a sales rep who works out of his car, I'm assuming he must have one. A place to fill out paperwork and phone clients. A place that's off-limits to the rest of the family.

I start at the end of the upstairs hallway and move toward the front of the house, opening doors as I go. I find two more bedrooms. The first is clearly Brian's. There's a colorful poster of the periodic table pinned to the wall above the bed, and the floor-to-ceiling bookcase is loaded with hardback science encyclopedias. The second bedroom is for guests. The mattress is bare, and the pictures on the walls look like the kind of nature photos that come with the frames—a waterfall, a half-moon, a blooming cactus.

Shaun's study is the last room on the right at the top of the stairs. It would be a corner office if this wasn't a row house. It isn't particularly large or well furnished, but there is a skylight he could use as an escape route if the Feds ever came knocking. The decor is ninety percent work related. Plaques hanging on the wall beside the door honor Shaun as Boston Rx's salesperson of the year in 2008, 2012, and 2016. What they tell me is that Shaun's held the same job for a while now. Stability must be part of his cover story.

His desk is a simple Ikea drafting table, a flat laminate surface with no drawers for me to search. A printer sits on one corner. The computer is missing, which means Shaun carries his laptop with him while he's working. Apart from a single ergonomic office chair, there's nothing to sit on. This isn't a place where Shaun entertains guests.

The room's only eye-catching feature is a trio of floating shelves affixed to the wall opposite the desk. Each shelf is approximately three feet deep and two feet wide. A thick pharmaceutical bible sits on one, travel guides to East Coast American cities on another. I wonder if Shaun's sales territory extends beyond Boston, or if he uses the guides for his other out-of-town business. The third shelf showcases an MVP trophy for Boston Rx's softball team and a framed family portrait that, like Laura's Facebook photos, doesn't include Shaun.

I start by thumbing through the drug bible and the travel guides. I find lots of dog-eared pages and highlighted passages, but no hidden compartments or sheets of paper with coded messages. No handwritten confession addressed to Laura, beginning with "In the event of my death . . ." Not that I was expecting one. I pick up the trophy. It's hollow and made of aluminum. When I shake it next to my ear, nothing rattles around inside.

I flip through a stack of envelopes on his desk, find nothing but work-related invoices and university-related bills. I open the closet door. The interior is empty. No office supplies. No file boxes. Not so much as a piece of lint. I get on my knees and check for loose planks. I crawl around the room tugging on baseboards and peering in air ducts. No secret chambers. No hidey-holes of any kind.

I move on to the bathroom. There's still some lingering steam from Shaun's shower. I search the medicine cabinet for a false backing. I lift the lid off the toilet tank. I rifle through the contents of the vanity. There's nothing the least bit incriminating anywhere. All I learn is that Shaun has a penchant for Old Spice and shaves with a straight razor.

I give Brian's room a cursory search. He's as much of a geek for science as his brother is for Japan. There are glow-in-the-dark constellations on the ceiling, posters on the walls that look like abstract art until you realize they're diagrams of molecules. There's a series of microscopes arranged in order of sophistication on a shelf above his desk. Again, nothing points to murder. Nothing suggests that anyone but Brian and the housekeeper have paid this room any attention.

I hold out some hope for the guest room, but in the end it's another bust. I search under the bed. I search between the mattress and the frame. I search the mattress itself, looking for a zipper or a patch of fabric that doesn't match the rest. I move on to the dresser, check the empty drawers for false bottoms. Nothing. I walk back through the second floor, looking for a door in the ceiling that might lead to an attic or crawl space. There isn't one.

Downstairs, I start with the master bedroom, where a garish, nearly life-sized oil painting of Mr. and Mrs. Hadlow hangs above their bed. Laura is sitting on a golden armchair and wearing a strapless red dress. Shaun stands behind her in a tux and bow tie, his hands resting on her shoulders. There's a crown-shaped halo of light encircling each of their heads. A forensic psychologist would have a field day. I'm no expert, but someone who kills for profit has to be a narcissist on a grand scale. That explains the crown on Shaun's head, but what about Laura? The painting makes me question again whether she's her husband's partner in more than marriage.

When I turn my attention to the room itself, the first thing I notice is that the bed's made. Shaun must have made it after all those alarms went off. It seems like an oddly fussy morning ritual for a contract murderer. I wonder if he spent time in the military. Or maybe a boarding school.

I comb every inch of the room and discover just a single item of interest: a stash of chocolate edibles in a nightstand drawer. The packaging boasts 100 mg of premium THC. Shaun's medical marijuana card is lying there next to the package. I guessed wrong: Shaun the Pharma Rep uses pot, not Ambien, to get him through the night.

I move on to the den, a windowless room that's done up as an entertainment hub. The flat-screen covers most of one wall, while the remaining walls are dedicated to vintage movie posters: *Casablanca, Gone with the Wind, Duck Soup*. There's a video game console, a pair of plush reclining chairs, even an old-fashioned popcorn maker. I open the closet door and find a column of shelves lined with CDs, vinyl records, board games, video games, and box-set DVDs. I take down the box set for *The Sopranos* and check the cases. There's nothing in them but DVDs, but the box itself catches my attention. It's the same shape as the floating shelves in Shaun's study. I hadn't thought to check if those shelves were solid or hollow, if they were supported by brackets or soldered to the wall. It's a long shot, but somehow it feels right.

I make sure everything is just as I found it, then head back upstairs.

THIRTY-SIX

The trio of shelves in Shaun's office are arranged in a horizontal line at roughly eye level. I start at the center. I set the big-pharma bible on the floor, then take hold of the shelf on either side and pull. There's some give, some wobble, but that could just be the result of shoddy installation. I tug a little harder, then harder still, and nearly go tumbling backward as the shelf slides free and its contents hit the floor with a heavy thud.

There's a stainless-steel case, a little larger than an old-fashioned school lunch box, lying at my feet. It's gleaming, even in this dim light. Not a scratch or a smudge anywhere. I kneel down, expecting to find some kind of security feature, either a combination lock or a fingerprint ID. But Shaun must think his hiding place is all the security he needs. I flip open the latches and lift the lid. Inside are two identical revolvers set in foam casing. My heart rate ticks up a few notches. I have to remind myself that a pair of guns doesn't advance my cause. For starters, Nolan wasn't shot. More importantly, they don't tell me who wanted him dead. Still, the discovery feels like a major step in the right direction. I shut the case, slide it back into the hollowed-out shelf, and reattach the shelf to the wall. I position the pharmaceutical bible exactly as I found it.

One down, two to go . . .

I step over to the shelf nearest the door. I set the softball trophy on the floor, then work the casing free. This time I'm prepared. I don't go stumbling backward. I don't spill the contents. Instead, I reach inside and pull out a leather bag roughly the size of a shaving kit. I zip it open and lay it out on the floor. One side is lined with syringes held in place by a nylon strap. The other side is covered with rows of small leather pouches. Each pouch holds a small vial of clear liquid. The vials are sealed, and their labels have been peeled off.

I can make a pretty well-educated guess as to what the vials are used for, but I don't know what chemical or potion they contain. I hesitate, then pull one out and slip it into the right pocket of my running jacket. I figure I'll be long gone by the time Shaun notices. *If* he notices. With any luck, he'll be in cuffs before he gets the chance.

Two down, one to go . . .

In the third shelf, I find a generic leather-bound photo album—the old-fashioned kind, with self-adhesive pages and transparent plastic coverings. I open it and discover that, instead of family snapshots, it's full of newspaper clippings. The first, titled "Multi-Millionaire Triathlete Dies of Heart Failure," dates back to October 20, 2001. It was printed in the *Miami Herald*. Jesse Mobley, founder and CEO of Mobley's Sports Apparel, died while on the phone with a 911 operator. His last words were *God help me, I can't find my pulse.*

I turn the page. The next article, from the *Portland Press*, is dated January 5, 2002. It's another extended obituary. A neurosurgeon turned hedge fund tycoon died in his sleep at the age of sixty-one. The cause, again, was heart failure. I keep turning pages. Shaun's scrapbook is a chronologically arranged who's who of the East Coast's wealthiest heart attack victims. This is Shaun's portfolio. These are his kills. He's done a steady business over the last twenty years.

I'm closing in on the last page when I'm stopped cold by a name I recognize. Joseph Moore. A textile magnate. A bit eccentric. In his late seventies when he died, but still, people were shocked by his passing. He was a vegan who prided himself on hiking the perimeter of his thirty-acre Pennsylvania property every morning. No history of heart disease in his family. I remember when he died. I remember because he was in a bidding war with Robert Langley over the new Wilmington Convention Center, the one that ultimately became part of the Downtown Development Project.

This is it, I tell myself. The connection to Nolan. Robert Langley might be the DDP's largest financial backer, but it's Olivia, his daughter, who represents him on the board. Olivia, whom Nolan was blackmailing by default when he threatened Dax with those photos. Dax must have told Olivia; that isn't the kind of secret you keep from your lover. The question is, Did she tell her father? Or did she reach out to Shaun on her own? Maybe Shaun did such a good job with Joseph Moore that he became the Langleys' default problem solver. Or maybe Joseph wasn't the first. Maybe other names in this book tie him back to the Langleys.

My mind is swimming with questions. Is Dax involved after all? At least as part of the cover-up? If Olivia killed to protect their affair, then what are the chances she did it without his knowledge? But there's a bigger, more puzzling question. Nolan's death doesn't fit Shaun's MO. Nolan didn't die in his bed of seemingly natural causes. He wasn't on the phone with 911. He was murdered and dumped in a river. Police are already sure of that much. So what happened? Did Shaun, after two successful decades, suddenly decide to change things up? Or did something go terribly wrong?

I turn to the final page of his scrapbook. I know what's coming, but still it knocks the wind out of me. The last article is just two days old. It was printed, in color, from the *Cape Gazette*'s website. A body washed up on shore, the victim and cause of death yet to be identified, though detectives are treating it as a homicide. The only recognized homicide in Shaun's book of the dead. I'll make sure that changes. I'll make sure Shaun pays for every murder he's committed—just as soon as I've identified his most recent employer.

I work backward through the pages, snapping pictures with my phone. I'm tempted to tuck the entire album under my arm and walk right out with it. It's not like Shaun could report it stolen. I imagine the shock he'd get when he discovered his prized possession was missing. He might have his own heart attack. But it's best for now that I leave the smallest trace possible. I don't want to spook him. I don't want to give him a reason to be extra cautious.

Once I have the shelves back in order, I take a picture that includes all three. Together, they represent Shaun's primary occupation. The guns are for protection. The syringes and vials are for assassination. The photo album is a kind of resume. I have a sample of the poison he uses to induce cardiac arrest. I have the names of people he's killed. And I have a link between him and Nolan. My work in Boston is done. What's left to do is waiting for me in Wilmington.

THIRTY-SEVEN

Twelve hours later, I'm back in Rehoboth. I've eaten and showered and am nowhere near as tired as I should be. My vision board is full to the max. I take a picture of it, then start tearing it down. I wipe the chalkboard clean with a damp cloth. I unpin the Eagles ticket, the photo of Shaun standing outside the Borgata, the map of DE, PA, NJ. When I'm done, I have a clean slate to work with, but I doubt I'll need all that space. This is the final chapter. I've built the base of the pyramid; now I just need to figure out who's sitting on top.

I download the photos of Shaun's trophy articles onto Nolan's computer, then carry the laptop into my study and hook it up to the printer. My ink supply is running low, but I get passable printouts of Joseph Moore's obituary and the article about the John Doe (Nolan) who washed up on Lewes Beach. I cut the white space from around both photos and take them back into the kitchen.

I tape the Moore article to the center of the board, then circle it with chalk and draw two arrows—one leading to the name Robert Langley, the other to the name Shaun Hadlow. Next, I tape up the Lewes-Beach-cadaver article and draw arrows to Shaun Hadlow, Robert Langley, and a third name: Olivia Langley. Beneath the articles and the names, I make a fresh *WHAT I KNOW* column. I know a lot. I know that Nolan was blackmailing Olivia's lover, Dax. I know that Shaun killed Nolan, and I'm all but certain that Robert Langley hired Shaun to kill Joseph Moore.

I scribble a second heading: *Suspects*. Beneath it, I write *Robert Langley* and *Olivia Langley*. But there's a third name, a name I might have been too quick to dismiss. There's every chance Dax hired Shaun Hadlow through the Langleys. And if he didn't, then I can't believe Olivia hasn't filled him in by now—not after the corpse washed up on Lewes Beach.

So I'll start with Dax. Because I know him. There's a weakness beneath his swagger that should be easy enough to exploit. It's called self-interest. Dax didn't make his fortune by worrying over who he might crush along the way. His image, his bottom line—that's what matters to Dax. He might believe he's in love, but threaten him with hard time, and he'd slap the cuffs on Olivia himself. The fact that his blackmailer was killed by an assassin on the Langleys' payroll should be more than enough to make Dax fear for his freedom.

———

The next morning, Dax passes through the gates of his driveway and finds my car blocking his path. I'm leaning against the driver-side window, arms folded across my chest. The McLaren's doors rise like wings, and Dax jumps out, his face already turning colors.

"That's it," he shouts. "You're off the rails. Harassment, stalking, trespassing—whatever charges I can press, I will. A restraining order won't cut it. I want you behind bars. A couple of phone calls and—"

I wave my hands for him to stop.

"Give it a rest," I say. "I'm here to talk about the body on Lewes Beach."

If nothing else, I've broken his momentum. He looks confused, flustered.

"What about it?"

"I think you know who it is."

I watch the news sink in. Dax sits down on the hood of his car, suddenly very pale.

"Nolan?" he asks.

"The man who was blackmailing you and your lover. I saw the corpse myself."

"I told you, I—"

"—didn't even know he was missing. I remember. But I'm not sure your story holds water. Who hires a PI to track down his blackmailer, then does nothing about it?"

"I didn't have to do anything. The demands stopped."

"Because Nolan was murdered. That's not a coincidence the cops are likely to gloss over."

"Jesus, Christian. *I* didn't kill him. Or have him killed."

He sounds distracted, as though his mind's racing on two tracks at once. It's clear he has more to say; the trick will be getting him to say it to me.

"The kid was a junkie," he continues. "He probably wasn't murdered at all. He probably OD'd."

"Maybe, but if he did, he had help."

"Meaning?"

"Someone else stuck the needle in his arm."

Dax shakes his head. "That's wild speculation. You have no way of knowing—"

"Oh, but I do. What I don't know yet is who gave the order. But if I were the DA, I'd think I had a pretty strong case against you.

You're right—Nolan was an addict. And a gambler. And you were his proven cash cow. Addicts are always looking to pay for their next fix. Gamblers rack up debts. He would have come back at you sooner or later. Or maybe he would have tried his luck with Olivia."

Dax stands back up and clenches his fists, ready to come to his true love's rescue.

"I never told Olivia about the blackmail," he says.

The lie is so unconvincing that I don't bother to call him out on it. Instead, I decide to test deeper waters.

"Joseph Moore," I say. "The man who would have outbid Olivia's father for the convention center."

Dax looks at me as though I've lost him. I don't buy it. He knows exactly where I'm headed.

"What about him?" he asks.

"His death was almost as convenient as Nolan's."

"There's nothing convenient about a heart attack."

"Not if it's the natural kind."

"You're talking in riddles. What the hell does Joseph Moore or his death have to do with anything?"

"Ask Olivia. Better yet, ask her old man."

"I'm not going to do that. I'm not going to dignify your idiocy by repeating it."

I figure it's time to bring out the big gun.

"You don't need to ask," I say. "You don't need to repeat a word. Olivia's already told you all about Shaun Hadlow."

"Who?"

The question comes too quick, and Dax's eyes are just a little too vacant. It's a practiced look. His poker face.

"Come off it, Dax," I say. "The same man who killed Joseph Moore killed Nolan. He's on the Langley payroll. The only question is whether you knew in advance or were told about it after the fact. Either way, you're involved."

I'm close. I can feel it. If I push Dax hard enough, he'll jump ship. He'll save himself and let the Langleys drown.

Or so I think . . .

"If you had any proof," he says, "you wouldn't be talking to me. You know how ridiculous your little theories sound. So why are you here? What is this? Some kind of twisted fun at my expense? I take away your flagship restaurant and now you want to ruin me? You need help, Christian."

Which is more or less what I knew he'd say. I've got my rebuttal ready to go.

"I do have proof," I tell him. "It just isn't conclusive yet. But I know an investigative journalist who'd be happy to run with what I've gathered. And he's demonstrated a particular interest in you. Remember Ed Motley? The reporter who was forced to swallow his story about your Jersey mob connections? I'm sure he'd love to take another swing at you."

Dax steps forward. I expect him to hit me or kick me or maybe even spit on me. Instead, he laughs in my face.

"Whisper in that hack's ear all you want," he says. "I'd feel safer confessing to him than to a priest."

"You sure about that? You might have shut Motley down, but not before he put one hell of a dent in your reputation. You won't survive another scandal."

I realize as I say it that I'm serious. Either Dax comes clean and tells me what he knows or I go straight to the fourth estate. I've collected plenty of evidence, probably as much as I can hope to collect on my own. Motley will know how to package and sell it. He'll know where to look for any missing pieces.

Dax steps up to me so our toes are touching.

"Fuck you, Christian," he says. "You have no idea. You're so far out of your depth you don't even know you're drowning. Now move your fucking car before I make your life more miserable than it already is."

———

Motley's a creature of habit. At exactly noon, I find him sitting in Rodney Square, biting into an overstuffed hoagie with mayo leaking out the sides. He sees me and does a double take.

"What happened to you?" he asks.

I'd almost forgotten about the state of my face. The swelling is gone and the bruises are fading, but the skin around my eyes is still an off-putting mix of dullish yellows and blues.

"I hit the brakes a little too hard," I say. "You should see my steering wheel."

I take a seat beside him on the steps.

"I've got a scoop for you," I tell him. "A reward for the lead you gave me on Dax."

"What kind of scoop?" he asks, his mouth crowded with cold cuts and bread.

"Remember Joseph Moore? The man who would have bought the convention center if he hadn't died?"

Motley nods.

"What if I told you his heart didn't stop all by itself? What if I told you he was murdered by the same people he was planning to outbid?"

Motley's eyes widen. It must be dollar signs he's seeing. A story that big would have to bump him up a pay grade or two. There might even be a book in it. Motley's credit is running thin. He has a kid to feed. He told me as much the last time we met.

"You have anything to back this up?" he asks.

"I do," I say. "It's circumstantial, but there's a lot of it. A pro like yourself should have no trouble building a case that's fit to print."

He puts aside his hoagie and pulls a small spiral notebook from his jacket pocket.

"Where do I start?"

I spell *Shaun Hadlow* for him.

THIRTY-EIGHT

The next day, I replace the ink cartridge in my printer and print out photos of every page from Shaun's scrapbook. I'm putting together a box of evidence for Motley. We're meeting tomorrow at noon in his office. Part of me wonders if I could, technically, be arrested for breaking into the home of a man with a few dozen murders under his belt. But then I dismiss the idea. I'll be Motley's anonymous source. Sources are protected.

I'm sliding the final article from Shaun's collection—the *Cape Gazette*'s write-up about the body on Lewes Beach—into a thick manila folder when my phone rings. The Caller ID reads EVELYN.

Before I can get out a greeting, she says, "Nolan wasn't murdered."

"What do you mean?"

"I just got off the phone with a detective. The toxicology report is in. Nolan did it to himself. He OD'd. Heroin."

I can't say what I'm thinking out loud. Dax knew about Nolan's addiction, down to the name of his dealer. He knew Nolan had been arrested for possession. It was all in the PI's file. Is that why Dax was so smug this morning? Because he knew Shaun had been given a special set of instructions? *Fill your needle with heroin, and no one will look twice.* But then why push Nolan's body into the water? If you were staging an overdose, wouldn't you want the corpse to be found?

"I don't know what to think," Evelyn says. "I don't know what to feel. Should I be relieved? Does this mean that Nolan didn't die in pain? That he wasn't afraid? That he . . ."

I wait for a beat after her voice trails off.

"If you want company," I say, "I could—"

"No, thank you. My neighbor is on her way over. I'll be fine. I just need time to process."

I want to tell her that two things can be true at once: Her son could have overdosed *and* been murdered. I want to prepare her for the news to come. But I can't because, even now, I'm not one-hundred-percent sure.

"Good night, Evelyn," I say.

She thanks me, then ends the call. I carry the articles and my boxed-up vision board out to the garage and stick them in the trunk of my car. Back in the kitchen, I uncork a bottle of Pinot Noir and pull a wineglass down from the rack above the counter. I take the bottle and glass into the den and switch on the television. I'm two episodes into an *NYPD Blue* marathon when I drift off.

It's my bladder that wakes me. I don't have a sense of what time it is or how long I've been asleep. The digital clock on the stereo system is blank. The whole room is pitch dark. I don't remember switching off the overhead. Or the TV.

"Alexa," I say, "turn on the lights."

Alexa doesn't respond. I reach into my pocket and pull out my phone. I'm fumbling for the flashlight icon when I sense something moving in the hallway. I turn and spot a small circle of light on the floor just outside the den. Then I hear the quietest possible footsteps, like someone's walking with pillows strapped to their feet.

Shit, shit, shit . . . Turnabout is fair play. I broke into his home, and now he's broken into mine.

My adrenal gland starts pumping double time. I seize up for a second, then shake myself to my senses. Shaun is just steps away. It's too late to dial 911. There's only one door in and out of this room. My best hope is the element of surprise. I shove my phone back in my pocket, grab the neck of the wine bottle in my right hand, and drop back onto the couch.

My heart's pounding so hard I imagine he can hear it. I shut my eyes just as the light finds my face. I let my mouth hang open. I raise the volume on my breathing. It's as though I'm inviting him to plunge the needle into my neck. I wait until I feel him leaning over me, then swing the bottle with all my strength.

My aim is off. I'd been hoping for a knockout blow, but I only graze the top of his head. He stumbles back, more stunned than hurt. I hear what must be the syringe clatter against the hardwood floor. As Shaun crouches to pick it up, I ram him with my shoulder and dart past, but not quick enough—he grabs my ankle and sends me sprawling. I kick him in the jaw as he starts to climb on top of me, then scramble to my feet and run.

The front door isn't an option; he'd be on me again before I managed to undo the locks. Instead, I'm headed for the kitchen—for the block of knives beside the stove. I hear Shaun sprinting behind me. I'm reaching for a steak knife when he grabs me by the hair and jerks me back. I throw out an elbow, feel it connect with bone. Shaun curses, loses his grip on my hair.

I start to back away, but now I'm cornered. The island in my kitchen is more of a peninsula; it runs right to the wall. My only option is to square up and face him. He's silhouetted in the moonlight coming through the window above the kitchen sink. His gun is out, and I see that he's grinning.

"Turn around," he says.

I can't make my legs move. Shaun aims the barrel of the revolver at my right knee. I throw up my hands.

"All right," I say.

I pivot and face the wall, knot my hands behind my head, get down on my knees. I feel my resolve harden. I'm focused on one thing: the handle of the frying pan sticking out from the stovetop. Shaun can't wield the gun and the syringe at the same time. He'll have to put the revolver down, either in his pocket or on the counter. I wait until I hear metal click against the Formica. I let Shaun take one step closer, then leap up, grab the handle, and swing.

Shaun raises both arms just in time. The base of the pan catches the knuckles of his left hand. He yelps and jumps back. I grab the revolver off the counter. I've never so much as held a gun before. Shaun can sense it. He's weighing up whether or not to lunge. I square the barrel with his chest, thumb back the hammer.

"Drop the—"

He rushes forward. I fire a single shot. His momentum sends us both careening into the wall. I feel him clinging to my shoulders. I feel his blood soaking through my shirt. I drop the gun and try to push him off me. He resists until he can't any longer, then staggers, teeters, and falls backward, his hands clutching at the hole in his chest.

I drop down beside him. I kneel in his blood, grab his face in my hands.

"Who?" I say. "Who hired you to kill Nolan?"

He lets out a muted gasp, then goes still. I sink to the floor with my back against the island. I'm trembling all over. My mind shuts down for a beat. Then it starts racing. Everything I've done since the moment I spotted Nolan lying in those reeds is for nothing so long as I don't know who hired Shaun. I look over at his corpse. More than one person has accused me of playing detective. I know damn well what a real detective would do.

I lean forward, open the cabinet under the sink with one pinky finger, then slide out a pair of latex gloves. I'm shaking so hard I have trouble pulling them on. I crouch beside Shaun's body, my feet straddling a pool of his blood. I find his phone in the right front pocket of his jeans. It's a burner. A simple flip phone with no fingerprint ID or access code required. There's a single number listed under Contacts—the person Shaun planned to call once the job was done. He filled in the Name field with a string of asterisks, but that doesn't matter. It's a number I know by heart. A number I've dialed countless times.

Impossible, I tell myself. *This has to be some kind of setup*.

But I know it isn't. Deep down, I've known for a while. I just didn't want to believe.

THIRTY-NINE

At 7 a.m. I open the door to Gloria's office and walk in unannounced.

"Christian," she says, shutting her laptop and yanking off her glasses. "What in the world . . ."

I watch her take me in. I changed out of my blood-spattered clothes, but I haven't showered, slept, or eaten. My hair is matted, my eyes rimmed with red. I must look part wild animal.

"I killed a man last night," I say.

At first she doesn't seem to understand. Then her mouth falls open and her hands white-knuckle the edge of her desk.

"Oh my God," she says. "Christian, are you okay? Are you hurt? What man? Tell me what happened."

I cross the room, pull out my cell phone, flip to a headshot of Shaun's corpse, and hold it up in front of her.

"Recognize him?" I ask.

She makes a show of studying the picture, then shakes her head.

"I've never seen him before in my life," she says.

"His name's Shaun Hadlow. He's a contract killer. Or he was. He broke into my home and tried to give me a lethal injection. He's the same man who attacked me outside the BBC Tavern while Dax was having drinks inside."

"Dax?"

I stick my phone back in my pocket, then sit down opposite her.

"You think Dax hired this man?" she asks.

"That's what I'm trying to figure out. How well do you know Ed Motley?"

"The journalist who nearly lost his career going after Dax? I know his reputation. Or what's left of it. Why?"

I lean forward, lower my voice. "Motley's involved. He knew I'd be at the BBC Tavern the night Hadlow jumped me. He's the reason I was there in the first place. He'd given me a tip about Dax. Roughly a week later, I go to him with a scoop. I tell him Joseph Moore didn't die of a heart attack—he was murdered. If Moore had lived, he would have outbid Robert Langley for the convention center. The Downtown Development Project would have been finished before it started. Next thing I know, Shaun Hadlow is standing over me with a syringe in his hand."

Gloria gives me a conspiratorial nod. "So you're saying . . ."

"Motley's been talking to someone. And that someone paid Hadlow to kill Joseph Moore, Nolan Styer, and me."

Gloria shakes her head, sinks deeper into her chair.

"I never thought he'd go so far," she says.

"Who?"

"Dax. He must have bought off Motley. That explains the retraction. You were right all along, Christian. I just didn't want to see it. I didn't want to believe it."

"Believe what, exactly?"

Her expression shifts. She looks embarrassed and bereaved at once.

"I've kept things from you, Christian," she says.

"What things?"

"Dax and Olivia Langley."

"You knew about their affair?"

Gloria looks up at the ceiling, then down at her desk. She looks everywhere but at me. "And the blackmail. Dax told me. He was so matter-of-fact about it, as though it were some minor administrative hiccup. But a scandal would have stopped the DDP in its tracks. Our backers would have fled. Dax promised he'd handle it. I thought he meant with money. If I'd believed for a second that he was capable of murder, I never would have—"

"I'm not sure he is capable of murder," I say.

Gloria cocks her head. "What are you saying? You've suspected Dax from the beginning. Now you have proof. You've solved your case, Christian. And it nearly cost you your life." She reaches for the landline on her desk. "I'm calling Chief—"

I put my hand on hers before she can lift the receiver from its cradle.

"There are things that don't add up," I say.

"What things?" she asks.

"For starters, I have a hard time believing Dax hired someone to kill Joseph Moore. Dax is a parasite. An opportunist. He goes wherever the money comes easiest. That's all the DDP is to Dax: easy money. He doesn't care about the future of this city. Not enough to risk a murder charge."

"I think you underestimate the man's ego. He may not care about saving this city, but he'd like nothing more than to be seen as its savior. And he's desperate to restore his reputation after the Jersey debacle."

All valid points. They might even be enough to make me reconsider if it weren't for one nagging fact.

"Less than a half hour before Hadlow jumped me outside the BBC, I got a call from you," I say. "You were worried about me. I'd developed an unhealthy obsession. You were going to put the city's resources at my disposal, but only if I came over right then."

"I *was* worried about you. And obviously for good reason. Never mind the beating you took—a man tried to kill you last night."

"I think there's more to it than that."

"I don't follow."

"I think your conscience got the better of you."

"What are you talking about?"

I go quiet, let her draw her own conclusion. More than rage, I feel a kind of dull sadness. Gloria's been a constant in my life going back to grade school. She was the first girl I kissed. We went to junior and senior prom together. She was the first customer at my first restaurant. I spoke at her wedding. I catered her every inaugural event, from city council all the way to the mayor's office.

"Are you seriously accusing me of . . . of what, Christian? Hiring someone to kill you? Not just you, but Joseph Moore? And Nolan Styer? Why on earth would *I* kill Dax's blackmailer?"

Someone who hadn't known her for twenty years might believe her. All that time she's put in on the campaign trail and the debate stage has paid off; she's mastered the art of thinking one thing and saying another.

"Because Nolan got in your way," I tell her. "The DDP was your ticket to the governor's mansion. It had to be unimpeachable. Scandal free. You couldn't have the head of the committee caught in an affair with the principal backer's daughter. It would all start to look unseemly. Reporters more honest than Motley might start poking around. You know better than me what they'd find. *Ambitious* doesn't begin to describe the DDP. Even with Langley and Dax as investors, the budget must be tight. I'm guessing corners were cut. Bribes were made. Funds misappropriated."

Gloria reaches across the desk, takes my hand. I let her.

"This attempt on your life has you rattled, Christian. You aren't thinking straight. This is *me* you're talking to. We grew up together. I sat next to you at Jon's funeral. You spoke at my wedding. A man tried to murder you last night, and someone paid him to do it. The world must seem like an ugly place. But it can't be *that* ugly. You're the last person I'd betray, Christian. You have to know that."

It's true. I remember resting my head on her shoulder at Jon's funeral. Every fiber of me wants to believe her. But somehow I'm more convinced now than when I first walked into her office.

"I know it was you," I tell her, pulling my hand away. "I know because Shaun Hadlow said your name while he was bleeding out on my kitchen floor. If ever anyone had no reason to lie . . ."

It's a bluff that would have made the poker player in Nolan proud. Gloria slumps down in her chair. I lean forward, lock eyes with her. Her expression tells me that she's done lying, but she isn't about to confess either. I fall back on our friendship.

"How could you, Gloria?"

She breaks eye contact.

"You backed me into a corner," she says. "I had no choice."

I stand, turn my back to her, and walk out of the room. I keep going down nine flights of stairs. In the lobby, I cross paths with Detective Dunne. He's accompanied by a quartet of uniformed officers and a man in a pin-striped suit. Dunne raises a hand when he sees me, and the procession stops in unison. I walk over to him. I reach under my shirt, rip off the wire, and drop it in his open palm.

"Was that enough?" I ask.

He gives me a slow nod.

"It's enough," he says.

The man in the suit pushes Dunne aside and steps to me. I recognize him now. I've seen him on the news, holding press conferences in front of the courthouse. He answers every reporter's question like he's out to crush a defendant on the witness stand.

"The question," he says, "is whether or not the recording will be admissible. What in God's name were you thinking? You had to kill a man before you involved the police?"

"I tried to involve the police," I say. "I went straight to Wilmington's highest authority: the mayor."

He stalls for a second, then plows ahead as though he hasn't heard me. "I have zero tolerance for vigilantes. Expect to see charges filed. Obstruction of justice, failure to—"

"You won't do that," I say.

"Oh, you bet your ass I will."

He looks like he wants to pummel me. The hand that isn't holding a briefcase is clenched in a fist.

"Mayor Calloway kept an assassin on the payroll," I say. "You have no choice but to prosecute. Otherwise, your entire office looks complicit. Corrupt, even. Charging the guy who got the confession would jeopardize your case. You need me. I'm your number one witness."

"Listen, you smug little shit . . ."

But I don't listen. I step past him and keep walking. I've been awake for thirty hours straight, and in that time I've shot a man through the heart and sent my best friend to prison. If the Wilmington DA wants to finish dressing me down, he can arrest me or subpoena me.

"This isn't over," he shouts.

But I'm pretty sure it is.

"I'll just be a minute," Evelyn says. "Make yourself at home."

She leaves me in the living room and goes down into the basement, into what had been Nolan's apartment, in search of some mementos she wants to display beside the casket at the service. The wake was well attended, but apart from Ashley, Nolan's sort-of girlfriend, the mourners were all in Evelyn's camp; they weren't there to grieve the deceased so much as support the mother who'd lost her son.

It's cold in Evelyn's house, almost as cold as it is outside. The day so far has been appropriately grim, with low-slung clouds and a temperature just shy of forty degrees. I go over and take a seat on the couch. Evelyn has the room set up for the handful of friends and family who will accompany her home after the funeral. There are flowers and photos and tins of cookies spread out on the coffee table and end tables. There's a strong odor of cleaning products, which explains why the window is open a crack.

I take a framed photo off the coffee table and hold it carefully by the edges. It shows Nolan, somewhere between eight and ten, sitting on a pony, decked out cowboy-style, with a red bandanna around his neck and an imitation Stetson hanging halfway down his back. It's a typical photo of a typical boy. No hint yet of who

Nolan would become or how he'd end. I imagine that if Evelyn could go back in time, knowing what she knows now, she'd choose this moment. This is where her do-over would begin, in the waning days of her child's innocence, when his future was still a blank slate.

The sound of Evelyn rummaging through drawers in the basement is suddenly stifled by a deluge outside. In a matter of seconds, water begins streaking down the wall beneath the open window. I run over and slam the window shut, then head into the kitchen in search of a dish towel.

I'm on my knees, wiping off the sill and the wall, when I hear Evelyn's voice behind me.

"I'm sorry," she says. "It took me forever to find—"

She stops short when she sees me mopping up the small flood under her window. I get to my feet and turn to face her. The towel in my hands is soaked through. For a long beat, Evelyn says nothing. There's a look on her face like she's just witnessed a car crash. It isn't shock—it's what comes after shock. That gut-punch moment when denial quits working and you realize the tragedy is here to stay.

"Just stop," she says. "I can't have you mopping my floor. Not after everything you've . . . It's too much. I can't stand it anymore."

She's talking to herself more than to me. Her energy has turned manic. I watch her dart over to the sofa, drag one end away from the wall, then disappear from view as she crouches down. I hear the sound of a zipper opening. I can't believe what I'm seeing. Bundles of cash come sailing one by one over the back of the couch and land in a pile on the cushions. When her secret compartment is empty, Evelyn stands, catches her breath, and leans against the wall.

"Now you know," she says.

I stare back at her. There must be $100,000 in small bills lying there between us. Nolan's blackmail money. Evelyn was her son's partner in crime.

All I can think to say is "Why?"

A question I seem to be asking a lot lately. Evelyn steps out from behind the couch, forces herself to look me in the eyes.

"Opportunity," she says.

"Opportunity?"

"At first, I thought it was fate—Nolan getting hired at Scotched Up. But the man owns half of Wilmington, so *fate* is the wrong word."

"Dax Morelli?"

She gestures to the black-and-white photos hanging on the wall above the television.

"I had to close the studio," she says. "Almost six months ago now. Morelli bought the building just as my lease was about to roll over. He doubled the rent. It was his way of evicting me. His wife wanted a second location for her fashion boutique. So I had to go. After twenty years."

The rest of the story writes itself. Nolan told Evelyn what he saw at Scotched Up. She had Nolan follow Dax and Olivia, snap some pictures. She saw a way to hurt Dax while clearing Nolan's debt and giving herself a little cushion.

"I thought I was taking justice into my own hands," Evelyn says. "I can't believe I was so stupid."

She presses the heels of her hands against her eyes, unleashes a single keening sob. It falls on deaf ears. I've been out there searching for answers day and night. I nearly got myself killed. Twice. And the woman I've been fighting for was in on it from the beginning. I don't hate her. I'm not even angry. My anger is all used up. So is my sympathy.

"You could have told me you'd enlisted your son in a felony," I say.

"I never believed for a second that he'd been murdered. Not because of what we did. That was over and done with. A onetime thing."

"You handed Nolan a way to score six figures at the drop of a hat, and you really thought he wouldn't try it again?"

"He promised me," Evelyn says. "He promised."

Her voice breaks over the words. There are thin lines of mascara spilling down her cheeks. She looks at me like she's expecting some kind of solace. I don't have any to give.

"I'll turn myself in," she says. "Just let me finish burying my son."

Shaun is dead. Gloria's behind bars. I'm numb. I don't care why Evelyn did it. I don't care if she's punished. I want to go home and climb under the covers. I want to sleep Evelyn and her son out of my system. I want to wake up in my old life. My *real* life. My restaurants, my staff, my friends. I remember what Jon's mother said to me before she left Wilmington: *Jon won't be the last person you see wronged.* I kept my promise. I did all I could to set things right. It's over now. I'm done.

I turn, start toward the door.

"Wait," Evelyn says. "Just wait."

She runs after me, grabs my arm.

"Take the money. All of it. I don't want it in this house another second."

I yank my arm free.

"Please," she says. "Spend it. Bury it. Burn it. I don't care."

She turns back to the couch, starts gathering the bundles in her arms. She's moving quickly, frantically. For every bundle she secures, another tumbles to the floor.

I take one last look, then pull the door shut behind me.

FORTY-ONE

Six weeks later, I'm sitting on the balcony of my Miami condo with my brother Michael. We're drinking a round of Michael's favorite cocktail: Aperol Spritz, light on the Aperol. It's a balmy, sun-drenched afternoon. Our view includes the beach below, then nothing but sky and ocean stretching out to the horizon. Back in Delaware, there's frost on the trees.

Michael has gained a few pounds in the months since I've seen him. There's a new patch of gray in his beard, and he's wearing, of all things, an Eagles jersey. He looks carefree and content in a way that makes me wonder why I don't just move down here permanently.

"The outcome was never in your control, Christian," Michael says. "You couldn't choose the guilty party. The best you could do was solve the case. And you did that."

My look tells him I'm not ready to declare victory.

"Let me ask you something," he says. "Did you feel more or less alive while you were hunting for Nolan's killer?"

I didn't have to think for very long.

"More," I say. "A lot more."

"Of course you did. You were doing something you're good at. Something that matters. You got justice for Nolan. That's important, Christian."

He raises his drink.

"To the crime-fighting restaurateur. Lord knows you've always been full of surprises."

We clink glasses.

"No more surprises," I say. "I want my life nice and normal from now on. Regular hours. Full days off. More time down here. I might even get a dog."

"Does Quinn fit in that picture?" Michael asks.

I shake my head.

"She's gone," I tell him. "If I met her now, I think things would be different."

"Meaning?"

I take a moment to find the right words.

"This case changed me," I say. "I've seen up close what people do to one another for money, status, power. Our priorities are out of whack. I don't want that to be me. I'm ready to let someone in. I'll do what it takes to make room."

"Good for you," Michael says. "There's more to life than work."

As if on cue, my phone, which is sitting face down in front of me, pings three times in quick succession. I flip it over, find a trio of texts from Claire. Of all the people in my life, I think she might be the happiest to have me back. She was left holding the bag while I went out searching for Nolan's killer. I owe her, which is why she and her husband will be spending February here in my Miami apartment.

Michael clears his throat, a not-so-subtle hint that I'm being rude.

"Want to tell me why you're smiling?" he asks.

"We've hired a bar manager for the convention center location," I say. "My top pick."

Claire's third message reads *Ashley is a go*. Nolan's onetime girl-friend and coworker has agreed to leave Scotched Up and join Big Ocean.

"I never thought that convention center would see the light of day," Michael says. "Old man Langley really came through."

"Twice," I say.

When the news about Gloria broke, the Downtown Development Project looked to be dead in the water. But Robert Langley, who's pushing eighty and wants to be remembered for something more than his personal fortune, stepped in and brought it back to life. He wiped Gloria's name from the books and delegated her responsibilities to his daughter, Olivia.

Then it was Dax's turn to make the tabloids.

The week after Gloria's arrest, a young man walked into a Wilmington pawn shop carrying a hundred-year-old Stradivarius violin worth a small fortune and proudly declared that he wouldn't part with it for less than fifty bucks. The shop's owner excused himself, stepped into a back room, and called the police. The violin, it turned out, had been stolen from my neighbor the night our homes were broken into. The young man was given a choice: name his coconspirators or face more than thirty counts of felony theft. He promptly rolled on the middleman, who in turn rolled on Dax. The "flash robberies" were an elaborate cover cooked up by Gloria. Dax used his mob connections to supply the muscle. He thought he could prevent any future blackmail attempts by destroying Nolan's laptop; Gloria hoped that eliminating key evidence would force me to abandon the hunt. Dax's wife posted his bail, but the case against him is open and shut. The only question is how long he'll spend behind bars. If he'd confessed prior to Gloria's arrest, he might have been able to negotiate a plea deal.

Now it's too late. The district attorney has everything he needs to prosecute Wilmington's former mayor.

Most people, including me, doubted the DDP could survive a second scandal, but once again Robert Langley came to the rescue. He reached into his pockets and bought out Dax's share. And in the process, I got my 5,000 square feet back.

I've just finished replying to Claire when my phone starts ringing. Detective Dunne scrolls across the screen.

"Hello, Detective," I say.

Michael shakes his head. I signal that I'll only be a minute, then walk inside and close the sliding door behind me.

"Did I catch you at a bad time?" Dunne asks.

"No," I say. "But I do have company, so—"

"I'll get right to it. I have a proposition for you."

"A proposition?"

"Well, more like a case. It involves a restaurant, if you can believe it."

His cousin, he tells me, is a homicide detective in Houston. He and his partner arrested a sixteen-year-old busboy for bludgeoning a sous-chef to death. On paper, the case is airtight. The boy's fingerprints are all over the weapon. A restaurant full of people saw him running from the scene. But the kid insists he's innocent, and Dunne's cousin believes him.

"Which in itself is a small miracle," Dunne says. "My cousin's stubborn and difficult. All suspects are guilty until proven innocent. So if his gut tells him the kid didn't do it, then chances are the kid didn't do it. But his lieutenant won't sink any more man-hours into a slam-dunk case. And the public defender doesn't exactly have an investigative budget."

Neither, Dunne tells me, do the boy's parents, which is why a half dozen local PIs have refused their services.

"Given your success on the Styer case," Dunne says, "I thought you might want to keep the ball rolling. I know it's asking you to work for free, but a win would be high-profile, and—"

"Money isn't the issue," I say. "I'm just not sure I have the bandwidth to go through all of that again."

"You're not sure? Or you don't?"

I glance out at Michael. *No more surprises*, I said. And I meant it, so why am I hesitating now? Why, instead of *No thanks*, do I hear myself say, "Can I have a day to think about it?"

"Yeah, all right," Dunne says. "But don't take *too* long. The kid's trial is coming up fast."

I end the call, then scroll through my apps until I find American Airlines. I type *Miami* in the From box, Houston in the To box. Seat 3A is available on the 5 a.m. flight. I slip my phone in my pocket, head back out on the balcony. Michael takes one look at me and hangs his head.

"Know any good hotels in Houston?" I ask.

ACKNOWLEDGMENTS

This book has been a long time in the making. As an owner and managing partner in multiple restaurants and businesses, finding and dedicating time to a passion project was challenging. COVID was the catalyst that allowed me to finally take this story across the finish line. In trying to find the silver lining during such a difficult time for us all, I decided to use my forced solitude as an opportunity. I realized it was now or never. It was time to see if I had what it took to publish a fictional crime thriller—I am now so glad that I did.

I would like to thank Nicole Plivelich for listening, helping, and encouraging me to pursue this dream. Your continued efforts helped me get this process started.

Thank you to my team at Kevin Anderson & Associates and especially Chris Narozny, who spent tireless hours helping to create a fun, exciting read. You are a very talented and special person!

To Greenleaf Book Group, who worked diligently to help me finalize all the book details and publish this first piece of the dream.

To my wife, Laura, for her support and understanding of this dream.

To Tina McIntosh, who passionately helped me stay focused, diligent, and organized throughout this process. I would not have been able to complete this book without you.

I would certainly like to thank the readers. Thank you for taking a chance on my first book. Hopefully with your support, more exciting adventures from Christian Stone will find their way into your lives and hearts.

Lastly, I would like to thank Zachary Busby for his relentless work in helping to create this special book. All of your time and effort did not go unnoticed. You are an incredibly smart, creative, and ingenious individual. This book, without question, would not have happened without you. I hope you have gotten as much joy out of this journey as I have.

ABOUT THE AUTHOR

ERIC SUGRUE is a successful Delaware restaurateur and entrepreneur with a love for crime fiction. He was inspired to write a mystery of his own when, in seat 3A on a flight from Philadelphia to Miami, he looked out the window and spotted what, at a glance, seemed to be a body. He was quickly able to determine that it wasn't a body, but the possibility stuck with him and became the inciting incident for *Seat 3A*. When not juggling his varied business responsibilities, he enjoys cooking, entertaining friends, honing his golf and tennis skills, and reading and watching crime thrillers. He resides in Rehoboth Beach, Delaware, with his wife, Laura, and their adorable dog, Wally. In the winter months, they spend as much time as they can in Miami Beach. *Seat 3A* is his first novel in what he hopes to develop into a series of Christian Stone adventures and a movie.